Brushed by Moonlight

Book 1
Château Nocturne

Anna Lowe

Contents

Free Books

Get your free e-books now!

Sign up for my newsletter at *annalowebooks.com* to get three free books!

- *Desert Wolf*: Friend or Foe (Book 1.1 in the Twin Moon Ranch series)

- *Off the Charts* (the prequel to the Serendipity Adventure series)

- *Perfection* (the prequel to the Blue Moon Saloon series)

Chapter One

MINA

Morning sun streamed through the trees, breaking into dozens of separate beams. Mist drifted under the lowest boughs, and pine needles crunched beneath my running shoes. A bird called from overhead, but otherwise, the only sounds were my short, steady breaths as I jogged along.

It was a beautiful, if overcast, morning. So beautiful, I could almost convince myself I'd done the right thing by moving to France. Inheriting and refurbishing a château in Burgundy — the chance of a lifetime, right?

I glanced back over my shoulder, and there it was, Château Nocturne, all the way at the end of a tunnel of trees. From a distance, the manor house was gorgeous, even postcard-worthy. But up close...

I turned away, doing my best to outrun the doubts, debts, and cobwebs.

The previous day had brought a deluge of autumn rain, so I slalomed around puddles for most of the way. The first mile took me through the deep, dark forest, and the second, along rolling, open fields. By the third mile, I was jogging through the little village of Auberre, with its town hall, church, and *boulangerie.*

I stopped and stretched before the scent of freshly baked bread and croissants lured me inside. The bell over the door chimed, and three people turned to greet me.

"Wilhelmina!" Madame Martin, the baker, called cheerily.

I preferred Mina, but my grandmother had always used my full name, and most older folks in town — and hence, most folks in town, period — stuck to that.

Madame Fontaine, the former schoolteacher, echoed her, then tut-tutted good-naturedly. "Running again? You're always in such a rush."

Jogging was more like it, and the only *me time* I could fit in to my schedule these days, but I didn't try to explain.

"And so thin," Madame Martin agreed. "No wonder she still hasn't found a man."

I opened my mouth, then closed it again. Back in Maine, I was the outspoken one who didn't shy away from gently calling out comments of that nature. In rural France... Well, I'd learned to cut the locals some slack, as they did for me.

"The usual for you?" Monsieur Martin asked.

I nodded. "A baguette and *pain au chocolate*, please."

"What about that big order you placed yesterday? Are your sister and cousin finally joining you?"

I forced a smile. We three had jointly inherited the château, though the other two were still untangling themselves from commitments at home.

"Unfortunately, not yet. But soon, I hope."

Mesdames Martin and Fontaine glanced at each other, and I steeled myself for rumors to fly. Something along the lines of us arguing over a huge inheritance, no doubt. Too bad that huge inheritance didn't exist. We were the stressed — er, proud — new owners of a château, but the estate hadn't come with enough cash to pay for basic upkeep, let alone the long list of urgent repairs.

I waved at my tiny backpack. "I'll leave the rest for Madame Picard to pick up later today."

Madame Picard was my grandmother's housekeeper — *my* housekeeper, technically — and as much of a fixture as the fireplaces, paintings, and furniture. My childhood memories of summers with my mother's family in France all featured a middle-aged version of Madame Picard. Now she had to be positively ancient, though she moved with the energy of someone half her age.

It's the eagle shifter in her, my grandmother used to say.

Yes, *shifter*, as in capable of changing into animal form and running — or, in her case, flying — away.

A shifter, like we used to be, something inside me mourned.

Our family had lost its fortune almost a century ago, and the ability to change forms had petered out at about the same time.

I'm all for a healthy mix of new blood, but somewhere along the line, the different species canceled out each other's powers, my grandmother used to lament. According to her, our family line held a blend of dragon, wolf, and eagle shifters, along with a number of magic-wielders.

But the only supernatural traits we had these days were, well…not much. We healed quickly, possessed incredibly acute senses, and could mind-speak to each other. But that was about it.

Madame Picard, on the other hand, came from much purer blood.

Maintaining two staff — Madame Picard and Monsieur Girard, the *winzer*/groundskeeper — might seem a little extravagant, but with forty-plus rooms and 120 acres to manage, they were more like a must. But even with their best efforts — and mine — the once-grand château was fading fast. The roof leaked in nineteen of the twenty bedrooms, and the place counted more rodents than human residents. Shutters hung askew, and the plumbing hadn't been updated since the early twenties — the *nineteen*-twenties, that is.

"I suppose you're expecting company, then?" Madame Fontaine asked.

Madame Martin leaned in. In small towns, everyone knew everyone's business, and the baker was always the first to find out.

"Not company," I said. "Clients."

"Oh! Did you finally find some tourists or a wedding party to rent rooms to?" Madame Martin asked.

That was the long-range plan — to make the huge property pay for itself, because I sure couldn't. Not on a teacher's salary, and especially not now that I'd taken time off to try to save the place. Château Nocturne had been in my family for eleven generations, and I refused to be the one who gave it all up.

"Not exactly. Just a small retreat group. But it's a start," I said, going for an upbeat note.

"It will take more than a start to save that money pit," Madame Fontaine muttered, using the French term, *gouffre financier*. A sinkhole, in other words.

I slipped my backpack from my shoulders, paid, and packed the baguette and bun away. I loved these straight-talking townsfolk, but this was the one hour of the day I declared free from constant fretting.

"Well, thanks. I'm off." I whirled for the door.

The bell jingled — too late for me to avoid bumping into the next customer. I had a fair bit of momentum, so the bump wasn't just a bump. It was a full-on, chest-to-chest crash. Which would have been mortifying if that had been Jacques, the portly, fifty-plus farmer who hit on me every chance he could.

But it wasn't Jacques, and it wasn't mortifying. Quite the opposite, in fact.

"Oh, sorry," the man said, grabbing my arms to keep me from wobbling back.

"My fault," I started, then stared into his warm brown eyes. "Clement?"

He broke into a huge smile. "Mina?"

My cheeks heated. My girls parts too.

"Wow. Good to see you," was all I managed to sputter.

And, double wow. The boy I'd played with as a kid was now filling in a police uniform very nicely, indeed.

His eyes shone in an unmistakable way, and I felt a little giddy too.

He whipped off his hat. "Good to see *you*."

"Finally, a young man who shows some manners," Madame Fontaine murmured.

"Finally, a young man, period," Madame Martin chuckled.

Like many rural towns in France, Auberre had an age demographic that leaned heavily to the senior side, so young blood was always cause for celebration. But ooh la la. Clement wasn't just young blood, but stunningly handsome young blood. His neatly trimmed, blondish-brown hair had a slight, natural wave. Caramel-colored eyes were set off by slightly darker brows and absolutely, totally focused on me. The faint brackets around his mouth could lift into a heart-melting smile, as they did now — or fall into a grim, law-and-order line, I supposed. Like Jacques, he was a local farmer's kid — but unlike Jacques, Clement kept his body sculpted like a god's.

The French custom of trading three kisses in greeting often felt like a chore. Not this time, though. I used the cheap excuse to grasp his shoulders — nicely muscled shoulders — while his lips gently brushed my cheeks each time.

I inhaled his scent — sage and lavender, like he'd been running through the surrounding fields. All kinds of warm feels went through me, and I barely remembered to step back.

"I didn't know you were back in town," I finally managed.

"I just transferred from Marseille."

"Trading big-city crime for the boredom of a small town?" Monsieur Martin joked.

"Trading crowded streets for space to roam," he murmured, keeping his eyes locked on mine.

My lips parted in realization, and I sniffed again. This time, I caught another, underlying scent. The scent of something wild, loyal, and fiercely protective.

Wolf, the back of my mind said.

Clement's eyes glowed with pride, and he puffed out his chest a little.

See? the little boy in him announced. *All grown up. I can shift and everything.*

There weren't many supernaturals around these parts, so we tended to congregate — or avoid each other at all costs. Clement's great-aunt had been friends with my grandmother, so I'd been privy to his family secret for a long time. As kids, we'd played together in the woods, and while I always wanted to be a knight, he'd eagerly looked forward to shifting someday.

And now, he could.

I flashed a warm smile to say, *Go, you.*

His grin widened, revealing a row of perfect teeth.

"I haven't seen Clement's mother this happy in years," Madame Martin said. "Her little boy, back in his childhood home again..."

I nearly burst out laughing. Did he fit in his old bed, or did his legs hang over the end?

"Just until I find my own place," he rushed to say.

I grinned at that glimpse of the bashful little boy he'd once been.

"Wilhelmina is back in town too." Madame Fontaine waggled her eyebrows. "Really back, for good."

"Really?"

His eyes sparkled, and a flurry of hopes — and misgivings — raced through my mind. I had my hands full with the château, and the last thing I wanted was a town gossiping about my love life. But, hell. They would gossip, regardless. I might as well have a love life, right?

On the other hand, I'd never seen Clement as anything more than a friend. As sweet — and hot — as he was, he had a hugely possessive, protective streak. Even as a kid, I'd had to fight for a little breathing space. A guy like him was fine as a friend and perfect law-enforcement material. But as a partner for life...

I'd toyed with that fantasy often and discarded it every time.

On the *other* other hand, I was thirty-five, and no man was perfect. And wasn't he great in every other way?

Including in bed, a naughty corner of my mind speculated.

The clock on the town hall struck, and I checked my watch. Yikes. Where had the time gone? My new clients were on their way, and I had to get moving.

"Oh! I have to go." I reached for the door. "I guess I'll see you around."

The three older folks traded sly winks as Clement nodded eagerly. "I guess you will."

My heart raced — and that was before I set off at a run. Was destiny offering me an unmissable opportunity or a complication I couldn't afford?

Chapter Two

MINA

Rain started to fall as I ran home, quickly turning into a down-pour. My footsteps sent up splatters of cold water that oozed into my shoes, and when a van passed, it hurled a curtain of water at me.

"Dammit," I muttered — only to be drenched a second time by the sports car that rushed up behind the van, then overtook it.

"Assholes," I muttered, watching them race onward.

Red brake lights flashed a moment later, and both vehicles took a hard left.

I stared, because the only thing down that road was Château Nocturne.

I checked my watch again. The clients referred to me by my godfather weren't due for another two hours. But, shit. A van and sports car would fit a group of four — the number I'd been told to expect. Were they early, or had I mixed up the time?

I'd run my best 5K times a decade earlier, but I felt on track to set a new personal record now, following the road rather than the winding path through the woods. When the château came into view at the end of the tree-lined road, I cringed, spotting two vehicles parked there.

I sprinted the home stretch, practically crashing into the front door. Panting, I pushed it open, whipped off my cap, and toed off my running shoes, cursing the whole time. Apparently, my clients had let themselves in. Crap. I pictured a group of older businessmen drumming their fingers impatiently.

I squeezed my ponytail, and rainwater ran out of my long brown hair.

"May I come in?" A man stepped out of the shadows of the entryway.

I jumped, barely holding back a yelp.

His dark eyes and slicked-back hair gleamed as he stared down at me from an inch or two above my five foot nine.

"Gordon sent me," he explained. "And the others." He motioned upstairs with disdain.

His accent was that of a man who'd mastered half a dozen languages and forgotten which one he'd started with. His bearing hinted at old European nobility — or plain old arrogance. Something about him set off all my inner alarms, though I wasn't sure why.

"Apologies for running in like this, but I wasn't expecting you until later today," I explained.

"Obviously," he sniffed.

I nearly gave him a piece of my mind, but heck. A client was a client — especially one in such a crisp, pricey Louis Vuitton blazer and shirt. And while this group was small, they could make or break my hopes of attracting more lucrative business in the future.

So I stuck out my hand, trying to maintain a sense of dignity despite the rainwater dripping into a puddle at my feet.

"Welcome to Château Nocturne. I'm Mina."

"Henrik," he said, shaking briefly, then dropping my hand.

And, yikes. His touch was cold and clammy. Or, shoot. Was that me after running three miles through the rain?

"Please, come in." I waved him in.

The main doors opened to a grand entrance hall with a huge chandelier. Twin stairways curved up either side to a mezzanine, making for an impressive sight. But Henrik set off up the right-side stairs without so much as a second glance at it all. Was he used to even grander surroundings?

I followed as my inner alarms screamed wildly. A split-second later, I realized why.

The stairs creaked under my feet but not under his.

My heart revved, and I stared as he continued over the next few steps.

No sound. Not so much as a whisper. No warmth in his voice either, and no scent. All that, plus cold, pale skin and asking for permission to enter despite acting like he owned the place.

Vampire. I'd just let a vampire into the house — er, château.

My grandmother had been quite the socialite, hosting huge parties attended by all manner of supernatural beings. As kids, my sister, cousin, and I would spy on the grown-ups from beneath tablecloths and work out what kind of supernatural each was, aided by acute senses and instincts passed down to us through the family line. We'd only ever seen a few vampires, though.

Henrik glanced back, arching one cocky eyebrow if to say, *Ha. What are you going to do now?*

I did my best to appear nonplussed. Vampires came in two varieties — *lethal* and merely *dangerous*. I was banking on the fact that Gordon wouldn't have sent me the former. Not that the latter gave me much peace of mind.

I would be giving my godfather an earful later, that was for sure. Yes, I was desperate for business. But vampires?

On the very small plus side, the other three weren't vampires. Otherwise, they couldn't have let themselves in.

But let themselves in they had, and, like fleas drawn to a mangy dog, they'd homed right in on the most comfortable room in the house. The *only* comfortable room, one might say — the grand drawing room on the upper floor.

A switch flipped in me, and I went from patient to pissed off.

I pushed past Henrik, who had paused at the threshold of the room. This was my château, dammit. And I was going to seize back control.

A tall man paced just inside the door with a phone glued to his ear, exuding *I'm in charge* vibes. Light brown hair, amber eyes, bright and cool as gemstones. Carefully tended, three-day shadow of a beard, and close-cropped hair. David

Beckham with a military twist and without the smirk. Oh, and an olive tint to his skin that hinted at the Near East.

"Excuse m—" I snipped, stomping up to him.

He stuck up a hand, like I was a waitress offering a refill of his coffee. *No thanks,* the gesture said. *Now, please toddle off. As you can see, I'm very busy.*

He paced right by me, as if I was part of the goddamn furniture.

The earthy, herbs-of-the-jungle scent behind his cologne hit me, and I did a double take. Tiger shifter?

My inner detective corrected *Near East* to *India,* but only a splash, perhaps from one of his parents or grandparents. That would explain the *tiger* part. But, yeesh. The guy might have a body to die for, but the dismissive attitude just wasn't doing it for me.

"Roux, meet Mina," the vampire murmured, ghosting past us and into a corner of the room, where he started inspecting the small items on display. An antique snuff box. A nineteenth-century porcelain clock. A music box with an exquisite lid of inlaid wood. One by one, he studied each treasure, then set it down — in the wrong place, despite the dust-free footprint clearly marking its home base.

I stomped over and snatched a brass candlestick out of his hands.

"Don't touch."

He scoffed. "You're worried about these knickknacks?"

They were heirlooms, dammit, not knickknacks. There was a difference.

"Don't touch," I growled.

The tiger was still pacing, intent on his phone. Intent on everything, in fact — in contrast to the blond flopped on the couch with a coffee in one hand and his feet on the Louis XVII table, looking all the world like an off-duty lifeguard. One I'd be tempted to ogle from behind a pair of dark sunglasses if I happened to be on his beach.

But I wasn't on his beach, dammit. He was in *my* drawing room, and his boots rested on the spot reserved for my grandmother's tea service.

I snapped my fingers in front of his face. "Feet off the table. Now."

"Well, hello to you too." He chuckled, lowering one foot, then the other, to the floor. Every move he made was lazy and confident, and no wonder.

Lion, my sixth sense told me. King of the jungle, at least in his own mind. I knew the type.

If Henrik, the vampire, was straight out of *GQ*, this guy was a vision from a teen fangirl magazine. Roux, the tiger, fit somewhere between *Guns & Ammo* and *Field & Stream*. All were in roughly the right — er, my — age bracket.

"Bene — short for Benedict. Nice to meet you," the blond on the couch said in an accent that was hard to place. South Africa? England? North America? Every syllable visited a different continent. He raised his mug in a toast, sipped, then grimaced.

"Mina," I grumbled, though I was drowned out by the tiger shifter complaining to the person on the other end of the line.

"Well, that's just not going to work," he said. "We need twice the gear you've supplied. A better vehicle, too."

"And a decent coffee machine," Bene called out.

I wished. Did he know how expensive those were?

I turned to the fourth man in the room — the tall, brooding one staring out the window and into the very gates of hell, it seemed. I had the impression he was looking in more than out, though. All in all, he would make a good candidate for the cover of *Bikes, Booze & Tattoos* magazine, if there was such a thing. Definitely the tortured soul type. I stepped closer, then halted, glimpsing bright, swirling flames in his midnight eyes.

That man was a dragon shifter, and he was not in a good mood. I turned away. Quickly.

"This place is just not suitable," Roux ranted into the phone.

I glared. Not that he noticed.

"Also," the tiger went on in rapid-fire English delivered in a slight French lilt, "you need to contact this Wilhelm guy and tell him to get his ass over here now."

I stalked closer, not amused.

"Say again?" Roux frowned into the phone. "Wilhem-who?"

Six inches away from his broad chest, I crossed my arms and tapped my foot. His eyes caught on me, and he made one long, drawn-out sound. "Ohhhhh."

He looked me up and down. Slowly. Disapprovingly — and frighteningly approving — at the same time.

"Wilhelmina," I growled.

"She goes by Mina," Bene called out, like we were old friends.

"Oh," Roux said. Again.

Finally, he shrugged and spoke into the phone. "I'll call you back." He clicked it off, stuck it into the thigh pocket of his cargo pants — as if the bulging muscles underneath didn't provide a sufficiently sculpted landscape — and gave me his undivided attention. Finally.

"Uh, hello. I'm Roux."

"Pronounced like kangaroo, but spelled funny," Bene interjected.

"He's implying he can spell," Henrik observed in a dry aside.

"Of course I can, Mr. T-R-A-N-S-Y-L-V-A-N-I-A."

"Livonia. I come from the Duchy of Livonia," Henrik corrected in a long-suffering tone.

Bene shrugged. "Whatever."

I kept my arms crossed and my lips sealed. Twelve years of teaching middle school had helped me get *angry silence* down to a science, and dealing with guys like this wasn't much different from teaching fifth grade. I was used to handling unruly, immature, self-centered (and surprisingly lovable) little beasts. The trick was immediately establishing that I would not take any crap. I could be nice later. . . if I were so inclined.

"Uh, no offense," Roux murmured, motioning around the *unsuitable* room.

Much taken, but I didn't say that. I didn't say anything.

"So. . . uh. . . " He struggled to fill the silence.

I spared him no mercy, letting the awkward silence stretch.

"Gordon said you were expecting us," he tried.

I made a show of checking my watch.

He frowned, then looked at his own — one of those massive man-watches that could withstand a spacewalk or a dive to the depths of the Mariana Trench. The male version of a handbag, as my sister liked to joke. With that and the Swiss Army Knife he probably kept in one of those cargo pockets, he would feel prepared for any occasion.

"Told you we were early." Bene motioned to Roux with his mug. "He's always early."

"Tigers," I grumbled, as if we'd traded complaints about Roux for months on end.

Roux's eyebrows shot up. Obviously, he'd assumed I was human. But I wasn't — not entirely, that is. I was a relic — or *brushed by moonlight,* the old-fashioned term my grandmother liked to use. We could no longer shift or perform magic, but we did have a few mystical qualities that came and went like the moon on a cloudy night — fleeting and unpredictable. They visited us in random, weirdly splintered bursts, like we'd pulled a card from a deck. Most of the time, we came up with nothing special, just extra-sharp vision or the ability to leap unusually far. But once in a blue moon, we would draw a joker. Something rare and startling, like Great-Grandmother Linda's ability to detect lies or Great-Great-Granddad Toby's trick of walking through walls. But ninety-nine-point-nine percent of the time, we were just plain human.

Bene raised his coffee mug to me in a silent toast and sipped. A moment later, he grimaced and shot the coffee machine a lethal look.

"So, ground rules," I announced, loud and clear.

Roux's brow furrowed. Clearly, he felt that was his job.

I turned slightly to face the other three, but they were all spread out.

"Henrik, if you please." I twitched a hand, directing him.

Roux's eyebrows shot up, and even the broody dragon shifter turned to look.

Yes, I was ordering a vampire around. I didn't normally flirt with death. I didn't flirt, period, and certainly not with clients — especially this bunch. But if I didn't grab the upper hand now...

Pinpoints of red lit Henrik's eyes, but he glided silently over to stand between Roux and the couch, where Bene sat.

"And you..." I motioned to the guy at the window.

"Marius," Bene provided when the guy didn't.

"Would you join us, please?" My tone wasn't as forgiving as my words.

The dragon shifter turned slowly, clearly annoyed. When his fiery eyes met mine, my stomach flipped. I'd gone from not even registering on his radar to being smack dab in his crosshairs. The vampire might be the obvious danger here, but this guy was downright lethal — and with a much, much shorter fuse.

Tread carefully, little lady, his burning eyes warned.

My knees wobbled, but I held my ground. If I caved now, I would never win their respect, and respect was the only route to keeping safe around this gang.

Finally, the floorboards creaked. Marius took one step forward, then another, exuding *rebel with no goddamn need for a cause* vibes. Then he stopped and folded his arms.

Muscles bulged. Testosterone flared. A millisecond after he passed, his scent caught up, and oh, that scent! I nearly closed my eyes and savored the fresh, airy blend. A thousand hopes and dreams flooded my mind, and I nearly swayed on my feet.

Then I caught myself and launched into a much-less-friendly version of the speech I'd rehearsed over the past week.

"So, welcome to Château Nocturne. This is my home, and I expect you to treat it as such."

I was way off script, which had called for something like *Mi casa es su casa.* But that would be courting disaster, and I knew it.

"In a moment, I'll show you to your quarters in the west wing. I'm sure you'll find them comfortable."

Well, I was only somewhat sure, and I really, really hoped the mild weather would hold, because the heating didn't work. But no need to mention that now, right?

"The rest of the house is off-limits, except the dining room directly below us." I pointed. "Madame Picard will serve lunch and dinner there at one and seven p.m."

Henrik's eyes drifted to my neck at the mention of meals. I glared at him and went on. "I'll set out breakfast at six-thirty and a midmorning snack at ten."

Bene chuckled. "Just like preschool."

"Yes. Very much like that," I said in a flat tone.

Henrik raised one thin eyebrow, while Roux's weary expression said he could relate. As their leader, he knew all about herding cats, I supposed. Very big, very dangerous cats, not to mention vampires and dragons.

"Can we use this space?" Bene asked. "It's, like, the only half-decent room in the house."

Ha. *Wait till you see your bedrooms,* I nearly said. I'd done my best to spruce them up, but I hadn't had time to deal with peeling wallpaper and paint.

Bene stuck up his hands. "No offense."

I pursed my lips.

Roux shot a pointed look at Bene's dirty boots. "Looks like it's off-limits."

"No, but it will be if I find bootprints anywhere but in the entry hall," I snipped.

Bene winced and leaned forward, brushing dirt off the tea table. He looked up, all sunny, like that would surely make up for it.

It didn't, as my expression made clear.

He frowned, then started picking dirt from the rug. "Sorry."

"In terms of. . . um, exploring in your free time. . . " I continued, aiming for a delicate way to say *shifting into wild beasts,* "You can use the surrounding fields and woods. No hunting permitted except in the woods within this property. The farmer's fields and the village are strictly no-go zones as far as such activities are concerned." I paused for emphasis, and also because I needed a nice way of saying, *Don't let anyone catch you in animal form.* I finally settled on, "I expect the highest discretion from each of you."

I shot Henrik a pointed look that said, *especially you.* If he tried to sate his bloodlust with anyone in the village, he would be out of here *tout de suite.*

Unless, of course, that someone was me. Then I would be the one who was gone — permanently.

Making a mental note to stock up on cloves of garlic and wooden stakes, I led them toward the west wing.

"Now, if you'll follow me. . ."

Chapter Three

MINA

Herding cats definitely fit the process of moving the men to the west wing. Marius stalked ahead, while Henrik lagged behind, inspecting every vase and painting in the hallway. Roux started out beside me, but his long, businesslike strides quickly put him several paces ahead. Then he would glance back, annoyed, pause for me to catch up, and repeat the process, like a tall, musclebound yo-yo — or a caged tiger.

Bene ambled along, peeking into each of the rooms on the left. "What's that? And that?"

I pointed. "Music room, smoking room, card room."

He whistled. "A whole room for playing cards, huh?"

"Off-limits," I growled, picturing his dirty boots on the tables and cushions. "All of them."

"I guess the roof leaks, huh?" he asked, noticing the buckets I'd done my best to hide.

I made a face. "A little, but I got an estimate, and the roof tops my repair list."

Bene chuckled. "Literally."

I wasn't so cheerful, because that list was about as long as the driveway. Part of me yearned to be setting up a classroom back in Maine instead. It was September, and twelve years of teaching was telling me it was time to migrate back to the classroom.

On the other hand, I had been starting to get into a rut at home. Teaching could be incredibly rewarding, but I couldn't help thinking the next thirty years of my life ought to hold more than the same predictable cycle of school days, weekends, and summers. Something more exciting. More adventurous, even.

Fixing a château might not be adventurous and exciting, but it was unpredictable, for sure. Especially with my new houseguests.

Bene indicated the one, long room on the right. "And that is...?"

"The library."

"Let me guess. Also off-limits?"

I nodded firmly.

My attention was only half with him, however. The rest was focused on the wide shoulders already disappearing down the far end of the hallway. Marius. The man moved like a thundercloud, both fascinating and frightening. When he turned the corner, out of sight, I felt a strange mix of relief and disappointment.

Relief, I told myself firmly.

I put the *disappointment* part down to his bad-boy aura. His type had a way of reeling women in. Foolish women, that is. Certainly not me.

I did my best to puzzle out the others. Bene was curious. Henrik, appraising. Roux was a bundle of pent-up energy. Energy that had to be harnessed and directed to a constructive purpose.

I hurried to catch up to him and lowered my voice. "Gordon said I could trust you to keep these guys in line."

Gordon had said no such thing, but I wasn't above stroking egos when I had to.

Roux's chest inflated another quarter inch, and he nodded briskly. *Of course I can.*

"Good." I kept my voice to a secretive whisper. "I think they'll need it."

"Believe me, I'm on it," he rumbled. "We'll get our training area set up before lunch."

I pictured one of those courses where dogs ran under, over, or around various obstacles. Whatever it took, I was all for it.

Still, I had to wonder. What were they training for? Gordon had been vague about what these men did for him, but that was par for the course with my godfather, who ran dozens of businesses in as many countries. He'd mentioned something along the lines of elite bodyguards he hired out to various associates. And, hell. It would be hard to beat a vampire, tiger, dragon, or lion shifter in that role.

"Excellent," I said, mimicking the clipped tone of a military commander. Something Roux was definitely familiar with.

As for the other three... Well, *discipline* clearly did not top their résumés.

We reached the west wing — a boxy annex connected to the central part of the building by the long hallway. That construction was mirrored on the east side of the château, where my suite of four rooms was. A distance I was doubly glad for now.

Before heading down the spiral staircase to the ground floor, I pointed out the window.

"In terms of outdoor space, you can use the courtyard of the stables and the grounds outside the west wing."

Everyone peeked out. Bene moved a curtain for a clearer view, and I prayed it wouldn't tear. The fabric was that old.

"Oh! A hedge maze! Can we use that too?"

I nearly said no, but maybe they would lose themselves in there for a while.

"Sure."

"What about that lake?" Roux asked.

I considered, then conceded. "Just don't bother the ducks." Then I motioned over my shoulder to the opposite end of the house. "The croquet lawn and gazebo are off-limits."

Bene sniggered. "Croquet lawn?"

I shot him a look. I was neither a rich snob nor hopelessly old-fashioned. But, heck. A château was a château. It had more than one lawn, and one of them was for croquet.

"What can I say?" I shrugged. "It was a thing in the old days."

We spiraled down, where I showed them around the lower level of the west wing, made up of four huge, airy rooms, two to the front and two to the back. I waved around the first room facing the south lawn.

"The rooms on this level are your quarters. A shared living room..."

A worn couch faced the fireplace. I'd set up a kitchen niche in one corner, with a mini fridge, microwave, and a few other necessities.

Bene made a beeline for the coffee machine, inspecting it while Henrik peered out a window, taking in the wide lawn and fringing forest. I did my best to keep them moving, directing their attention to the beautiful oak floors instead of the sagging wallpaper.

"The other three rooms can be configured as you like. I've put two beds in each room and left the third as an additional lounge, but you can rearrange any way it suits you."

This was the only part of the château that wasn't cluttered with mementos and furniture. My grandmother had cleared everything out years ago in hopes of renting the space, though she'd never followed through. I'd picked up where she'd left off and had busted my butt to make it habitable. I'd only dragged in the fourth bed and mattress the previous evening, in fact.

Boy, did I deserve a coffee, my *pain au chocolate*, and some downtime. I sighed.

"Bathroom?" Bene asked.

The château had over forty rooms, but only a handful of bathrooms. Luckily, my grandmother had had two installed in this level of the west wing...in the 1980s.

"They're a little dated," I admitted, flicking on the lights in one, then the other.

Bene and Roux crowded in to peek over my shoulder, and all that prime man-flesh made a warm flush spread over my cheeks. Clearly, I'd had far too long a dry spell.

My mind wandered to Clement, while my eyes drifted over Roux, Bene, and Marius. Not that I was considering my options. Just, er...fantasizing a little.

Then Henrik leaned in, instantly quelling my libido. His eyes focused on my neck rather than the bathroom fixtures, and my skin crawled.

"I've seen worse," Roux announced.

"I've seen better." Bene sighed, checking his hair in the mirror.

"Well, updating these bathrooms is on the list, and that's where you come in," I said. "I assume Gordon briefed you on our arrangement?"

Roux nodded. "An hour of work a day from each of us."

I echoed the movement. "Exactly. But I have a proposal."

Bene's eyebrows jumped up.

Not that kind, I let my grimace say. "Instead of an hour each day, I suggest you all give me six hours in a single day. Starting at the end of this week, all right?"

No one looked too enthusiastic, but no one protested either.

Gordon had been generous in his terms — not just in paying double the rent I'd proposed, but also providing me with my own, in-house workforce. Then again, my godfather had always been kind to me, and he knew about the sad state of the château.

"Well, I'll let you settle in while I check on lunch. Madame Picard should be here any minute. She'll ring at mealtimes."

I indicated the tarnished bell by an aperture near the ceiling. The system had been state-of-the-art in the 1930s and was about the only thing in the house that didn't need repairing.

"Any questions before I go?" I asked once we returned to the staircase.

Roux and Henrik shrugged. Marius scowled silently out a window. Bene waggled his eyebrows.

"Where do *you* live?"

Everyone looked over expectantly — even Marius.

I crossed my arms and socked them with my toughest, bitchiest expression.

"At the opposite end of the building. And guess what?"

"Off-limits?" Bene ventured.

Bet your ass, it is, I let my firm nod tell them. Then I pointed down the hallway.

"Lunch at one, in the dining room."

With that, I marched away. The only sound was the pad of my soggy socks over the oak flooring — and the creak from behind as the men leaned into the doorway to watch me.

Just three months, I reminded myself, sensing their eyes on my back. Gordon had offered a slick $15,000 per month for me to house and feed these men. I only had to share my leaky roof with these strangers for three months — and afterward, I would have enough money to replace (most of) it. Plus, the château was bigger than many apartment buildings.

You'll barely notice them, Gordon had assured me.

And, silly girl, I'd actually believed him.

∞∞∞∞

Madame Picard arrived shortly after — thank goodness — with all the fixings for a three-course lunch. In no time, she'd filled the kitchen with mouthwatering aromas.

"You're soaked," she scolded me. "Now, shoo."

I headed to my room in the upper east wing for a quick shower, then dried off. The windows of my bedroom overlooked the back lawn and forest, so I rarely bothered covering up before getting dressed. But my new houseguests had such presence that I remained acutely aware of them, even at this distance.

Safely wrapped in a towel, I peeked out a window.

We'll get our training area set up before lunch, Roux had said.

And, wow. He wasn't kidding. They'd already created a weight-lifting area with old paint cans raided from the garage, along with two rows of tires to run through. Roux was doing his best to direct the others, but it seemed more like an every-man-for-himself operation.

Henrik had hammered a series of knee-high posts into the ground and was stretching wire between them, creating one of those low, crawl-through-the-mud obstacles the Marines used. He stuck to shaded areas as much as possible, like all vampires. The *creatures of the night* myth only applied to recently turned vampires. The older they were, the better they could tolerate sunlight.

Marius was combining several old horse-jumping standards into one tall structure. Was he planning to shimmy over or leap in a single bound, like Superman?

Then again, he was a dragon shifter. Why even bother, unless to train his human body?

Not that it appeared to need much training. He'd stripped out of his jacket and was down to a snug black T-shirt that showed off line upon line of muscle and a broad chest that tapered down to—

—a place I was not interested in, I reminded myself and whirled away to dress.

A thud sounded, and I peered along the length of the building, where something dangled.

My mouth fell open. Bene stood casually at the very edge of the roof, not at all concerned by the drop-off. Turning his back to the forest, he grabbed a thick rope and rappelled down. No safety equipment, no belay buddy. He touched down smoothly, then stood beside Roux and gestured back at the roof. Had he discovered how saggy it was or was he suggesting anchor points for more ropes?

Backing away from the window, I speed-combed my hair, pulled it into a ponytail, and headed to the kitchen just as Madame Picard chimed to summon everyone.

The men filed into the dining room politely, then devoured the meal like ravenous animals — except Henrik, who took neat bites and dabbed his lips like a seventeenth-century gentleman.

Madame Picard hmpfed, reading my mind.

Sixteenth, at least. That is, before he became what he is now. You watch yourself around him, she warned, shooting her harsh whisper directly into my mind.

Not exactly a news flash.

I will, I assured her.

Then Madame Picard sighed to herself. *I'll add more meat to the menu.*

Apparently, the more meat a vampire consumed, the longer he could go without blood. The rarer, the better.

Good idea, I agreed. As in all the carpaccio and steak tartare we could get our hands on. But for now...

The meal started with onion soup topped with hearty Gruyère, followed by a main course of fresh-out-of-the-oven quiche Lorraine — two huge ones the men devoured within minutes.

"Good thing I held back a smaller one for us," she murmured as we passed, bustling in and out of the kitchen.

Happily, lunch was a hit, right down to the cheese platters served — and decimated — for dessert. But food was going to take a bigger chunk of my budget than I'd anticipated.

"Delicious." Bene kissed and flicked his fingertips.

"Quite good," Henrik agreed, folding his napkin.

"Can't wait for dinner." Roux leaned back from the table.

Marius jerked his chin in a faint nod. That was it. But, hey. He looked slightly less disgruntled than usual.

They lingered around the table for a long time, sipping drinks and generally settling into a post-meal stupor, like lions in a savanna surrounded by the bloody carcass of their latest meal. Marius's eyes took on a faraway look, and Henrik stared into his wineglass. Even Roux looked a little sleepy.

Bene, bless him, scored major brownie points by helping carry dishes into the kitchen.

"Wow. Is this place for real?" He looked around the massive space.

I grinned. "Nice, huh? It's the oldest room in the house."

"You could film a medieval banquet scene here."

I laughed. "They did, back in the 1950s. *Le Fripon de Rougemont.*" Sadly, the grainy, black-and-white epic was now forgotten except by members of my family.

Bene nodded, translating the title. "*The Rogue of Rougemont.* Love it."

"You speak French," I observed.

He nodded. "I do."

"But you're not French?"

He shook his head. "My parents kept moving. Zimbabwe, Canada, France, England... But I've never seen a kitchen like this."

I moved to the sink, which was big enough to rinse several grouse in — something I'd witnessed Madame Picard do when I was a kid. A stone fireplace with space to roast an entire ox took up most of the far wall, where a chain still hung, part of a mechanism to turn the spit. Wooden counters ran the length of each wall, while pots and ladles hung over the center island.

"I'm hoping to rent the space out for filming," I said. "Movies, commercials, whatever."

Madame Picard looked scandalized, but Bene nodded readily.

"Good idea. This is amazing." Then he shot me a wry look. "If only it came with a half-decent coffee machine."

I ignored that, using his previous comment to segue into a different topic.

"Where are the other guys from? Roux is French, right?"

He nodded. "Marius is Swiss-German, but he's lived all over."

Now that was a surprise, but maybe not such a surprise. I loved the tidy perfection of Switzerland, but I knew it grated on some people — especially people who didn't like to play by the rules.

"And Henrik... He said, the Duchy of...?" I asked.

Bene shrugged. "Part of the Polish-Lithuanian Commonwealth that no longer exists," he said, inching toward the macarons cooling on a counter.

Madame Picard smacked his hand. "Those, young man, are for after dinner."

"Yes, ma'am." He hung his head and retreated to the dining room.

I sighed. I could do bossy, but Madame Picard could be downright menacing.

"It comes with age," she chuckled, reading my mind. "Now, run along and leave me in peace."

That was one of many qualities that made Madame Picard a godsend — she was happy to rule the kitchen single-handedly, and I was happy to leave her to it.

I took off for a round of errands in my battered old Citroën afterward, stocking up on more groceries, more napkins... more *everything*, including enough red meat to feed an entire coven of vampires. I even wandered through the appliance section of the huge Hypermarché in Auxerre, the nearest town of notable size. But one look at the price tag of the espresso machines had me scurrying back to the discount aisles.

I made a last stop for more bread at the bakery in Auberre, then halted on my way back to the car.

"Shit," I muttered, spotting Clement beside it. He pulled out a little notebook and checked the license plate. Oops. Had I parked illegally?

"It's mine." I hurried over, adding a meeker, "Sorry!"

Clement looked up and broke into a smile. And I mean, a *smile*. One so radiant, it made my heart flutter.

Apparently, he was just as single as I was and just as lonely.

"Mina." Just two syllables, but they rolled off his tongue like poetry.

"*Bonjour.*" I waved, suddenly self-conscious. "I guess I was in a hurry. No parking here, huh?"

He put away his notebook. "Now you know."

"You're not going to ticket me?"

"Now, what kind of welcome home would that be?" His sparkling eyes implied he would be happy to welcome me into his home just as warmly.

Tempting, but I had a house full of shifters — and a vampire — to tend to. And Clement was a police officer, while my guests were definitely on the sketchy side.

My stomach clenched when he eyed the bags rammed into the hatchback.

"Expecting company?"

I gulped and tried to wave it off. "Just a small group renting a few rooms. You know, to offset costs."

He nodded unenthusiastically. That was the thing with wolf shifters. They were very loyal and very territorial. Inconveniently so, especially since *territorial* covered places *and* people.

The way he looked at me made heat pool in my core. That was another thing about shifters — they drew you in, especially when they wanted you.

And, wow. Clement Dulaire, chief of police and studly homegrown son of Auberre, wanted me. There was no mistaking it.

Did I want him? Yes? No? I wasn't sure.

Either way, my godfather had made it clear he wanted his group to fly under the radar. I couldn't afford to get involved with the local police chief — a shifter, no less — at a time like this.

"I guess I should go. Unless you're going to book me," I joked, jingling my keys nervously.

He grinned. "Not this time."

But next time... His eyes danced, telling me he wouldn't give up easily.

Yikes. I sensed trouble, not just over the horizon but galloping right up to the front steps of the château.

"*À bientôt.*" *See you soon,* I said, opening the car door.

Clement stepped aside, keeping his eyes locked on mine. "See you soon."

∞∞∞∞

I barely had time to unpack the car before dinner — another feast, thanks to Madame Picard. It started with *potage Crécy* — carrot soup with fresh herbs — followed by a main course of *steak au poivre* served extra rare, paired with our vineyard's very own Pinot Noir, and chased down with *mousse au chocolat.*

Even Roux smacked his lips when it was over. "Delicious."

"Is there more?" Bene asked after two helpings.

There was, but I was saving some for myself, dammit.

"No." I shook my head sadly.

Bene consoled himself with half a dozen macarons.

"Sublime," he announced, stacking his plate with another four and following the others to the drawing room. I cringed, picturing crumbs all over the furniture.

Too tired to protest, but too wary to leave them unsupervised, I followed. But the guys must have been equally tired, because they were surprisingly quiet, each quickly settling down to his own pastime.

Roux and Henrik played chess. Bene looked on, munching away. Marius stood gazing out the window, pointedly ignoring me.

Clearly, he hated me. Which shouldn't have felt like such a blow, but it did.

I sat for a while, flipping through a faded art picture book while surreptitiously keeping an eye on him — er, them.

The book was one of my father's — a picture book on masterpieces of post-Impressionist art — and marked by scraps of paper with notes in his tight, slanted script. I ran my finger over one note, drifting away on memories. Then I sighed and stood to go. I couldn't keep an eye on my guests twenty-four seven, and I had to rise early to set up breakfast.

"Good night. See you tomorrow," I called from the doorway.

"See you," Roux murmured, barely looking up from the chessboard.

Bene waggled his fingers. "Nighty-night. Don't let the bedbugs bite."

Or other things, I thought, spotting Henrik.

"Good night." His lips curled in a small, dangerous smile, and his voice was as smooth as the fine whisky he'd helped himself to.

Whisky I would definitely add to the running tab Gordon had okayed for incidentals.

Marius didn't so much as look away from the window.

"Good night," I grumbled, staring at him.

Something I instantly regretted, because the moment our eyes met, a warm, pulsing force throbbed through my chest, and my lungs squeezed. Time stretched, and warning lights flashed in my mind, blinding me to everything but the bluish-black of his eyes.

Blue like the sky at twilight. Like fresh ink over parchment.

Blue like a day-old bruise, something in the back of my mind whispered. *Tread carefully.*

And yet, my foolish heart beat wildly, and an inexplicable yearning resonated in my soul — far, far more than Clement had ever inspired.

Far, far more than Clement ever will, my heart whispered.

I blinked, and Marius looked away, grunting, "Goodnight."

So, there it was. The very first — and only — word he'd ever uttered to me.

I unwrapped my fingers from the doorframe and walked mechanically down the hallway. Fifteen minutes later, I was in bed with a book I didn't bother opening.

Chapter Four

MINA

That night, I tossed and turned, unable to sleep. My mind was too busy blending the events of a hell of a day. When I eventually dozed off, I was plagued by unsettling dreams.

In one, I ran down an endless hallway, chased by beasts. I turned to sleep on my side, but that only set off different dreams. A lion stalked me from behind the maze hedge — or was that a tiger? A dragon swooped overhead, blotting out the moon with his huge, leathery wings. A man with fangs followed me up the front stairs...

I jerked out of that dream, panting in terror. Then I flopped back, heart thumping wildly.

Think of something nice, my mom used to say.

Clement popped into my mind, and I decided to treat myself to a little fantasy of him.

And, ha. A fantasy probably shared by every woman in Auberre.

It worked, and soon, I was dreaming far more satisfying dreams. But the details of the man exploring my body were hazy. Was that Clement or someone else?

All I knew was that he filled me again and again, bringing me right to the highest rung on the ladder of ecstasy, then pushing me off it — and catching me so smoothly, I kept moaning in unbridled pleasure.

A damn good dream, until something in my subconscious yanked me out of it.

I jerked upright, then sank back into my pillow, determined to revisit that dream. But my eyes snapped open again, and I held my breath.

Something was stalking me. For real, not a dream.

Not daring to move, I cast my eyes around. Moonlight streamed through the slot between the curtains, playing charades with the clothes I'd heaped on a chair. The faint sound of nocturnal residents filtered in from the woods. A drop of water fell from the tap in the bathroom sink. . . and a long minute later, another.

But otherwise, there was silence. Eerie silence.

I closed my eyes, tuning in with my other senses. Highly sensitive, supernatural senses gifted to me by my ancestors. Bit by bit, I homed in on that creepy *something* and stared at the ceiling.

That's where he was — whoever *he* was. In the attic, directly above me.

A scream built in my throat, held back by a wall of sheer fear.

It took everything I had to back away from the brink of panic and think. Maybe it was just a really nasty dream?

No, I decided. I was wide awake, and his — or her — presence loomed over me.

A presence that emitted no scent, no sound, no nothing. Which meant. . . ?

Finally, it hit me. *Vampire.*

Henrik?

My pulse revved, and I cursed. The more my blood pumped, the more it would call to him. My sensual dreams had already tinged the air with the scent of desire. Rushing blood would only intensify the draw on him.

I did my best to lie still, slow my heart rate, and think.

The attic was filled with small rooms used as staff quarters in the old days. A long, dim corridor ran the entire length of the house, meaning a person — or vampire — could creep from the west to east wing without encountering any obstacle, apart from cobwebs.

So, yikes. Henrik had been out exploring and found his way to the space directly over my bed. Coincidence?

I doubted it.

The question was, what would he do next? Could a vampire move through walls — or ceilings? Was he liable to burst through at any moment, or would he be content to quietly savor the scent of my life's blood like secondhand smoke from a nice, relaxing joint?

I doubted that too.

Then another thought struck me. Vampires could enthrall with their voices. Could their mere presence enthrall in a similar way?

My skin crawled as I pictured offering myself to him willingly. I imagined his body pressing against mine... The punch of his fangs... The suction in my veins as he gulped one mouthful of blood after another—

I clenched my hands, cutting off such thoughts. How likely was Henrik to come after me in his very first night at the château? Vampires were parasites. It made no sense to kill off his host, right?

I grimaced at the unintentional pun. *Host* certainly fit.

So, maybe he didn't intend to kill me. Maybe he just wanted a sip of his favorite drink every night. Was he already trying to enthrall me into wanting that, and possibly more? He could come back again and again, wipe my memory, and I would never know.

My stomach churned.

One thing was clear. The longer I lay there, the more I would be at his mercy. A strange buzz was already building around my mind. The early stages of his thrall?

I had to get away, and fast. But moving would let him know I was onto him. Worse, it could even excite him.

I thought hard. Option One — to yell *Fuck off, Henrik!* at the top of my lungs — didn't seem wise. Option Two — hightailing it out of bed — was no better, because where would I go?

That left Option Three. I gulped, desperately searching for a better plan.

The buzz in my mind increased from the level of a single bumblebee to a dozen hornets.

I forced a few deep breaths. Fine. Option Three. To move without moving. A trick my great-grandmother had been proud of mastering, but that I had only ever tried twice. Once, it had gone perfectly. The other time, I'd nearly "moved" myself right out of existence. Was I really ready to risk that?

The hair standing on my skin yelped, *Risk it! Risk it!*

I closed my eyes and pictured myself in bed. The angle of my limbs, the shape of my body. I memorized the feel of the sheets, the pattern of wrinkles in the blanket. I cataloged tiny eddies in the air above and around me.

Then, picturing exactly that scene, I slid silently out of bed, tiptoed to a corner of the room, and looked back.

My body was still in bed, slumbering peacefully. The blanket was wrinkled, and air wafted around my huddled form exactly as it had before.

I was there, but I wasn't there.

I concentrated hard, maintaining the illusion while the real me hunched silently in the corner. My great-grandmother had claimed it was easy, but I could only pull it off with head-splitting focus.

Shadow-walking, she'd called it. But if you weren't careful, you risked distancing yourself too far from the illusion. In that case, the illusion could crumple, or the real you would — in the most final way possible.

Death by crumpling didn't sound too painful, but I'd ventured too close once, and it had scared the hell out of me.

I held still, minimizing each breath, staring at the illusion in bed, then up at the ceiling. Was it working? Had I fooled him?

I exhaled, because those buzzing hornets kept circling over the illusionary me in bed.

Then, shit. The buzz took on a puzzled note, and instead of humming close to the sheets, the hornets started spreading out. They ventured farther and farther away, seeking.

My heart pounded. I could sense, if not see or hear, that imaginary cloud move. More angry than puzzled now, the hornets searched the room, buzzing over the clothes in the chair... the wardrobe... the book on the bedside table...

Holding my breath, I inched quietly along the wall, working my way over toward the bathroom. I crouched, sensing that force invade the space I'd just vacated.

The buzz intensified.

Ice formed in my veins. But maybe that was a good thing, helping conceal my body heat.

My hopes rose, then plummeted as the buzzing crept along the wall, tracking me to my new hiding place.

I balled my hands into fists, desperate enough to consider Option One again.

The words *Fuck, off,* and *Henrik* formed on the tip of my tongue.

But the curtains billowed inward on a sudden gust of wind, and the moonlight was blotted out by something huge. Shutters rattled, and a mighty *whoosh* sounded overhead. Dead leaves tumbled over the roof. The attic floorboards creaked for the first time, and I heard a man curse under his breath.

The buzzing sensation evaporated, and moments later...

I searched the ceiling with my eyes, though it wasn't sight I was relying on. Was he gone?

A full minute later, I decided yes, he was.

The human-shaped blanket on the bed fell flat as I sat down hard, gripping my head with both hands. Damn, did my head ache.

The vampire was gone, and my shadow-walking had worked, so I should have been glad. But I was too busy shaking — and nursing a pounding migraine — to celebrate.

I curled into a ball on the floor, whimpering, and stayed there for a long, long time.

Chapter Five

MINA

"So, uh...breakfast?" Bene waved at the empty sideboard in the dining room.

Madame Picard had set out plates and silverware the previous evening, but it was my job to set out breakfast. At least, it was until my sister and cousin arrived or until I found someone from the village to take over the task. For now, I was juggling a dozen daily tasks on my own.

And boy, did I feel alone as the men filed into the dining room one by one. I patted the garlic cloves I'd stuffed in my pockets and took a deep breath.

"Good morning," Roux said, entering the room shortly after Bene.

I crossed my arms and glared. Sometime in the early hours of morning, I'd decided my best tactic was to go on the war path and attack my vampire problem head on.

"Maybe not such a good morning," Bene mumbled.

Roux stopped in his tracks, frowning at the empty platters on the sideboard.

"Um..." he started.

"No breakfast. I think she's mad," Bene stage-whispered to Roux.

Oh, he had that right.

Roux eyed me, then leaned toward Bene. "Mad at what?"

He shrugged. "No idea."

Roux raised an eyebrow at me. "Did we do something wrong?"

I kept my lips sealed and my glare at DEFCON 1.

"I told you we shouldn't have moved in to those extra rooms," Bene murmured.

I stared. They'd *what?*

"Just a few," Bene hastened to add, catching my expression.

I closed my eyes, telling myself, *one thing at a time.*

I did snatch my favorite mug out of his hands, though — the chipped one with a picture of Franz Marc's *Blue Horses.*

"Hey!" he protested. "Are mugs off-limits now too?"

"Just that one," I muttered.

A scuffing sound heralded the arrival of my next hungry guest, and I didn't have to open my eyes to recognize Marius. His thundercloud presence made the air pressure in the room drop abruptly, the way it did before the heavens opened in a deluge.

Yeesh. What was his problem? And how the hell did he manage to intimidate and arouse me at the same time? Just being around him made my nipples go hard.

A second later, a wave of ice-cold air heralded the arrival of Henrik. I socked him with my bitchiest glare.

His smug look evaporated, and he took a step back.

You could cut the tension in the room with a knife — or better yet, a garlic-smeared ax.

Everyone stared at Henrik, and Bene murmured, "Uh-oh."

Uh-oh was right. But silence was my best weapon, and I wielded it like a sword.

"What did he do?" Roux asked me.

I ignored him the way he'd ignored me when we'd first met.

"What did you do?" he tried Henrik next.

The vampire stuck his hands up. "Nothing."

Marius snorted.

For an instant, my eyes flicked to him, surprised to find him halfway engaged in a conversation. Then I flicked my gaze — er, glare — back to Henrik.

"I said, what did you do?" Roux's voice dropped to a snarl.

Henrik moved his icy gaze to Roux, and I couldn't help wondering who would come out on top in a fight between a vampire and a tiger shifter.

I would be cheering for the tiger, that was for sure.

"Let me guess," Bene cut in. "Someone went exploring last night. Somewhere off-limits."

Twin pricks of red shone in Henrik's eyes. "And you didn't?"

Bene put a hand on his heart. "Absolutely not." His offended tone suggested he would never, ever consider such a thing.

I doubted that, but Bene wasn't my problem right now.

Henrik pinned me with a glare, like I'd been the one disturbing *his* sleep last night.

Asshole, I let my eyes say.

"To solve this issue, it would help to know what happened," Roux said rather reasonably.

But I doubted vampires reasoned, so I refused to respond.

"We have to play fucking charades now?" Marius grumbled.

I turned my glare to him — and nearly wobbled backward when his glowing eyes met mine. Clearly, his dragon side was worked up about something. But what? I doubted rules violations offended him. Maybe a violation of an honor code? Even bad-boy dragon shifters had to have those.

The longer I gazed into those midnight eyes, the more I settled on *violation of an honor code.* And if that was true, well... Huh. Whose honor was at stake here?

Then it hit me, and my knees wobbled. Mine?

Finally, I yanked my gaze away. If I didn't, it would stay with him all day. The man was like lava spurting from a volcano — dangerous but so mesmerizing, you forgot to drag yourself to safety.

Henrik. Focus on Henrik, I reminded myself.

I had him on the back foot, so it was time to show my hand.

"If you want to stay here — all of you — you have to play by the rules," I barked.

"Who says I want to stay here?" Henrik grumbled.

Exactly what I'd spent the morning mulling over. Vampires only answered to one boss — themselves. And most vampires lived comfortably from assets amassed over centuries-long lifespans. So why would one stoop so low as to work for Gordon?

Because he has to, I'd realized in the wee hours of the morning. Whether his motive was financial, a favor owed, or some other reason was a moot point. Henrik had had no choice in taking this job. Therefore, he couldn't afford to lose it.

I put all my eggs in one basket and hurled it at Henrik.

"What you want isn't the point, is it?" I said. "You're here because you have to be here, correct?"

Henrik glared.

Definitely a *Yes.*

"You cannot afford to fail, because you know there will be consequences," I powered on.

All four men stared at their feet. So, ha. I was right. Pretty dire consequences, I figured, because none of them was the type to shy away from breaking the rules.

"Yes, I need Gordon's business," I admitted. "But I am prepared to call off this deal if you don't respect my rules. And not just you." I pointed at Henrik. "All of you will be out of here..."

Bene's throat bobbed in a heavy gulp.

"...and it will be up to you, Henrik, to explain to Gordon why," I finished.

As a teacher, I'd rarely called on the principal to assist with discipline because that undermined my own credibility. But Henrik was a vampire, not a fifth grader. Whatever power I could hold over his head, I sure as hell would.

It seemed to work too, because Roux, Bene, and Marius all glared at Henrik. Especially Marius, I noticed. Interesting. What did a man like him have to lose?

A low, menacing growl built in Roux's throat — aimed at Henrik, not me, thank goodness.

"Now, I suggest you four head outside and hold a little powwow," I said. "That way, you can consider your priorities and decide on the course of action you'd like to take."

That would also keep my grandmother's china safe if a fight broke out — and keep the Persian carpet clean if blood happened to be spilled.

God, I should have known Gordon's deal was too good to be true.

"I'm sure that won't be necessary," Roux rumbled in his best commander's voice.

But a commander needed followers, and the other three were not the *following* type.

"Will it?" he barked at Henrik.

Henrik socked me with a nasty, red-eyed glare — until a deep snarl made him blink.

Me too, because that was Marius, not Roux, warning him. Clearly, the dragon shifter was just as desperate to keep this job as the other three.

"I said, I'm sure a meeting is not necessary. Is it, Henrik?" Roux demanded.

When the vampire shifted his gaze to the tiger, a weight dropped from my shoulders. Whew.

"No, it won't," Henrik finally muttered.

I exhaled very, very slowly. For a long, awkward minute, silence reigned. Then Bene spoke up.

"So, about breakfast..."

I regretted ever letting Henrik in, but thank goodness for Bene — the sole ray of sunshine in this otherwise surly gang.

"Fifteen minutes," I muttered, walking to the kitchen. On the way, I called over my shoulder to Bene, "Ten if I get a little help."

The lion shifter flashed a sunny smile and fell into step beside me. "Always happy to assist, ma'am."

I strode away, as regal and unperturbed as a queen. But the moment I reached the kitchen, I slumped, bracing myself on the counter with both hands.

"You okay?" Bene whispered.

I mustered a weak smile. Who knew a lion could be so sweet?

"Just wondering if I took things too far."

"Just about right, I'd say." He patted me on the back, then moved to the pantry. "Now, about breakfast. May I suggest you leave the coffee to me?"

I laughed out loud. Maybe I would live to see the end of this day. Maybe I could keep this desperately needed contract from falling apart. Maybe calling on my bitchy side hadn't been a mistake.

And maybe, just maybe, I could accept a little help from time to time.

"It's all yours." I grinned, waving Bene to the moka pot. "It's all yours."

Chapter Six

MINA

The confrontation over breakfast had drained me, so I spent the morning on an easy, mindless task — painting the last third of the hallway leading to the east wing an off-white color called *Antique Lace.* Madame Picard arrived at eleven to manage meals, and thank goodness for that.

I tiptoed into the kitchen an hour after the men had lunch, not ready to face them yet.

"Sit. Eat. You work too much," Madame Picard recited her usual refrain.

I slid into a stool, gratefully accepting the *tarte flambée* she'd saved for me. One bite of the creamy Alsatian flatbread, and I groaned.

"So good."

"It is," she agreed, all matter-of-fact. "Your guests liked it too."

Your guests, not *ours.* She'd been skeptical of my income-generating ideas from day one, but this was the twenty-first century. I had a château to maintain without a family fortune or crew of servants.

I munched quietly away, watching her chop vegetables for soup.

Bene wandered in just then, and Madame Picard pointed at him with a knife.

"Out of my kitchen."

He stuck up his hands. "Just looking for a snack."

"You just had lunch," Madame protested. "A big lunch that you devoured like ravenous wolves."

"Ravenous lions," he corrected earnestly.

She waved the knife again. "Out."

He gave her his best lost puppy look — er, lost cub? — with wide, sad eyes, but she didn't relent.

"Out, I said."

His hurt expression said, *Hey, that works with everyone else.*

Ha. Not with her.

He slunk away without another word.

A minute later, an idea struck me. I took another huge bite of *tarte flambée*, grabbed two scones, and raced after Bene.

"What's that?" Madame called after me.

I winked. "A bribe."

It took me a good five minutes to track Bene down. The building was that big, with multiple staircases and hallways to disappear down. Eventually, I found him sunning himself on the south lawn.

"Bene," I called.

He cracked one eye open, then closed it. "What?"

"I need help."

"I'm busy," he said, not bothering to open his eyes.

Obviously.

I used the reset trick that worked like a charm with fifth graders. "I need help."

He yawned a mighty lion yawn, letting his teeth extend. "Help with what?"

I crossed my arms. "Help with the house."

He snorted. "You mean, the *château*."

I rolled my eyes. "I'm trying not to sound pretentious. Besides, *house* works better than *château*."

He cracked open one eye. "How?"

"You don't tell someone, *come on over to my château*, or *my château is your château...*"

He laughed, and I held up the scones.

He licked his lips, then shot me a suspicious look. "One for you, one for me?"

I shook my head. "Both for you. For an easy half hour of work, max."

A grossly overoptimistic estimate, but he didn't need to know that.

I crooked a finger and led him upstairs. *Way* upstairs, into the attic.

"So, you inherited this whole place, huh?" he asked as we climbed the stairs.

"My grandmother left it to me, my sister, and my cousin."

"Not your mother or father?"

"My mom and aunt both refused it. They said they didn't want to die with a mountain of debt and responsibilities." I sighed. "I'm starting to see why."

He chuckled. "I guess there's a good and a bad side to everything."

We wound around the next set of stairs.

"So, you have a sister, huh?" Bene asked. "I guess she's the nice one?"

I glared, communicating, *No scones for you, buster.*

"I mean, is she as nice as you?" He hurried to correct himself.

I decided not to grace that with an answer.

We reached the attic hallway, where I pointed out the tools and materials I'd prepared earlier, handed him the scones, and explained the task at hand.

"You want a *what*?" he asked, wiping crumbs from his mouth.

"A partition," I repeated, reaching across the narrow hall-way. "Right here."

He rubbed his chin. "Why?"

"I have a problem with... er... "

He raised an eyebrow, not getting it.

"Bats," I finally said.

His eyes widened. "Oh. Big bats?"

I nodded. "Very big."

"I see." He studied the space. "Do these bats need a door to pass back and forth?"

I shook my head. "Definitely not."

"Not very practical," he pointed out. "For anyone other than the bats, I mean."

"Not my priority."

"And what is?"

Staying alive seemed too blunt, so I settled for, "Getting a good night's sleep."

"Gotcha," he said.

Lions — especially males — weren't known for being overly zealous when it came to anything other than sunning themselves or scoring dates. But I had to hand it to Bene. He turned out to be a damn good assistant. With me measuring and sawing beams and him hammering them into place, we had a frame up in no time.

It was warm up there, though, and soon, his gray T stuck to his chest with sweat. A welcome diversion, I had to admit. One I allowed myself because I'd had a shitty night and a tough morning. I deserved a little pep-me-up.

All very innocent, of course. Lion shifters were notorious womanizers and definitely not my type, even if this one had the body of a Viking.

Bene made surprisingly good company too, happy to chat about anything but himself.

"All those places you've lived... Do you have more than one passport?" I asked.

"I do," was all he was willing to divulge.

"And you decided to work for Gordon because..."

"Oh, you know. Time for a change."

"From what?"

"From my previous job."

Okay, I got the point. No talking about personal stuff.

I turned back to my circular saw and continued cutting planks to size.

"How was your night?" I asked as Bene held the first one in place. A perfect fit.

"Great. We made a few changes, though."

I wanted to ask, but I didn't want to ask.

"Got my own room now," Bene went on without prompting.

I couldn't help myself. "So, the other guys are sharing, then?"

"Nah. We each got a room. Marius and Henrik moved upstairs."

"They what?" I squawked.

"Well, you know how it is," Bene said, then dropped his voice to a growly bass, imitating Marius. "Dragons need space."

I clicked my jaw. That had not been the plan.

"So, we have cats on one level, the dragon above, and the vampire above that," he said.

My blood went cold. "Above, where?"

"Roux and I are on the ground floor, just where you put us." Bene held his hand flat, then put the other hand above it. "Marius is one flight up, same level as the drawing room." Then he moved the bottom hand to the top, marking another story. "Henrik took the top."

"The top, *where*?" I demanded.

Bene jerked a thumb over his shoulder. "Down there."

I stared into the darkness at the end of the hallway.

Bene must have caught my expression. "You did tell us to rearrange if we wanted to."

"The *furniture*. I said, rearrange the *furniture*."

He made a face. "Okay, okay. But, hell. Would you want to room with a vampire?"

"No." I slapped a hand against the partition frame. "I wouldn't."

"Smart." He chuckled. "Not that this will hold him if he really wanted to get through."

"No, but it will remind him he's not wanted."

"Good luck with that," he muttered, then caught himself. "I mean, good plan."

"Do you have a better one?"

"No. But for whatever it's worth, I think he'll play by the rules from now on."

I snorted and got back to sawing planks. Enough for a double layer.

Just in case.

∞∞∞∞∞

Thanks to the partition — and the thick string of garlic *and* the massive crucifix I'd dug out of storage to hang on my side of the structure — I slept slightly better that night, and even better the next. Over the next few days, things settled into something like a rhythm, and at the end of the week...

"Roux," I said as breakfast wound down the following Saturday.

"Yes?" He turned, waiting.

A big improvement over our first meeting. These days, he actually noticed me.

Good. I was starting to make an impression. Even if that impression was *grouchy*, I would take it.

"Are you ready?" I asked, bracing myself for a decisive *no*.

Roux looked less than thrilled, but he did nod. "We're ready, as promised."

"Yeah. Put us to work, boss," Bene chirped.

I led them out to the north stable block, where I pulled the double doors open and motioned around.

"We need to make the property earn its keep by renting it out for events," I explained. "You know — weddings, retreats, photo shoots..."

Bene shot Henrik a look, muttering, "Funerals..."

I ignored him the way I did when kids cracked jokes in class. "The plan is to start here, so we have a big, multipurpose space that we can start renting soon — next spring, I hope. When this is done, we'll move on to creating accommodations and developing other venues."

"We?" Roux asked, sounding a little worried.

"Not you guys," I chuckled. "We have a three-year plan."

"She means her, her sister, and her cousin," Bene filled in.

So, ha. He'd actually listened. The only gold-star student in an otherwise challenging class.

"Why aren't they here to help?" Roux asked.

"They're coming as soon as they can. Dora is finishing her master's degree, and Gen is... um, getting her affairs in order."

Affairs in every sense of the word, but I didn't elaborate.

I waved at the junk that had been heaped inside the barn over the years — everything from decades-old farm equipment to building supplies, furniture, and two beautiful old carriages.

"So, all this needs to be sorted or binned." I motioned to the dumpster I'd had trucked in the previous week.

Henrik looked affronted. "You mean to say, you expect us to perform unskilled labor?"

I nodded firmly. "Yes — unless you have relevant skills. Does anyone know anything about plumbing, for instance?"

When no one moved, Bene raised his hand. "I know how to flush."

I sighed and made a mental note. Maybe no gold star yet.

"Roux and Bene, please start there. Marius, over there, please. And Henrik..." I shot him a thin smile and pointed up. "You get the loft — or should I say, the attic?"

Bene snickered.

"I'll circulate to let you know what we're discarding and what we'll keep," I continued. "The goal is to eventually clear this central space."

That area was big enough to rig up both of the carriages at once, and the roof was highest there. Someday, it would make a hell of an event space, with stables branching out in two long wings. Right now, though, it was a hell of a mess.

Roux whistled, spotting the classic car in one corner.

"Is that what I think it is?"

I nodded. "1936 Jaguar SS100. We called it Chitty Chitty Bang Bang when we were kids."

Judging by their expressions, I'd just committed classic car blasphemy akin to calling the *Mona Lisa* a doodle.

"This is at least a decade older," Henrik sniffed, probably speaking from personal experience in that era.

"We want to use it for weddings, but we'll have to get it fixed first. Right now, it's—"

"Off-limits?" Bene guessed.

I nearly said *You bet your tawny ass it is*, but a lightbulb went off in my head.

"Yes — off-limits *except* to the person who clears the most junk today. I'll let him sit in it when we're done."

"Just sit?" Bene pouted.

With offended looks and grumbles, they set about work. But boy, did they work. Quickly. Efficiently. Effortlessly — lifting and moving items I would barely have been able to budge by myself.

Apparently, a chance to outcompete one another and sit in a classic roadster was motivation enough.

I spent a few minutes directing Bene and Roux, then moved to the corner Marius had claimed.

He held up a six-foot steel lamp with one hand. "Trash or keep?"

Three new words uttered just for me, all in a low, gravelly voice that electrified my girl parts.

"Trash," I said. "Please."

He chuckled. "That ugly?"

I nodded. "Hideous. Unless you want it for your room."

He shook his head. "Got everything I need. Or, almost."

His voice dropped an octave, and I might have suspected some kind of cryptic innuendo if he hadn't cleared his throat and whirled away.

I grabbed a box of appliances to sort through later and moved on to check in with Henrik... but having no desire to join a vampire in the shadowy attic, I returned to Roux and Bene instead. After a few minutes, I wandered to my own area and checked a pile of boxes stacked as high as my eyes.

Thomas — books and notes, the top one was labeled in my grandmother's neat print.

A lump formed in my throat, and I reached for it. It was heavy as hell, as I realized when it started to tip out of my hands.

Ugly visions flashed through my mind — visions of my dad's books lying all over the dirty floor and me crying among them, the last, precious reminders of a lost loved one. Items that deserved better than to be packed away and forgotten in a barn.

I grunted, trying to stabilize the box over my head. But I wobbled, and it did too, tipping far enough to crash.

At the last possible second, though, it floated out of my hands, and a warm, firm presence pressed against my side.

"Got it," Marius murmured.

I skittered away before the box fell on my head and patted another box at knee level. "Over here, please."

I had no idea what the box weighed, but it was a lot, though Marius swung it down with barely a grunt.

"Thank you. Thank you," I murmured again and again, running both hands over the cardboard.

It's just a box, his expression said.

Not just a box. A treasure chest.

"Thank you," I whispered again.

Well, I meant to. But our eyes met, and I went all tongue-tied. Marius, too, and for a moment, we stood quietly, trapped in time. Henrik thumping around the attic... Bene cracking a joke to Roux... Everything faded away, and all I saw was the universe in Marius's eyes. A softer, gentler universe than the dystopian view I expected to find, with a warm breeze and a peaceful landscape of vineyards and forests as seen from high, high above.

Then Roux called out, breaking the spell.

"Hey, Mina. Where do you want this table?"

I blinked, then gulped, because I'd just been brushed by moonlight. It felt like it, at least — one of those rare moments when an ancestor's gift briefly emerged, giving me a power I didn't ordinarily have — in this case, glimpsing the state of someone's soul at a given moment in time.

Or maybe my mind was just muddled by the rush of emotions my father's things had set off. Marius certainly didn't look as gobsmacked as I felt. And the scene I'd imagined was peaceful, while Marius was anything but.

So, just wacky emotions, I decided.

"Over there, please," I called to Roux. Then I nodded to Marius as casually as I could.

"Thanks," I said, more businesslike this time.

He replied as cooly as ever. *"De rien."* — literally, *it was nothing.*

I watched his back as he moved away. Was it really nothing, though?

52

Chapter Seven

MINA

By *eventually clearing this space*, I'd meant *in a few weeks*. But Roux and his crew cleared enough room in the stable to U-turn my little Citroën in, all before lunch. By the end of the day, the entire area was clear, and they'd even made a dent into the first few stalls.

Maybe even a dent in my heart.

"Good work, everyone," I said, calling it a day with a broad smile.

For the first time since the guys arrived, things were starting to look up.

"Who won?" Bene asked, indicating the roadster.

Roux looked at me just as eagerly.

I chuckled. "It's a tie. You all win today."

Bene groaned. "Just like fourth grade."

"Fifth," I sighed as he and Roux elbowed each other, rushing to get to the Jaguar first.

They took turns sitting in the driver's seat. Bene took selfies. Roux didn't actually make *vroom, vroom* sounds when he got behind the steering wheel, but he didn't look far off. Marius and Henrik showed a little more restraint, but I could see the happy sparkles in their eyes.

I would definitely be dangling the classic-car carrot in front of them on their next workday.

Too bad that was a whole week away. I worked alone for the next few days, painting, plastering, and plugging leaks.

Madame Picard arrived an hour before lunch each day and stayed until dinner, churning out meal after delicious meal.

I'd finally found extra help in the form of Claudette, a young woman who'd recently returned to Auberre. Her departure and return had both come under mysterious circumstances, making her the hush-hush talk of the town. Then again, having more than your ears pierced could fuel the rumor mill in Auberre — and rumor had it that Claudette's nose and ears weren't the only parts of her body that had been pierced. *Quel scandale!*

She wore her hair short and stylishly messy, along with extra-short shorts and tank tops that revealed enough tattoos for a crew of pirates. What she lacked in feminine curves, she made up for in heavy chains and sheer attitude.

I would have preferred not to throw such a young, nubile, flirty thing into the shark tank of my clients. But there wasn't anyone else, and Claudette was old enough to make her own decisions. Or so I hoped.

As expected, she was an instant hit with the guys, who would have stretched breakfast out into brunch if it weren't for Roux's insistence on discipline.

Thanks to him, they trudged off at eight a.m. to keep busy with their thing. Training, they called it, though it was unclear what they were training for.

I cared less and less, though, because the sight was pretty...er, impressive.

"One...two...three..." Claudette tapped her finger on the window, admiring Bene's six-pack — or, as the French so aptly put it, *tablette de chocolat.*

The obstacle course had doubled in size, and they raced around it, leaping, hopping, and climbing like Olympic athletes. They even made crawling look good.

After a round or two of the course, they would disappear into the woods for who knew what. Every once in a while, an earsplitting roar or yowl would explode and trees shook.

"Better not to ask," Madame Picard sighed as I stared out the window.

Claudette didn't seem concerned. She was human but had spent her years away from Auberre hanging with a supernatural crowd in Paris — the *wrong* supernatural crowd, according to Madame Picard. So, shifters and vampires didn't faze her.

Roux and Bene raced each other over the next circuit, and the winner — Roux, by an inch — raised an arm in triumph.

Madame Picard sighed dreamily. She, Claudette, and I didn't have a lot in common, but we were united in our mutual appreciation for *tablette de chocolat*.

Eventually, the men would move on to a few rounds of weights. Very big, very heavy weights. It was mesmerizing.

"My favorite part," Claudette breathed.

I left the kitchen, detouring unnecessarily through the dining room to grab one more peek before hurrying on to my latest task — tracing a leak in the east wing.

The next time I peeked outside, I stopped to stare. A lion leaped over the tires in a single bound, landing as agilely as — well, a cat — then bounding toward the next obstacle. Sunlight dappled over his golden pelt, and his tail flicked playfully. Pure Bene — different packaging, same *joie de vivre*.

The striped tiger went around the course with his teeth clenched, exuding intensity and sheer power. His coat shimmered as he sailed gracefully over the length of the crawling pit, and he landed soundlessly.

Marius was nowhere to be seen — but maybe that was a good thing. The man was overwhelming in human form. As a dragon, he would be downright terrifying.

Henrik leaned against the shaded barn wall, looking bored.

A split second after I located him, he turned directly toward me. I jumped back from the window, making the curtains sway, then cursed myself. Not a good look.

My heart pounded for a long time afterward. It was one thing to know that your houseguests were shifters. Quite another to see them prowling around as beasts.

And as for the vampire... I touched the wooden stake I'd taken to carrying up my sleeve.

All in all, everyone settled into a routine, and we even developed a level of trust.

Well, maybe *trust* was an overstatement.

I trusted Bene to maintain a positive attitude and not to go out of his way to kill me. But trust him with any real responsibility? Not a chance.

I trusted Roux to lead by impeccable example, whether the others followed or not.

I trusted Henrik... er, no. I didn't.

And as for Marius, well... I could count on him to scowl and be aloof, but I couldn't figure him out beyond that — or why my heart skipped when he stomped into or out of a room.

He always skulked in to meals and training sessions a minute after everyone else — but never actually late. He grumbled at any task assigned to him — then slaved away until it was perfectly done. He ignored me to the point of rudeness ninety-nine percent of the time, but I could feel his gaze on me when my back was turned.

And if our eyes happened to meet... Well, the world seemed to grind to a halt for him too. Everything narrowed to a long, dark tunnel with him lit brightly at one end and me at the other, and a warm flush would creep into my cheeks.

Inevitably, one or the other of us would tear away and pretend it had never happened. But it did happen. Again and again.

Which was terribly confusing, because he hated me, and I had no interest in surly dragon shifters.

Claudette did, however, and boy, did that grate.

To my intense satisfaction, Marius ignored her.

To my intense annoyance, the other men did not, and she lapped up their misplaced attention.

"You know they're just looking for fresh meat, right?" I dragged her aside to whisper.

She winked at Bene while chuckling to me. "Maybe I'm doing the same thing."

Madame Picard was scandalized. Especially when Claudette put her moves on Henrik.

"Careful. He's a vampire," I warned, pulling Claudette aside a second time.

"Oh, I know," she practically purred, eyeing him. "Believe me, I know."

Now I was the one who was scandalized.

"Thank goodness you hired her to help with breakfast and lunch and not dinner," Madame Picard observed.

At least there was that — the timing made it difficult for Claudette to disappear to enjoy "dessert" afterward.

But other than the jealousy — er, annoyance — Claudette stirred in me, things finally settled into a relatively peaceful routine.

Or so I thought, until the sound of shattering glass made me sprint to the drawing room one evening. What was going on?

I rushed in to find Henrik and Roux huffing, puffing, and generally going for each other's throats while Bene and Marius looked on.

"I've had it with you!" Roux growled, shoving Henrik.

Henrik shoved back. "I've had it with *you!*" His fangs extended.

I saw that as clearly as I saw Roux's facial hair thicken in a prelude to shifting. But more than anything, I saw how perilously close they were to my grandmother's china cabinet.

I stomped over to separate them, but Bene stuck out a hand. "Wouldn't get mixed up in that if I were you." He steered me — and his wineglass — to safety.

I twisted out of his grip, barking, "Stop that!" when Henrik threw a punch at Roux.

Roux ducked, and my heart leaped, because Henrik's momentum nearly carried him into the china cabinet.

"Stop it right now!" I yelled.

Henrik had his back to me, and I grabbed his shoulder.

"Watch it," Bene called from behind, though the words were lost in Marius's roar of warning.

A warning I didn't heed, because that was my grandmother's china. I'd promised her I would care for it as diligently as I cared for the château. I had to. My family's legacy depended on me now.

"I said, stop!" I cried, tugging Henrik back.

He spun and ducked just as Roux let out a vicious punch.

"Watch it!" Bene yelled.

Too late. Like a deer in headlights, I stared at the fist flying toward me in fast, then terrifyingly slow, motion. Then my head snapped back. My teeth rattled. An explosion thundered through my mind, and I was dimly aware of falling backward.

Dim was a fitting word, because darkness closed in around me. I remembered falling, falling. . . then hitting the floor.

And then, there was nothing.

Chapter Eight

MINA

Pain pulsed through my head. My skull seemed to have shrunk, squeezing my brain like a vise. My left eye screamed. Everything was blurry, and the only movement I could muster was a weak scratching motion over a rug. Was I sprawled over the carpet?

Voices erupted above me, every word a sledgehammer to my ears.

"Dammit, Roux!" someone yelled.

I winced.

"Crap." His voice wavered. "I didn't...I didn't mean to."

"Well, you did. You hit her."

"Fucking Henrik," someone else growled. "It's your fault."

"How the hell is this my fault?"

Boys, boys, I wanted to chide. *My head is already exploding. Do you have to add to the agony?*

But my lips didn't move, except to croak out a groan.

When someone stepped in briskly, I jerked an arm over my face. Would I be trampled next?

Someone leaned down, touching my forehead softly. Then he growled, and I felt two thick arms slide under me.

I tried to flail, but my arms wouldn't obey. I did not want to be touched. I did not want to be lifted.

Get away from me, I wanted to yell.

"Hang in there, Mina," I heard Bene say. Was he the one lifting me, or was he a few steps away?

Up I went, and the movement made my head swim. I groaned.

"Watch it," someone warned my valiant protector. Was that Roux? Marius?

My limp arm banged against a hard surface. The edge of the table?

"I said, watch it," someone hissed.

I can't watch anything, I wanted to yell. My eyes were too thick and heavy, and a piercing sound filled my head, like a fire alarm that rang and rang.

Put me down, I wanted to plead. *Leave me alone. Go away. Please.*

My limbs flopped around as I was lifted, and while I couldn't identify which way was up, I was way, way off-balance. My body shifted in Mystery Man's arms, and a moment later, I found myself cradled snugly against his chest.

And, oh. Just like that, the noise and pain ebbed away.

I sighed. Much better.

Inhaling his pleasant, earth-after-rain scent, I gave in to my fate.

"Fucking morons," Mystery Man growled, pacing away.

The movement was smooth and gentle, suggesting Mystery Man was one of the cats — Roux or Bene. Then again, Henrik and Marius moved with the same powerful, confident grace.

Please, please don't let it be Henrik, I prayed.

Not Henrik, I decided. I would know, because it wouldn't feel right.

Then again, nothing about this was right. Nothing but the hard, strong body I was snuggled against. I tried to count steps, but it was too much. Darkness crept over all my senses, then stole me away.

∞∞∞∞

The next time I came to, someone was fussing over me as I lay in bed. A blanket fell over my shoulders, and gentle hands tucked it into place. Close to my ear, a murmur promised I would be all right.

My pounding head said otherwise. I cracked an eye open, but everything was dark and blurry.

Mystery Man stepped away, and I whimpered, suddenly afraid. What if my brain was hemorrhaging? What if Henrik seized his chance to attack? What if—

Mystery Man wavered, then returned to my bedside. The mattress dipped behind me, and every muscle in my body tensed.

Oh God. I was incapacitated, defenseless. Totally vulnerable.

His movements were slow and cautious, his voice reassuring as he spooned behind me. All an act, I was sure. Any minute now, I would be groped, abused... maybe even raped.

But the arm he looped over my side stayed safely away from the front of my body, and his hand curled in the neutral territory of the sheets. And that was it, other than the caress of his warm, steady breaths.

So, huh. Mystery Man seemed to be more *valiant knight* than *marauding Viking*.

I exhaled and slowly relaxed into the mattress. Maybe he would protect me. Maybe I wouldn't die. Maybe he would keep Henrik away.

Maybe Mystery Man, whoever he was, had a good heart.

That, or I was truly up shit creek.

I drifted away again, falling into a fitful sleep.

∞∞∞

Sometime in the night, I sensed my valiant knight stir, then back away.

No, I nearly protested, reaching for his hand.

But it was too late. The warm, hard body that had guarded my back disappeared, and the blanket he tucked into that space was a poor substitute.

Please, don't go, I wanted to plead. But all that came out was a meek whimper.

He circled the bed, hesitated, then crouched down in front of me. I only caught a vague impression of wide shoulders before my eye slid firmly shut, like the hurt one. A hazy impression stuck, though — that of a big, burly angel backlit by pale dawn light.

Soft lips grazed my brow, and I sighed, settling back into the sheets. Maybe everything would be okay after all.

Light steps sounded, then faded away.

∞∞∞∞

The next time I opened my eye — singular — sunlight spilled around the edges of the curtains, and birds chirped. Morning, it seemed.

I rolled carefully to my back, groaning, then lay limp, taking a mental inventory. Right eye okay. Left eye gooey and thick. Every heartbeat echoed through my head, but the pounding was down to a more manageable pulse.

I felt around, tracing fabric all the way from my chest to my legs. So, whew. Mystery Man hadn't overstepped the boundaries there either.

I lay quietly for a minute or two, then rolled ever so slowly and eased my legs over the side of my bed. Sitting up made my head swim, but eventually, my limited view stabilized. Standing, I took one unsteady step, then another, toward the bathroom. There, I declared a time-out and hunched on the throne for a long, long time. Finally, I forced myself to stand and wash my hands. Only then did I look in the mirror—

—and gasped at the monster staring back at me.

I looked like I'd been in a train wreck. One eye was swollen grotesquely shut, and a bruise crept over the left side of my face.

I gulped, then forced myself to dab at my eye with cold water. Even the slightest motion hurt.

The digits on the clock beside the sink flipped, catching my attention. Cursing, I hurried to fix my hair, then rushed for the door. Seven o'clock. Breakfast. Clients waiting. Big-paying clients I couldn't afford to lose.

If I'd been thinking clearly, I would have realized how ridiculous that was. But I wasn't, so I rushed downstairs and into the kitchen, where I froze.

Bene stood over the stove, wearing one of Madame Picard's frilly aprons while cooking eggs, sunny-side up. The coffee machine percolated, and a bowl of sliced fruit stood beside the door to the dining room.

"Oh, hello. Didn't expect to see you up so soon," Bene said. He leaned in for a closer look at my eye, then winced. "Wow."

Moving quickly had made my blood pump, and now that I'd stopped, it all drained away from my head. I sank into a chair.

"I don't feel very wow."

When my head stopped spinning, I moved toward the refrigerator to set out milk and juice.

"Oh no, you don't." Bene blocked the way.

I studied him a moment too long, because he tilted his head. "What?"

I was too embarrassed to ask, *Were you the one who put me to bed and held me so sweetly?* but I did wonder.

Just then, Roux came in through the dining room door. He froze, gaping at my face.

"*Merde.* I'm sorry. I'm so sorry." His shoulders sagged, and his features fell.

"It's not so bad," I tried, fearing he might drop to his knees and beg for forgiveness.

"Liar." Bene snorted, then shooed me away. "Go sit. And you..." He pointed to Roux. "Get her some ice."

"Really, it's—" I protested, but Bene pointed with the spatula.

"My kitchen today. Out. Both of you."

I glanced around. "Wait. Where's Claudette?"

Bene shrugged. "No idea. She didn't show. Now, go sit."

My aching head got the better of me, and I obeyed. I made it to the plush chair in the corner of the dining room and sank down there. Roux kneeled by my feet.

"I'm sorry. I'm really, really sorry."

"It's fine." I tried waving him away.

"It's not, and I'm really, really sorry."

"Henrik's fault," Bene muttered, carrying in a platter of steaming eggs.

Henrik growled from beside the fireplace, startling me. "You expect me to stand there and take his punch?"

"Better you than her, asshole," Bene said cheerfully.

Henrik's scowl said he didn't agree.

My eyes drifted to Roux's hands, then Bene's, and even Henrik's, looking for a match to the pair that had held me so tenderly. But my vision had been so hazy, I couldn't be sure, except for eliminating Henrik. Other than the obvious — not a tender bone in his body — his hands were more manicured than the others', and *manicured* definitely didn't fit.

Then I snorted to myself. *None* of these guys had a tender bone in his body. I'd probably imagined the whole thing.

"I'm really sorry," Roux repeated, sounding truly miserable.

"It's fine."

Henrik pointed to my face. "That's not fine."

"Thanks," I grumbled.

"I think you look great," Bene declared as he set out plates. Then he caught my incredulous look. "Okay, maybe not. But it's what's inside that counts, right?"

Leave it to Bene to see the bright side of things.

I glanced around. "Where's Marius?"

"Yes. Where is Marius?" Bene echoed with a heavy subtext.

Everyone went quiet, and their eyes avoided mine. I looked from one to the other. Something had gone over my head. But what?

Roux shot Bene a look, then reached for the phone he'd left on the table. Henrik lunged forward, slapping a hand over it.

"Who are you calling?" the vampire demanded.

"Gordon, like I said," Roux retorted.

"No, you're not." Henrik pulled the phone away.

"Yes, I am." Roux raised his voice.

I covered my ears and leaned away. "Stop! Please. No more."

They glared at each other like a couple of gorillas, then finally stepped apart.

"Why call Gordon?" I asked.

Roux glared at Henrik. "To tell him we're leaving."

"Leaving?" I bolted upright, then slumped as a wave of nausea hit me.

"Leaving," Roux said firmly.

"Yeah, now that Catman here fucked up," Henrik snarled.

"You're the one who ducked," Roux growled back.

I stuck up a hand. "Stop. Just stop."

They turned to me with sourpuss expressions, like I'd ruined a perfectly good morning fight.

"Why would you leave?" I asked.

Roux's eyebrow shot up. "Not obvious?"

No, it wasn't. I didn't even know whether the notion made me alarmed or relieved.

"We messed up. We hurt you."

"*You* hurt her," Henrik corrected.

"You started it," Bene pointed out.

I put my face in my hands. Letting them leave definitely had its pluses. But if they left now, I would lose a sizable chunk of income — income I'd been counting on to stay afloat.

Plus, part of me liked having them around for reasons I couldn't quite explain.

I glanced at Henrik, then corrected myself. I didn't mind having three of the four around.

"You can't leave," I said.

Bene looked up from his eggs. "You're not going to turn this into a creepy Hotel California thing, are you?"

"Better not." Henrik showed his fangs.

"For once in your life, be nice," Roux snarled.

"Or is it, *for once in your death*?" Bene wondered aloud.

Henrik made a face and crossed his arms.

A pouting vampire. Now I'd seen it all.

"You can leave any time you want," I assured them. "But do you have a better option?"

Roux looked at Bene. Bene looked at Henrik. Henrik looked at the floor.

So, ha. My gut had been right about that.

"This isn't about us. It's about you," Bene said.

Henrik's grouchy expression said, *The hell it is,* but we ignored him.

"You were hurt," Bene continued. "What if it was worse? What if something else happens?"

Roux rubbed his face miserably, reliving that punch, no doubt.

"Are you saying something else will happen?" I asked, half alarmed, half in challenge.

Bene shook his head vehemently. "No. I mean, I hope not. But..."

His eyes slid to Henrik. Roux's joined his, and I added my own glare.

Silence fell and stretched for several heart-thumping moments.

Finally, Henrik relented, grumbling, "Nothing will happen." Then he motioned angrily. "Not as far as I'm concerned. But I'm speaking for myself, not for these cretins."

"Cretins?" Roux bristled.

"You're the one who punched her."

I rolled my eyes — er, eye. *Here we go again.* I lowered my pounding head back to my hands.

"Cut it out, ladies," Bene interrupted, putting a hand on my shoulder. "You're not exactly making a convincing argument."

Bene was close enough for me to whiff his scent, and it was nice and fresh, with a hint of lilac. I inhaled, trying to recall Mystery Man's scent. Did it match Bene's?

Steps sounded, and Marius stormed into the room. Even without looking, I knew it was him just by the sound and electrified sensation. He stopped abruptly, and I could feel his eyes burning into me. Then the steps resumed, moving in my direction.

"Jesus," he muttered, squatting down before me.

I covered my eyes, but his hands took mine and moved them gently aside.

When I opened my eye, my heart nearly stopped. Those hands...the gentle touch...the *earth after a summer rain shower* scent...

Mystery Man was Marius?

I gulped, staring into his eyes.

A soft glow lit them from within, and his breath caught.

I barely moved — barely breathed — as it all came back to me. The careful movements, like I might break. The soft reassurances. The *this is home* feeling I'd had snuggled up against his chest.

My heart thumped so hard, I was sure everyone could hear it.

A moment later, he spun around and stormed toward Roux.

"Wait!" I cried, an instant too late.

His fist was already flying at Roux.

Crack! Roux's head snapped back, and he staggered. Bene grabbed Marius, and Henrik, to my surprise, stood between the two combatants.

Roux straightened slowly, holding a hand over his right eye. Slowly, his fangs extended, and his eyes took on a scary yellow hue. Any second now, my dining room would be crowded by a tiger and a dragon.

"Don't even think about it," Bene warned them.

Marius rose to his full height, keeping his fists tightly balled.

Roux cursed, then sighed, and just like that, the tension broke.

"I deserved that," he grumbled.

"Yes, you did." Marius's voice was a glacier grinding over boulders.

"True," Bene agreed. "Are you even now?" He looked between them.

"We're even," Roux muttered, the model of fair play, at least in a world where fists solved problems.

But Marius wasn't so forgiving.

"I don't know. Are we?" He made a half turn, asking me while keeping his eyes pinned on Roux.

"Yes, but only if you agree to a new rule," I said.

All four looked at me, waiting.

"No fighting."

Henrik scowled. Marius looked like he'd been robbed of a prize possession, and even Roux looked skeptical.

"No fighting at all?" Bene scratched his chin dubiously.

"Is that so unreasonable?" I demanded.

"We *have* to fight occasionally," Bene insisted. "Otherwise, we'd kill each other."

The logic made zero sense to me.

"How about, no fighting indoors?" Roux suggested.

The other three nodded, suddenly united in a common cause. Men!

I relented, though a sinking feeling told me I would come to regret it.

"Fine. No fighting indoors — and nowhere near me."

"Deal," Bene announced, and they all shook on it in another *Men are from Mars, women are from Venus* moment.

I slumped back in the armchair, exhausted by it all. Exhausted and overwhelmed — especially when my weary eye met Marius's.

They swirled at me, and time slowed. Then he grumbled something, ripped his gaze away, and stormed out of the room.

Like a dust cloud kicked up by a car, my mixed emotions tumbled after him.

Destiny, a deep voice murmured in my mind.

I pretended not to hear, because that just couldn't be.

Of course, having a dragon protector could come in handy, especially with a vampire in the neighborhood. But a short-fused, intense dragon could also be a huge liability. And that didn't even begin to capture the potential complications.

Complications I felt racing toward me like a meteor shower.

Bene dusted off his hands and cheerily readjusted his apron. "Now that that's settled... Breakfast, anyone?"

Chapter Nine

MARIUS

I strode down the hall and out the rear door into the fresh air. A dozen outdoor aromas washed over me — damp grass, woodsy oaks, and the faint whiff of freshly cut hay. But Mina's rose-and-lilac scent clung stubbornly to me, pushing all that away.

Everything about her was like that — front and center in my senses, twenty-four seven — and I seesawed between hope and despair. Hope when she was close and the world seemed bright and sunny. Despair, because a bossy, stubborn woman was not entitled to mess with my heart, body, or soul.

But she did, and she had from day one.

I stomped along the outer wall of the west wing, keeping out of sight. My shirt choked me, and my skin itched as my dragon fought to emerge. Moving automatically, almost desperately, I tore off my jacket and dropped it. My shirt followed, and I barely took the time to peek around the corner of the building before kicking off my boots, stripping out of my pants, and stepping into the open.

No humans there to see me, luckily. Not with Château Nocturne situated in the middle of nowhere.

I sprinted across the lawn, the first steps quiet on bare feet. The next few were stiff, somewhere between man and beast. The final steps were scratchy as dragon claws pounded over the earth, tearing tufts of grass. Then, *whoosh!* I launched myself into the air and beat my wings.

Whoosh. Whoosh. Whoosh. Every powerful thrust created a whirlwind that spun away in my wake. I opened my mouth, letting fire blaze forth. I even released a roar, albeit a stifled one. Flying in broad daylight was already risky. Flying and roaring at the top of my lungs was even worse.

Let everyone see, my dragon side thundered. *Let them cower.*

I hurtled over the forest, pursued by a dozen twisted emotions.

For years, my soul had been buried under a heap of mistakes and regrets, and peace was an abstract term. But Mina had reached into that mess on day one, like it needed to be mended along with her crumbling château. She'd been reeling me in ever since, and holding her last night...

I'd never, ever felt so at peace.

I'd only meant to carry her to bed and let her rest alone. But I hadn't been able to resist sliding in beside her.

Just for a second, my dragon had promised.

Liar, liar.

I'd closed my eyes, but I couldn't close my nose, and soon, I was drunk on her heavenly scent. So drunk, I'd fallen asleep.

My dragon side snorted. *Real sleep. Real peace. That's not drunk. That's what normal feels like.*

How the beast could claim to recognize *normal,* I didn't know. I hadn't had a good night's sleep in years.

Which was pretty fucked up, because Mina had been hurt. But fucked up was my normal — and the number one reason I had no right to dream about her. Even if I wanted someone in my life, she wouldn't want me.

Oh, she wants, all right, my dragon side rumbled.

I huffed. Even if she did, she knew better. She deserved better too.

Leaves blurred as I skimmed over the trees, trying to outrun...what exactly?

Outrunning inner demons was futile. Outrunning what Mina did to me was downright impossible. The faster I flew, the more she stuck with me.

She's the one, something deep in my soul rumbled.

Well, I didn't want *one.* I didn't need one. I was fine on my own, keeping things simple and under control.

Sure. So under control, my dragon side scoffed. *And so wonderfully peaceful.*

The treetops formed a lumpy green carpet under a blanket of gray clouds, and soon, I spotted the spire of the town's church ahead. I'd flown over it several times since my first day here, but only at night and at a great height.

Dipping a wing, I swung into a turn to stay over the forest. Really thick, unbroken forest, except for a razor-straight line to my right. With a flick of my tail, I turned toward it, then adjusted course to fly directly over the tree-lined avenue leading to the château. The woods had been trimmed back on either side to let those century-old oaks stand out — a single line of order in a world of chaos.

Beautiful, my dragon side sighed.

The road, trees, and forest were like one of those perspective paintings where all the elements converged on one point — the château. I flapped my wings a few more times, then angled them to glide silently over the château. No need to draw Mina's attention now.

But my stupid heart thumped at the thought of it, and my dragon side preened.

Let her see. Let her admire.

The roofline of the château was broken up by windows and towers topped with spires. My heart rose a little at the sight, and a thrill went through me as I shot overhead. Then came a split second of open lawn with its cool updraft, and *whoosh!* Thick, leafy forest reclaimed the view under my wings.

Far to my right, the woods gave way to vineyards with parallel lines of grapes. But I remained over the forest and circled through that loop again — over the trees, toward the church, then along the tree alley and over the château. That time, however, I banked hard and flew over the entire length of the building.

Nice place, my dragon sighed, taking it in.

But man, did it need work. Roof tiles lay askew, gutters drooped, and paint peeled. I didn't know whether to admire Mina for trying to manage it all or laugh her off as a fool.

She's no fool, my dragon grumbled.

In terms of pure brains, definitely not. But when it came to common sense, I wasn't so sure. After all, she'd let three shifters and a vampire into her home.

I eyed the attic windows on my next flyby, cursing Henrik the whole time. A damn good thing I'd been out flying our first night here, when he'd snooped over to Mina's side of the house. Sensing something awry, I'd sprinted into a low, blasting flyover to warn him away.

My woman! my dragon had nearly roared in wrath.

I'd barely bitten the sound back, not wanting to spook Mina.

But man, had I spooked myself with that out-of-nowhere urge to protect.

I would have burned the roof off the house if Henrik had made a move toward Mina, but he'd stopped. Not solely because of my warning, however. Something else had surprised him at about the same time. One of the other guys, maybe?

My dragon growled. *If one of the other guys is after Mina, he's dead.*

I frowned at the word choice. I wasn't after Mina, and I never would be. I just had to figure out how to...to...

I struggled to fill in the blank. To get her out of my mind? My heart?

Too late, my dragon rumbled.

All that flashed through my mind in the seconds it took to fly along the château. Then I was soaring over the forest, washed by a thousand earthy scents from below. Damp, musky moss. Peaty bark. Fresh leaves, musty fungi...and something else.

My chin jerked down, because something didn't fit. I craned my neck to inspect the ground, then whirled around for another pass. The third time around, I cursed. A dragon's-eye view of the world had its advantages, but it didn't come with X-ray vision to peer through foliage. What I really needed was to inspect the area on foot.

Or get Bene to, my dragon decided. *Better yet, Roux.*

The tiger shifter might be an uptight asswad, but he wasn't bad at heart. Of course, he had punched Mina — by accident, but still. I would love to send him on a mission through the forest, and if that patch turned out to be boggy, even better.

Asshole, my dragon grumbled, though the target that time was Henrik. Mina's injury was as much his fault as Roux's.

Send him *through the bog,* my dragon grumbled.

I flew over the area several times, failing to pinpoint anything amiss. But that feeling of trouble creeping over the horizon was hard to shake.

I flew back to the château, touched down, and shifted to human form. Then I pulled on my clothes and stood by the corner of the house, staring into the forest.

"Now, wouldn't Gordon just love it if someone reported a dragon flying around in broad daylight?" Bene drawled, startling me.

I whirled to scowl back. "Good thing I don't give a damn what Gordon thinks or knows."

Bene snorted. "You give enough of a damn to be here."

I scuffed the ground, acknowledging the truth. Like Bene and the other guys, I'd made one big mistake, and the price of clearing my name was six months of working for Gordon. The guy had worked himself to the very apex of Europe's supernatural underworld, and what he said, went. If he declared the four of us forgiven, rehabilitated, or whatever other spin he used to gloss things over, we would be clear.

If he didn't, we were as good as dead.

And honestly, the thought hadn't fazed me much — until now. Until Mina.

Now, something in me yearned to live. To start fresh.

"Yes, I give enough of a damn to be here," I admitted. "Same as you."

Bene gave me that look that said some lion wisdom was about to pour forth.

I'd met a lion or two who had wisdom to share, but Bene wasn't one of them.

"Yes, same as me," he agreed. "But I figure, why make it hard on myself? Why not look on the bright side of life?"

Because life didn't have a bright side — not on the side of the tracks I was familiar with.

"The food is good, and we have space to roam," Bene went on. "The rooms aren't great, but I've had worse. And as for Mina..."

A low rumble built in my throat.

Bene grinned. "She might have a bee up her ass, but it's a pretty great ass. Also, an entire week has gone by without Gordon putting us to work. If we're lucky, he'll forget about us, and in a few months, we'll all be free."

I scoffed. "Dream on. Gordon will have something for us soon."

Silence reigned as we both considered what that *something* would be. Gordon hadn't achieved pole position by playing nice. The only use he had for guys like us was to keep his hands clean of his dirtiest deeds.

Plus, Gordon had only contracted for us to stay with Mina for three months. Where might he ship us off to when our time here was up?

"How bad do you think it will be?" Bene asked quietly.

Unbearable, my dragon lamented.

But Bene meant the missions we might be assigned.

I shrugged. "Something dangerous, for sure."

Bene flapped a hand, unimpressed. "I can do danger."

"Remember, we're expendable," I said.

"Speak for yourself, man."

I grimaced. "What I mean is, Gordon will only give us jobs he wouldn't risk his best men on."

Bene's eyes went wide in alarm. "You mean, *canary in a coal mine* type thing?"

"Yeah. Canaries in a coal mine rigged with explosives. Canaries deep behind enemy lines, outnumbered and on their own."

"What did I do to deserve this?" Bene started. Then he caught himself with a rueful shake of the head. "Okay, scratch that. I do deserve this."

I made a face. Each of us had screwed up, but none of our crimes warranted a death sentence. But, hey. Maybe we would get lucky.

Bene faked a cheery grin. "Well, maybe we'll get something to break up the monotony."

Yeah, right. He was starting to love this place as much as I did — but for different reasons, I hoped.

My claws strained under my fingernails as my dragon fought to emerge. *If Bene so much as looks at Mina the wrong way. . .*

The *great ass* comment was evidence that he already had, but I couldn't blame him for that. But if he got it in his big, blond head to get anywhere near that great ass — or any other part. . .

Touch her and you're dead, my dragon rumbled.

The message must have carried — a miracle, given the thickness of his lion skull — because Bene backed away with his palms up.

"Maybe not such a great ass after all."

My growl grew louder.

"Uh. . .I mean. . ." He backpedaled on the comment. "Just kidding. Anyway, you know me, man. All work and no play."

Ha. More like all play and no work, like most lions.

"Speaking of which, I think I hear Roux calling. . ." Bene inched away.

A lie, but it reminded me of the scent I'd caught in the woods, so I followed him inside. We found Roux going over his messages in the drawing room.

He looked up. "What?"

I jerked a thumb over my shoulder. "Round up Henrik. We need to check the woods."

"Trouble?" Roux's eyes lit in a mixture of hope and wrath.

I shrugged. "We'll see."

∞∞∞∞

Hours later, I leaned back in an armchair and sighed at the ceiling. We'd spent the entire day searching the woods with only a quick break for lunch. Now, it was just shy of dinnertime.

"Nothing, huh?" Henrik asked.

I shook my head. No. Nothing concrete, but I still couldn't shake that feeling of trouble on the horizon.

Of course, trouble was pretty much a permanent fixture on my horizon. The question was, what kind of trouble and how far — or near — it lay.

Trouble for me was more or less normal. But trouble for Mina. . .

My fingernails dug into the upholstery.

Henrik twisted his lips into a scowl. "Those cats wouldn't find a litter box if it were right in front of them."

I scowled up at the vampire. "Who's less useful — the guy who gets off his ass to search or the vampire who doesn't bother leaving his clubhouse in the first place?"

Henrik yawned, revealing his fangs. "Why bother if it's no use?"

I took a sip of whisky and went back to ignoring him. Nothing worse than a guy who didn't pull his own weight. But Roux and Bene had impressed me out there. As felines, they might not have the amazing noses of a bear or — next best thing — a wolf. But man, could they leap, climb, or slink their way into the most inaccessible places. And neither had complained the way the average dragon or vampire would.

If it weren't so muddy, this would almost be fun, Roux had even chuckled at one point. It came out in rumbly tiger-talk, but his words sounded in my mind.

Lions were fussier than tigers, and Bene had started out by daintily picking up his paws. At one point, I'd found him perched on a log, wetting a paw and patting his mane into place. But even he had been a good sport about it.

Definitely too muddy, but yes — kind of fun, he'd agreed in the end.

It had been fun — or, at least, invigorating. That sense of a hunt, of having a mission. . .

I gazed out the window. A mission was definitely a good thing. With any luck, Gordon would come up with something for us soon. Something not too suicidal, I hoped. That would also get me away from Mina and the sensations she stirred in me.

I downed another sip of whisky. Maybe that would help.

Bene entered the drawing room, freshly showered like me, but far more chipper.

"Heya." He dropped onto the couch and started lifting his feet to the coffee table. Before I could snarl in warning, he caught himself, grimaced, and put his feet back on the carpet.

"So, all that searching for nothing?" Henrik crowed.

Bene snorted and folded his arms behind his head. "Nah. It was good to be out. And now, we can rest easy that there's nothing there."

I pursed my lips. Maybe he could rest easy. I wasn't about to.

Roux joined us next, looking at his watch.

"Two minutes to go," Bene said, reading his expression.

An army marched on its stomach, and judging by the rumbling, the others were as famished as me.

Roux took the chair beside mine and looked out the window. "What do you think?"

I did my best to keep my voice casual. "Hard to say. I'll do a few more flybys tonight. Just in case."

I wasn't going to get much sleep anyway. Not with one corner of my mind fixated on Mina and another on what might be lurking out there.

"Did you tell Mina?" Henrik asked.

"Tell Mina what?" she demanded, appearing in the doorway.

I glared at Henrik, though the bastard just looked amused.

"Tell Mina about what we found in the forest," Bene said smoothly. "Biggest mushroom I've ever seen. You have some serious fungi out there."

I rolled my eyes. No way would Mina buy that.

But somehow, Bene pulled it off by chuckling. "I was going to bring it back and ask Madame Picard to bake some magic cookies for us, but I figured she might not approve."

Mina's expression said she didn't approve either, but whew. The comment had been enough to distract her.

"Should you even be up and around?" I asked, suddenly anxious. "Shouldn't you be resting? Concussions are serious, you know..."

I knew because I'd spent an hour on my phone researching it. Shifters didn't have to worry about such things, but humans did.

"I'm fine," she insisted. "Really."

"You do look better." Bene leaned closer to her in surprise. "Wait. You actually look good."

She stuck her hands on her hips. "Gee, thanks."

"No, I mean..." Bene stepped closer. "Your eye. It looks better. Much better. Wow."

I'd developed a habit of keeping my gaze glued to the floor around Mina, because anytime our eyes met, sparks flew. But now, I looked up — and did a double take.

Without thinking, I marched over and cupped her jaw, tilting her face gently to the light.

Her mouth fell open in a protest, but our eyes locked, and yep. Sparks. A whole Bastille Day's worth — plus everything we Swiss ignited on August first — along with a burst of heat that raced through my veins.

Her features mirrored her grandmother's fine porcelain, so my hand wrapped a long way around her face. And, hell. It took everything I had to fight the urge to kiss her.

"Wow. Much better." Roux was just over my shoulder, but his murmur came from miles away.

Mina's lips twitched, making my breath hitch.

Focus, I ordered myself.

Her eye was still bruised, but barely a shadow now rather than the bulging rainbow of ugly colors I'd expected. How was that possible?

Henrik leaned in and hooted. "Now I understand."

Mina's eyes cut from me to the vampire, making me hate him more than ever.

"Understand what?" Bene asked.

"She's not human." Henrik stabbed an accusing finger at Mina.

She jutted her chin defiantly. "Never said I was."

"Wait a minute. Not human?" Bene came closer, wrinkling his nose to sniff.

Mina stepped back, out of my grip.

Dragons didn't whimper, but man, did I come close.

"Do we have a problem, gentlemen?" she asked icily.

Bene stuck up his hands. "No problem. Not at all."

My head spun. If she wasn't human, what was she? I'd spent a night curled up beside her and hadn't sensed a thing. No trace of shifter, definitely not a vampire... Maybe a witch?

My gut roiled in a mixture of joy and fear.

If Mina were human, she would be marginally easier to resist. But supernaturals lived, loved, and lusted on a totally different level. If she was half as attracted to me as I was to her, the pull would be impossible to fight off — for both of us.

"Shifter? Witch? Psychic?" Henrik demanded.

I glared. He had no right talking to my woman — er, a woman — like that.

Mina turned on her heel and marched out of the room, muttering over her shoulder as she went.

"Dinner's in five minutes. Don't be late."

Chapter Ten

MINA

I piled my plate with food and exited the kitchen through the side door. Madame Picard gave me a sharp look but didn't say a word.

At least someone around here had a bit of sense.

The sound of the men filing into the dining room faded away as I spiraled up the stairs, then down the long hall to my private quarters in the east wing. I'd had enough of the men for one day. I'd had enough of Marius. Or not enough, maybe.

God, was I mixed-up.

I balanced my plate and silverware in one hand to dig out the key from my pocket. Yes, I'd taken to locking my door, just in case. Having a few other souls around beat being alone in all the potentially spooky space of the château. But since one of the other souls was a vampire — if a vampire had a soul at all — I was taking precautions.

Pushing the door open, I entered my private suite and continued out to the tiny balcony nestled beside one of the château's ornate towers. There, I sat in my bistro chair and lit a candle to dine by. Long after I'd finished eating, I sat quietly, letting my mind wander.

At first, it wandered to Marius. What was he doing? Did he hate me or like me? How did I feel about him?

Confused, I decided.

The moon was barely a sliver, and the stars were shining bright, so I did my best to gaze out and clear my mind — an effort that lasted exactly thirty seconds before Marius popped into my thoughts again. I glanced over to my bedroom. He'd carried me there and spent the night at my side. What did that mean?

He likes me! He likes me! a hopelessly juvenile part of my mind cheered.

Otherwise, he hadn't laid a hand on me. So, he was either a gentleman — an image completely at odds with his gruff exterior — or he was absolutely uninterested in me.

The glow in his eyes suggested the opposite, but it was hard to tell with dragons. From what I knew, any kind of extreme emotion could do that, from anger to hate. . . even arousal.

My pulse skipped a few beats.

An hour later, the candle had burned down to a nub, and my skin was starting to prickle with the night's chill.

Nothing like a good evening walk to clear the mind, my grandmother used to say.

We used to walk together, she and I, out to the gardens and around the lake. So I grabbed a sweater and headed downstairs. Detouring to the kitchen, I added an extra clove of garlic to the two already stuffed in my pockets, then stepped outside, wrapping my arms around my body and tilting my face toward the stars.

"Wow. Beautiful," I murmured aloud.

I wandered away from the house, remembering all the times I'd walked with my grandmother. The chirp of crickets rising from knee-high grass. . . The whisper of the wind over the forest. . . The bright, hopeful pulsing of the stars. . . It felt like nothing had changed since then or since the previous generation or even centuries past. But when I turned to gaze at the house. . .

I sighed. In my grandmother's day, the lights in every room had been lit, giving the place a grand air. She'd loved hosting old-fashioned soirées with live music, card games, and copious food and drink. Music and laughter had drifted outside, and the château exuded a positively regal air.

But electricity hadn't cost what it did now. And back then, maintaining a vibrant social circle didn't take as much effort — or maybe folks didn't consider it an effort. Back then, my family had had staff, though their number had dwindled over time.

Now, dark, empty windows gazed over the equally dark lawn, giving the building a soulless feel. I let out a long, hopeless sigh. No matter how much work I poured into the place, I would never be done. And even if I could somehow restore it all, I could never breathe life back into it. Not the way my grandmother had.

I gazed at the melancholy sight for another minute, then walked toward the tangle that had once been perfectly trimmed geometric gardens. It was more of a jungle these days, but I could still stroll the same path my grandmother used for her evening walks, and I could still enjoy the stars.

I meandered toward what had once been a magnificent fountain in the center of countless flower beds. Now it was a silent hulk, the three wedding-cake tiers empty, the hippocamp sculptures underneath dry and lifeless. I looked down at the faint reflection of the stars dotting the stagnant water in the basin.

Then I closed my eyes. If nothing else, my imagination could restore the faded glory of the château and gardens.

It worked, and I stood with a faint smile on my lips for a while, reliving better days. Then a finger of cold air touched my neck, and the crickets suddenly went quiet.

My eyes popped open, and I whirled. Was someone out there?

The hair on the back of my neck stood, and my throat went dry. When the bushes rustled, I jumped.

Then I let out a dry laugh and called, "Ha, ha. Very funny, Benedict."

I crossed my arms, bracing myself for a lion shifter to stalk into view, showing off his fangs and mane. But Bene kept up the ruse and crouched silently behind the bush.

"Could you not find another place to wander around?" I gestured toward the west wing. "Seriously. You guys have all that space, not to mention acres of forest. I'd really, really appreciate having a little time to myself."

Still nothing. A wispy cloud drifted over the moon, blotting out its dim light.

Muttering in Bene's direction, I set off, continuing my walk. The bushes behind me rustled as he followed. Stupid lion!

I continued another few steps then whirled to shout, "Enough already! I mean it, Bene. I really need some time alone."

I half expected an off-color joke about a woman like me needing exactly the opposite, though he didn't utter a word. He remained crouched just out of sight.

Well, okay. He couldn't speak in lion form, I supposed. That didn't mean he was allowed to be a jerk.

"You know, I thought you were the decent one of the bunch," I grumbled aloud. "The only one who—"

A lion appeared on the path beside me, snarling at the bushes before us.

I stared at him, then at the bushes. Oh. Oops. That hadn't been Bene trying to spook me.

I squinted into the darkness and called, "Roux?" as unlikely as that was. He didn't have Bene's juvenile sense of humor. In fact, he didn't have a sense of humor at all. So why was he hiding in the bushes?

Soft, warm fur pressed against my leg as Bene nudged closer. My heart skipped a beat, because wow. It wasn't every day you found yourself touching a full-grown lion. I inched my hand out, stroking the outermost wisps of his magnificent golden mane.

The ridge of hair along Bene's spine stood stiff. His long, tufted tail twitched, and his lips peeled back in a ferocious snarl.

I gulped, looking back at the bushes. Okay, that wasn't Roux out there. Henrik, maybe?

My hands curled into fists, and I called out again. "You know, I've really had it with—"

Bene swatted me with his tail. I blinked at him, then at the bushes. Clearly, Bene considered this serious — dead serious. He kept up that low, dangerous rumble, telling Henrik to back the hell off.

A shadow glided into my peripheral vision, and I turned to stare. It took ten long seconds to make out the outline of another feline. Thanks to his stripes, he blended into the foliage perfectly.

Roux. Like Bene, he faced the bushes and growled.

I gulped. This was definitely not good.

My mind spun, and the only conclusion I could come to was that Henrik had completely lost his marbles and was stalking me, either to scare me or to suck my blood.

"Psst. Mina," Henrik called from my right.

I whirled to find him on the overgrown path.

So, yikes. Henrik wasn't the one stalking me from the bushes either.

"Over here." He beckoned me with a terrifyingly serious expression that said, *Hurry but don't hurry, because whatever it is out there might pounce.*

Bene pressed against my legs, and the tone of his snarl changed as he communicated with me. *Back up. Slowly. Please.*

The blood drained from my cheeks as I took one unsteady step back, then another. Henrik stepped forward, passing me without so much as a second glance at my neck or any other body part. He was totally, utterly fixated on the bushes before us. Then he called out in a language I didn't recognize. Something my ear translated as, *Nahiva vol ijonni,* though I probably missed a syllable or two.

Not French, nor Italian, nor any other Romance language I knew. Not German, not Dutch.

Not that it matters, Bene's insistent backward push said.

The bushes rustled, giving the impression of someone — or something — backing away slowly.

Henrik advanced, chastising it bitterly the whole time. A moment later, he disappeared from view, and a moment after that—

Twigs snapped. Footsteps sounded. Henrik yelled.

Move it. Now! Bene growled at me urgently.

I stumbled backward. Roux slid smoothly between me and the rustling bushes, growling into the darkness where Henrik and the intruder tussled.

I said, move it, Bene ordered with another tap of his tail.

Still, I froze. Everyone was accounted for — except Marius. My heart dropped. That wasn't him out there, was it?

A deep sense of betrayal filled my gut.

"Hey! Hey!" Henrik yelled somewhere ahead.

I pictured the intruder sprinting through the bushes, toward the woods. Trying to escape.

Not Marius, my heart insisted. *He wouldn't.*

But who else would that be?

Mina... Bene's grumble hurried me along.

I took another two steps backward, then ducked when the air pressure behind me spiked.

Whoosh! A massive shape hurtled over my head.

Even Bene and Roux crouched and stared. And no wonder. I gaped at the missile-shaped body. The pair of huge, leathery wings. The long, thick tail.

"Marius," I whispered.

Then I yelped and ducked again, because he roared, shattering the tense silence. The flames he spat crackled nearly as loudly, cutting into the inky sky with long, fiery streaks.

Bene grunted something I interpreted as *Show-off* and nudged me back.

Marius flew so low to the ground, he immediately shot out of sight. Another roar shook the night, and another plume of fire illuminated the sky. Henrik reappeared from the bushes, a leaf stuck in his hair, and pointed to the house.

"Go, already! Go!"

I ran. Bene, Roux, and Henrik formed ranks around me like secret service agents. My heart pounded as I sprinted along. What was going on?

Seconds later, I shot onto the open lawn, feeling dangerously exposed yet protected at the same time. I raced across the driveway, flew up the stairs, and fumbled with the front doors. I practically fell inside, and a fleet of furred, fanged bodies tumbled in behind me. Henrik brought the doors together with a slam, and I twisted the lock, then yanked a crossbar down for good measure. Nothing short of a battering ram was going to break through those doors.

I took two steps back and stared, panting as wildly as my motley entourage.

A dozen questions whipped through my mind. Where was Marius? Was he all right? What was going on?

"What the hell was that?" I finally managed.

Bene and Roux looked at each other, then at Henrik.

He ran a hand through his hair, plucked out the leaf, and regarded it in disdain.

"You mean, *who* the hell was that," he grumbled, looking at Roux. "Hard to say. One of the usual suspects, I suppose."

My mouth hung open. *Usual?*

Then it dawned on me that the intruder might not have been here at random, and he — or she or it — might not have been here for me, but for my clients.

I bristled and stuck my hands on my hips. "You have exactly one minute to explain."

Chapter Eleven

MINA

Twenty minutes later, we were all in the drawing room — except Marius, who was still out "patrolling," as Roux put it.

I stood by the huge rear windows, studying the dark sky. Château Nocturne had never, ever needed patrolling. Not as far as I'd ever heard of, at least. But now...

I cursed Henrik under my breath, blaming him for no good reason. Well, other than being a vampire and for sneaking into the attic over my bedroom and freaking me out and keeping me on edge for the entire week he'd been here. But other than that...

I took a deep breath and reminded myself he'd just chased away an intruder — for me.

Then I frowned and glanced at him. Had that been for me... or some other reason?

That was the thing with vampires. Their allegiances constantly shifted, and it was impossible to tell whose side they were on — except their own, of course.

"Here." Roux pressed a glass into my hand.

I turned reluctantly away from the windows and absently sniffed the drink. "Thanks."

Bene was crouched by the fireplace, stacking kindling and logs. And wow, did the guy have a fantastic ass. Not that I was looking, but I couldn't *not* look, what with him crouched the way he was.

Henrik stood by the piano, staring pensively into his whisky glass. *Friend or foe?* I wondered for the hundredth time. *Friend or foe?*

Roux was — no surprise — pacing back and forth, back and forth. The man was a thundercloud, bouncing from one wall of the drawing room to the opposite side in an ever-unfolding storm.

"Perfect," Bene murmured, holding his hands toward the crackling fire.

Leave it to the sunny lion shifter to find a silver lining.

He and Roux had disappeared — one at a time, thank goodness, so as not to leave me alone with Henrik — to shift into human form and dress. Still, the scent of dew-moistened fur lingered and carried on the draft of the crackling fire.

Both felines were furious about the intruder and concerned for me. Apparently, they considered me part of their turf now. I didn't know whether to be honored or offended.

"So, who — or what — was that?" I asked, carefully maneuvering my drink as I crossed my arms.

Bene and Henrik looked at Roux, and I made a little mental note. Marius's absence seemed to give the tiger's authority a subtle boost, though I'd never seen Marius challenge Roux outright. I supposed the others recognized a top dog when they saw one, and that had the side effect of knocking Roux down a peg or two.

Poor Roux. He tried so hard to rule the roost. And he was good at it too — as long as the guys played along. Too bad discipline wasn't their strong suit.

Roux jutted his chin toward Henrik. "You got the closest. What do you think?"

Henrik scowled. "I didn't get a clear look, but my guess is it was Szabo."

The tussle in the bushes replayed in my mind, along with the sound of fleeing footsteps.

"Who is Szabo?" I demanded.

"A vampire." Henrik regarded his fingernails with distaste.

Which really didn't bode well — a vampire looked down upon by my sneaky, night crawler of a client.

"A Carpathian," he emphasized, as if that explained anything.

Roux rolled his eyes. Clearly, he'd heard this before.

"A vampire on a social call...in my garden?" I snipped.

"You call that a garden? More like a jungle," Bene chuckled.

I glared. "It's on the list."

He stuck up his hands.

"Also, I could have died," I said.

Henrik yawned. Apparently, my near-death experience hadn't been near enough for him.

"Well, it wasn't a social call," he said in a voice as dry as the decade-old roses stuck in a vase by the piano. "He was snooping around."

"Snooping around because...?" I stirred my hand impatiently.

Henrik shrugged. "Reading the mind of a Carpathian is like reading the mind of a human." He wiggled his hands in the air. "Nothing but a jumble up there, if anything at all." Then he spotted me and added a weak, "No offense."

I leveled a flat glare at him.

He stared into my eyes, then froze. "Wait. Why is it I can't read your mind?"

"Why is it that you're trying?" I shot back.

He shrugged. "Habit, I suppose."

"Well, break it," I muttered, then returned to the matter at hand. "How do you know Szabo?"

The door flew open, and Marius strode in. He'd shifted and dressed, but yikes. As far as *aura* went, that was still a dragon storming into my drawing room. A very big, very angry one.

His eyes swept over the room, then screeched to a halt on me. A wave of emotion followed, and *boom!* I grabbed the back of a chair before I stumbled.

My first instinct was anger, and maybe his too, because that's what ran on the heels of relief when you worried about someone close.

Wait. Someone close? I barely knew the man, and he barely knew me.

I let out a long, shaky breath, figuring now was not the time to examine that.

Everything is okay, I did my best to radiate cool, calm vibes. Because... Well, dragon shifter standing awfully close to my grandmother's china cabinet. And for other reasons, too, like that inexplicable ache in my heart.

Everything is all right. I pushed the unspoken words toward his mind. *I'm mad as hell, but everything is all right.*

"Did you get him?" Bene asked in a casual tone suitable for asking, *Did you get the newspaper?*

Marius turned his piercing look to the window. "No, but I swear, I will."

I wondered how many miles he'd flown — and how many acres of forest he'd torched in the process. I peeked outside and sniffed for smoke, picturing an apocalyptic landscape where my gardens had once stood. Overgrown gardens, but still.

Then I sighed. The château was probably worth more in fire insurance than it was in the flesh... if I'd made the last payment in time.

I made a mental note to check *tout de suite.*

"He took off in the direction of town," Marius growled.

"Who?" Bene, Roux, Henrik, and I all asked at the same time.

Marius shook his head bitterly. "I'm not sure. Maybe Szabo?" He shot Henrik a significant look.

Did the vampire and Szabo, whoever he was, have an ongoing feud? Had it caused trouble for this gang before?

Szabo, who? I wanted to scream.

"In any case, he went toward town," Marius concluded.

"And you didn't follow?" Roux barked.

"What, like this?" Marius held out his arms and bared his teeth, as if anyone needed a reminder of his second side. Then he hmpfed. "Sure. Great idea. I could have followed him right through town. Maybe even torched him as he ran down the street. You know, in plain view of everyone."

Bene cackled. "Not in this town, man. Everyone's in bed by nine."

True, but Marius's point still held, and I said as much.

"He did the right thing. We can't risk anyone in town reporting unusual sights."

Marius crossed his arms and shot Bene a smug look.

Bene snorted. "Like long plumes of fire in the sky?"

Marius loomed over him, sticking out his chest. The hair on Bene's chin thickened, and—

I stuck out my hands, sensing a shoving match brewing — or worse. "Oh no, you don't."

I did have the good sense not to step between them, though. That was one lesson I would never forget.

I jerked a thumb over my shoulder. "You want to fight, take it outside."

Roux sliced the air, using his hands as twin knives. "No fighting at all. We're not enemies."

Well, they sure acted like it.

"The enemy is out there," Roux emphasized, pointing outside.

A chill went down my spine. Having an intruder was creepy enough. Having an enemy was even worse.

But I didn't have enemies. Neither had my grandmother.

"Wait a minute," I growled. "Whose enemy?"

I looked from Bene to Roux, over to Henrik, and finally, at Marius.

"Whose enemy?" I demanded.

"His." They all said in unison, each pointing to someone else.

"Oh, for goodness' sake..." I muttered, throwing back a gulp of my drink.

Cognac burned my throat, making me choke.

Bene patted my back. Not all that helpful, but it was the thought that counted.

"Whoa, there. Take it easy with that stuff."

I composed myself and thanked him... then folded into another coughing fit.

Still patting me, Bene turned to the others. "Mina has a point. She's way too harmless to have enemies."

Still coughing, I formed a fist. I'd show him harmless...

But Roux was already nodding, dammit. "He's right. It has to be one of us."

To a man, they glared at Henrik, who stuck up his hands.

"Why is it always me?"

Bene shrugged. "Because you're you."

"Well, it could well have been one of your enemies." Henrik stuck a finger at Marius. "Like whatshername — Celeste."

Marius's eyes went dark, and he clenched his jaw. Clearly, those two had some kind of history.

My fists grew tighter. Celeste sounded rich. Beautiful. Seductive.

I hated her already.

"Or that colonel you pissed off." Henrik moved on to Roux.

"Corrupt colonel," the tiger grumbled.

"Or that black widow of a woman you were foolish enough to carry on with." Henrik started in on Bene.

My ears perked. It was hard picturing the good-hearted lion shifter making an enemy of anyone, except the fathers — or jealous husbands — of all the women he must have lured to his bed over the years.

Lucky girls, a dirty part of my mind sighed. Not that he was my type.

My eyes jumped to Marius, and my body heated.

A damn good thing that my phone rang just then. I'd left it on the coffee table, and the buzz made it jiggle in place.

Everyone froze, staring at it.

So did I. It was late. Who would be calling at such an hour?

I approached it slowly, imagining a hoarse voice threatening me with. . . what?

"Please don't let it be Gordon," Bene muttered as I looked at the display.

Roux's pained expression was a mirror of Bene's. Henrik's too. Marius looked downright murderous.

I frowned, then answered, keeping my eyes on the men before me.

"Hello?"

I froze at the reply, then composed myself, keeping my eyes on the men when I spoke.

"Oh hello, Gordon. How are you?"

Chapter Twelve

MINA

The room fell silent as I greeted Gordon, and everyone leaned in.

"Hello, Mina. How is everything?"

The phone wasn't on speaker, but my godfather's deep, aged-in-an-oak-barrel voice boomed through the line and carried across the room.

I shot Roux a glance and touched my eye. "Oh, just fine."

Marius growled under his breath, and the tiger bit his lip.

Henrik gave the antique clock over the hearth a pointed look, and I followed his eyes. Eleven p.m. Funny time for a social call.

"Hello?" I asked after a long pause on the other end of the line. Had we lost our connection?

"Sorry, still here," Gordon hastened to reply. "I was just..."

Surprised, his tone said.

"...distracted," was the word he chose. "And I wanted to check on, er...your guests. Everything all right there?"

I pictured Henrik creeping through the attic. Predators stalking around the obstacle course. Worst of all, that intruder — an enemy vampire — in the garden.

"Nothing out of the ordinary?" my godfather continued.

Ha. Where did I begin?

A dragon, a vampire, and two felines stared silently at me.

Then I frowned. Staring at me...why?

I swiveled away. This was my call, not theirs, dammit. My home, too. I'd had it with these guys getting mixed up in my business—

"Actually..." I started, but Bene sliced the air urgently.

I turned the other way, but that brought me right back to the others. Roux put a finger firmly over his lips.

"Um..." I stalled. Why didn't they want me to mention the intruder?

"I went for a walk in the garden tonight..." I continued.

Roux winced, and Henrik's eyes shone red. Bene wrung his hands.

I was ready to ignore all of them, but my eyes caught on Marius's, and for the first time, I wasn't catapulted away into a dream world.

Danger! Danger! his stormy eyes warned.

"Yes?" Gordon asked impatiently.

I swallowed hard, keeping my eyes on Marius.

He gave a curt shake of his head. *Don't. Please.*

"It was beautiful. All the stars..." I said.

Roux and Bene exhaled. Henrik looked slightly less murderous, while Marius gave me a nod. A teensy-tiny one that somehow made me feel ridiculously proud.

"It was so peaceful. Grandma used to take a walk every evening, and it reminded me of all the times I walked with her."

Bene gave me a thumbs-up, though I was still confused. Gordon was their boss. Wouldn't they want to inform him of the intruder?

I frowned at the thought. Not my intruder, dammit. *Theirs.* I had nothing to do with this.

Except, of course, I did, because the intruder had been lurking in *my* mess of a garden.

"The garden? At night?" Gordon practically shrieked.

I winced, holding the phone away from my ear.

Gordon was one of the steadiest, least excitable people I knew. He'd been visiting the day I'd told my grandmother I'd accepted a summer volunteer position in Senegal, and while she had flipped out, he hadn't batted an eye.

The girl has a good head on her shoulders, he'd said, perfectly calmly. *Let her go learn about the world.*

Senegal was all right, but my garden wasn't?

"My dear, the world isn't what it used to be," he cautioned.

"Gordon, this is rural France. And I have four big, tough boarders now."

Bene tapped his chest immodestly, while Roux hit a stiff, military pose that said, *Damn right, you do.*

"Boarders or no boarders, I urge you to be more cautious," Gordon said.

"On my own property?"

"A very large, very remote property," Gordon pointed out. "If anything happened there, no one would know."

Yikes. Now he was creeping me out. Large...remote...no one around to observe what was going on...

The very reason he'd chosen it as a base for his bodyguards, maybe?

"Well, I'll be more careful from now on," I said, as if I needed convincing.

"Regarding the boarders..." Gordon switched gears. "I trust they are behaving themselves?"

To a man, they all tensed.

I hesitated, letting them sweat for a few seconds, then chuckled into the phone.

"It's like I told you. Teaching fifth grade prepares you for anything."

Roux and Henrik looked affronted. Bene stifled a laugh.

Marius quirked his lips, and I grinned. Boy, would I love to see him flash a full smile.

But he wrestled it back, whispered something to Roux, and disappeared down the hallway. A mournful wolf howl went up in a corner of my soul, as it always did when he left the room.

"They've settled in," I continued, trying to concentrate on Gordon. "I think they have everything they need."

"And what about you? Do you have everything you need?"

I looked at the door Marius had exited through.

Yes? No?

"All fine," I fibbed, fiddling with the upholstery of my chair.

"Well, I'm happy to hear that," Gordon proclaimed.

Relieved was more like it. Did he have such low expectations of my boarders, or did his relief have something to do with the intruder?

Henrik made a cutthroat motion. I rolled my eyes. Only a vampire would hint at ending a call in the same way you'd hint at ending a life.

Still, I decided he was right.

"Well, thanks for checking in," I said, faking a yawn. "It's a bit late here, so..."

"Sorry to disturb you, sweetheart. You take care."

"You too. We'll talk soon," I assured him. "And thanks again. For everything."

I owed him so much. More than I could ever repay.

"It's my pleasure, sweetheart," Gordon said, sounding more like the man I knew.

"Good night," I said.

"Good night," he echoed.

I clicked off the phone and looked around.

"Well?" I finally demanded.

"Well, what?" Bene asked innocently.

I gave him a look, then shifted my gaze to Roux. "What was that all about?"

He looked at the floor in the manner of a man composing a full report. I glanced at the clock, then twirled my hand impatiently.

"The short version, please."

"Short version..." He rubbed his jaw.

"How much do you trust Gordon?" Bene filled in for him.

"Too much," Henrik grumbled, filling in for *me.*

"Says the night crawler," I muttered back.

Bene laughed. "Good one."

Henrik did not look pleased, but I was too annoyed to care.

"I trust Gordon with...everything," I said, just as Marius reappeared with a cookie tin in his hands.

"Maybe that's why Gordon chose you," he said, munching thoughtfully.

"Oh! Are those macarons?" Bene grabbed for one.

I laughed. "And here I'd been thinking comfort food was a girl thing."

Marius scowled. "Food for thought."

Ha. I bet.

I grabbed one the same color as his and made a mental note. Raspberry flavor. Marius's favorite?

Then my mind jumped back to what he had just said.

"What do you mean about why Gordon chose me?" I asked. "He's always been good to me. He stood by my family after my father died. He helped me get through college, and he even paid for Christmas flights for me to visit my grandmother here when I couldn't afford it."

"Why?" Henrik asked, clearly suspicious.

I snorted. It was sad, how some people lived with such a depressing world view.

Then again, he was a vampire.

"My father and Gordon were best friends," I explained. "I was fourteen when my dad died, and Gordon stepped in to help with a lot of things."

Bene's throat bobbed, and even Henrik's expression softened a little.

"If it weren't for him, my family would have struggled with so much more. He did me a big favor by renting the west wing for you four." I shook my head emphatically. "Gordon would never do anything to endanger me."

Marius snorted. "He sent us, didn't he?"

"Well, you haven't hurt me yet."

Bene snorted. "Other than the black eye Roux gave you..."

"It was the vampire's fault," Roux grumbled.

"Not to mention the night crawler here, sneaking through your attic," Bene pointed to Henrik, who huffed.

"Vampires do not crawl."

They did sneak, though.

"The point is, you wouldn't hurt me purposely, right?" I asked, then chilled. Maybe they would.

Never, Marius's eyes blazed.

"Of course not," Roux said. "But having us here puts you in danger."

"Wouldn't having a bunch of bodyguards here keep me safer?" I reasoned.

Roux and Henrik stared. Bene guffawed.

"Bodyguards? Is that what he told you?"

Now, that didn't bode well.

"Er...yes," I peeped.

Marius cursed under his breath. "Fucking Gordon..."

"Lady, we ain't no bodyguards," Bene quipped.

My mind spun. Not bodyguards? Then why did they train all day? Leaping over obstacles, practicing hand-to-hand combat, rappelling from the roof, working out various ways to force entry...

Then it dawned on me, and I yelped. "You're mercenaries?"

"I prefer *security contractor*," Bene said. "Mercenary sounds so..."

"Unethical? Illegal?" I supplied.

Roux and Bene looked chagrined, while Henrik and Marius showed little remorse.

"Who's unethical — us or the man who hires us?" Henrik asked.

"Both!" I blurted without thinking.

"Bingo," Bene pointed at me.

And, yikes. He meant my godfather.

"But... But..."

Bene patted my arm. "I'm sure he's a very nice guy..."

Henrik snarled, and Roux shifted uncomfortably in his seat.

"...to you, at least," Bene continued with a major qualifier.

"Why would Gordon need mercenaries?" I demanded. "He runs an import-export business—" I stopped short, then broke into a long, drawn-out, "Ohhh."

Bene handed me a macaron.

I'd never asked Gordon much about the business. All I knew was that he focused on rare cars and other luxury goods.

I winced, because *luxury goods* could encompass all sorts of things. And, huh. I'd always wondered why, for all Gordon's unwavering support, he hadn't offered me any of the internships he mentioned from time to time. He hadn't asked my sister or cousin either, though he'd supported us in every other way.

I gulped and clutched for straws. "Gordon has always been kind and generous. He wouldn't get me involved in anything bad."

Marius pointed toward the garden. "He has now."

"Strange that he chose to call at precisely this moment," Roux added quietly.

"Gordon often calls to check in!" I insisted.

"At this hour?" Roux pointed to the clock.

"No, but..." I ran out of steam there, and not even the macaron Bene pushed toward me helped.

The men looked around, daring one another to speak up.

What? I wanted to demand. What weren't they telling me?

"Here's the thing," Bene finally spoke — gently, like he was breaking bad news to a child. Something along the lines of, *the tooth fairy doesn't exist.* "Gordon sounded like he was expecting trouble. Like he was surprised you had nothing to report."

True, but why? And why had the guys been so adamant that I not divulge the truth?

"If he knew about an intruder, he would have warned me. Right?" I declared.

Bene scratched his temple. Marius looked out the window.

"He would have told me," I insisted, growing louder.

"Would he?" Roux asked gently.

I gaped. "Why *wouldn't* he?"

"That's what I'm trying to figure out," Roux admitted, reaching for another macaron.

I snatched the tin away. My macarons, my house, my godfather. I would not let these men malign any of them.

"I can't believe you suspect him of...of..." I stalled out there. "Of what?" I asked, genuinely perplexed.

No one spoke — par for the course with those four, especially when it came to touchy subjects — so I was left to puzzle it out for myself.

"You think Gordon knew the intruder was coming?" I tried.

Their expressions said no, and I threw up my hands. "Honestly. I would really appreciate a little up-front information for a change."

"Sorry. We don't do up-front information," Bene said. "Comes with the job."

Right. His *mercenary* job.

I put my face in my hands. I was harboring criminals. Murderers, for all I knew. Men who claimed my godfather had hired them and—

Then it hit me, and I jerked my head up. "You suspect Gordon of *sending* the intruder? That's ridiculous."

"Nah, but I'd bet the farm he knew someone was coming," Bene said, helpful as ever.

Henrik nodded, and Marius did too.

"I agree," Roux said, all matter-of-fact.

"An intruder sent by whom? To do what?" I demanded.

Marius crossed his arms and sent Roux a significant look. The tiger shifter nodded, and his words came in a clipped, military tone.

"That's what we'll find out. I promise you."

Chapter Thirteen

MARIUS

"So, what do you think?" Roux asked when we reconvened on the front lawn.

Bene yawned and scratched his belly. "I think it's been a long night. And, shit." He looked at the sun, now fairly high over the horizon. "A long morning, too."

"Fine. Go tuck yourself in while the rest of us figure out who nearly killed Mina last night," I snarled.

"Says the last guy on the scene. Want to know who got there first? Oh, right. That was me." Bene patted his chest.

"Because I sent you," I grumbled.

The truth was, if I hadn't been out stargazing/soul-searching/fantasizing about Mina last night, I wouldn't have picked up on the intruder at all, and Mina could be dead.

The thought chilled me to the bone.

A damn good thing something had prickled in my subconscious, setting off my inner alarms.

Not just something, my dragon reminded me. *Mina.*

That was the scary part — well, one of the scary parts. I could sense her emotions, at least the more extreme ones. Which shouldn't be possible, unless—

Destiny, my dragon hummed. *My destined ma—*

I tried cutting off the thought, but it stuck stubbornly in my mind and heart.

She's ours, my dragon insisted.

Well, that's what fate thought. But a guy like me wasn't cut out to be anyone's mate, least of all to a nice girl from a nice family — apart from the godfather, but he didn't count —

with an entire fucking château to her name. A sweet, slightly bookish schoolteacher, for chrissakes!

My dragon chuckled, sending all kinds of inappropriate images into my mind. Like her and me getting it on on a desk vigorously enough to make the apple there wobble, then tumble away. Pens, pencils, and notebooks would rattle too, and soon, she would be moaning my name in ecstasy.

We would be moaning too, my dragon assured me. *It would be that good.*

I had no doubt, because underneath that cool, collected exterior was a soul simmering with passion and desire. Passion and desire that tortured me every time I ventured too close — or too far.

"Whether it was Szabo or someone else, he wasn't after Mina," Bene reasoned.

Maybe not, but he couldn't have failed to notice the way we'd rushed to her aid.

"No, but if someone wants to get to us, he would target our weakest link — and that's Mina," Roux said, voicing my fears.

She's not weak, my dragon snarled.

No, she wasn't. The night Henrik had snuck through the attic had proven that. I had no idea what she'd done, but one moment, I could clearly sense her there, frightened in bed, and the next...

Vanished, my dragon whispered in awe.

Well, not quite, but blurred. There, but not there. I'd circled over the château countless times afterward, trying to puzzle out what she'd done.

Clearly, our hostess had a few supernatural powers of her own.

One of a kind, my dragon sighed dreamily.

Bene kicked the ground. "Let's say it wasn't Szabo. Who — or what — was it?"

"No scent. That points to a vampire," Roux observed.

Henrik grimaced but didn't protest.

"Getting this close wouldn't take any special skill." Roux motioned to the woods. "Not with zero security."

I bit back a growl. All four of us were highly trained, yet no one had been on watch last night — or any night over the past week.

Well, that had all changed now.

The morning was chilly, and the sun had just climbed into a layer of cloud. But a moment later, a brilliant beam broke through and warmed my back.

I turned, and oops. Still cloudy, but Mina marching toward us from the house made the whole world brighter.

"Watch what you say," Bene warned the others as she approached.

"Anything new?" Mina asked, coming up with a tray of steaming coffee mugs and croissants.

"God, I love France," Bene murmured, helping himself, though careful to avoid the mug printed with a painting of blue horses — Mina's favorite and strictly off-limits. "Tell Gordon I want all my future assignments here, okay?" Then he winced as Mina's expression fell. "Or maybe not," he mumbled.

I jutted my jaw. If lions had multiple brain cells, you could have fooled me. Or maybe ninety-nine percent were devoted to grooming, leaving one percent to manage everything else.

"Nothing new to report, unfortunately," Roux admitted.

Mina scoffed. "You've been out all night and most of the morning, and you haven't found anything? Either Gordon needs to fire all of you, or you're lying."

Bene sighed. "He's lying."

"No kidding." She thrust the tray into Henrik's hands and snatched her own coffee and croissant from it. Then she pointed the croissant at the garden. "Show me."

Show me implied someone else leading the way, but Mina was the one who marched us over at a pace that said she meant business.

I hid a grin and followed, taking my own coffee and pastry with me.

"Do I look like a waiter?" Henrik grumbled in our wake.

"You do now," Bene chuckled over his shoulder.

"Hey, where's Claudette?" Roux asked. "Isn't she supposed to help with breakfast?"

"Apparently, she left town," Mina muttered.

I exhaled. I'd had enough of Claudette hitting on me for a lifetime, not to mention watching her hit on the others. So, whew.

"Was it us?" Bene looked hurt.

Mina snorted. "A good guess, but in this case, probably not. Claudette has a reputation for being a little, er...spontaneous."

Leave it to Mina to find a nice way to say *unreliable*. It was easy to picture her composing understated report cards. What would mine say?

Must learn to harness his impulses... Social skills still developing...

Bene's would say, *Encouraged to develop his focus more,* and Roux's, *Strong leadership and responsibility, but recommend activities that are not directly linked to achievement.* As for Henrik, probably something like, *Should strive to interact with peers in ways that foster mutual comfort.*

Her pace brought us to the garden in no time, and she didn't let up until we approached the derelict fountain.

"So, I was about here..." She slowed, then stopped, and pointed into the bushes. "And he — or she — was over there. Have you checked that area?"

"Of course we checked," Roux groused.

Mina took another sip of coffee, placed her mug on the lip of the fountain, and charged off into the bushes.

"Feisty, isn't she?" Bene chuckled while Roux hurried after her.

"That's one word for it," Henrik grumbled, catching up at last.

I hurried after Mina and found her inspecting the ground behind the bushes.

"What about this?" She patted one trampled area. "Or this?"

Roux clearly didn't appreciate being questioned by a schoolteacher. She might know a lot about math, spelling, and social studies, but what did she know about tracking?

More than I expected, frankly, because the spots she indicated had also caught Roux's attention, and he was the best tracker among us.

"We checked those," he said. "Someone was there, but there's no scent."

"So, a vampire," Mina mused.

Roux and I traded surprised looks.

"You know more about supernaturals than I thought," he said.

"You should have seen the parties my grandmother used to throw," Mina muttered, still focused on the ground.

"Your grandmother, the...?" Roux tried.

Mina hesitated, leaving me to fill in the blank with my own guesses.

Fox shifter? She was that crafty. Wolf?

Dragon? my inner beast hummed hopefully.

"My grandmother, the socialite," Mina said, evading the heart of the question. Then she patted the ground again. "How heavy a vampire? Can you tell?"

Roux nodded. "Someone around my size."

Or my size, I nearly growled as she looked him over. Not that I was jealous or anything.

"So, probably not a woman," she concluded.

"Henrik passed through here too, so we're seeing two trails, which makes it difficult to judge," Roux said. "But, yes. Probably not a woman."

Mina followed the path of trampled vegetation. That took her — and us, in her wake — through the jumble of the garden and onto the north lawn.

"Any indication that he came from the road?" She looked toward the long, tree-lined driveway.

"No. He came and went through the forest," Roux said decisively. We'd all combed the area carefully and reached the same conclusion.

"So, he probably came alone," Mina mused. "No accomplice dropping him off, for example."

"That's what it looks like, Sherlock," Roux snipped.

Mina shot him a sharp look, and he stuck up his hands.

"Sorry. It's been a long night."

"And I appreciate you staying out so long to gather information," she said evenly. "But I'd appreciate you even more for *sharing* that information."

He nodded wearily and led her toward the forest, pointing along the way.

"His in- and outbound trails overlap. Traces here, here, and here, but no scent anywhere."

The bushes behind us rustled, and Mina whirled, raising her fists.

"Sorry, just us," Bene said, emerging with Henrik.

Mina lowered her hands slowly. So, being here did put her on edge, but that hadn't stopped her from coming to see for herself.

I doubt anything can stop this woman, Roux sighed into my mind, having caught my thoughts.

A good reminder for me to keep up a mental barrier.

So I don't find out you have the hots for the teacher? he goaded.

I do not have the hots for her! I snarled into his mind so fiercely, he took a step back.

Sure. Right. No feelings whatsoever, he muttered.

None, I told myself. Nothing I wouldn't soon rid myself of. . . somehow.

"This way?" Mina asked, oblivious to our silent communication.

Roux nodded and took the lead, indicating the trail we'd followed a dozen times in the past few hours.

"He came from that angle, but he fled, well. . ."

"Let me guess," Mina deadpanned, staring down a hundred-meter strip of charred forest. "He fled that way."

Everyone stood quietly for a good minute, taking in scorched skeletons of trees and clumps of smoldering vegetation.

I fidgeted.

"Did he, um. . ." Mina waved at the far side of the burned patch.

"Continue out the other side?" Roux said somewhat diplomatically. "Yes. We picked up his trail there."

Bene clapped my shoulder on his way past. "That's okay, man. Anyone could have missed a target that big."

My growl chased both felines and Henrik to a safe distance. That left me alone with Mina, overlooking the gash I'd burned through her forest.

She picked up a charred twig, inspected it, then waved to the torched strip.

"Not that I'm not grateful," she said, picking her words carefully. "But could you maybe next time..."

I raised an eyebrow. "Let you die?"

"Maybe just ask questions first, fire away later."

I crossed my arms. "You don't *ask* a guy who's lurking around your property. You *demand*."

Mina pursed her lips and turned toward Bene, who was picking through the ashes.

"Any evidence?" she called out.

He laughed. "Evidence? It's all incinerated." He gave me a thumbs-up. "Great job, big guy."

I rumbled in warning, then snapped my head left, toward the road.

Everyone tensed, picking up on the same thing.

"Incoming vehicle," Bene warned.

Mina bit her lip, and I touched her shoulder. I only meant to reassure her. But, *zing!* Even that minor contact sent fireworks through my veins.

Mina looked up at me through wide, shocked eyes, telling me she felt it too. And not just the fireworks, but also the wild hopes and fantasies.

My chest filled with a warm, heavy sensation, and the world around me blurred like it did when I flew and got in the zone. Especially here, around Château Nocturne, with its peaceful landscape of fields, vineyards, and forests.

Fields, forests, and Mina, my dragon whispered.

"Police car," Roux muttered.

His voice seemed miles away, but it was enough to tear us out of the moment. *Really* tear, like a wave ripping two shipwreck survivors apart, each to their own fate.

Or shared fate, my dragon murmured.

"All right, everyone." Mina hurried ahead. "Let me handle this."

We followed as she took a shortcut back to the house. The police car reached the main door before we did, and an officer emerged from the vehicle.

Just one, Henrik murmured into our minds. *We can easily take him down.*

We can, but we won't. Not unless I signal, you got that? Roux barked sternly.

Mina had the legs of a gazelle — hard not to notice — and loped right over. No surprise there. But the way she greeted him — well, that caught me off guard.

"Clem!" Her voice rose in glee.

When the policeman turned around, he lit up like a Christmas tree. "Mina!"

I froze as they practically threw their arms around each other. They stopped at the last minute, though, gripping each other's forearms and flashing goofy smiles.

Uh-oh, Bene murmured into the others' minds, loud enough for me to catch it. *Mina has a guy.*

A young, buff, blond cop. The kind too good to be true, like a Chippendales stripper.

Mina does not have a guy. She couldn't, my roiling gut decided.

And if she does, we'll kill him, my dragon chimed in.

The cop leaned in and traded kisses with Mina. And not just harmless air kisses. The bastard made full contact with her cheeks each time.

A snarl built in my chest even before the wind carried his scent to me.

Wolf shifter, my dragon grumbled.

A secondary scent clung to the first, and I nearly snarled. The scent of desire.

He wanted Mina. Bad.

Bene grabbed my arm before I could charge over and roast that ass alive.

"Nice of you to stop by," Mina said, all sweet and shiny-eyed. Not at all the way she treated us.

Yeah, well, the cop probably didn't torch her forest, sneak around her attic, or punch her, Bene whispered into my mind.

That was an accident, dammit! Roux grunted.

I slammed a wall over my thoughts and focused on that jerk of an officer, who looked like he ought to be starring in *Baywatch* instead of policing a tiny town in the French countryside.

Yeah, well, he'll be starring in his own mystery soon, my dragon growled.

I pictured him lying in a pool of blood somewhere behind a barn. Better yet, a haystack.

"Unfortunately, I'm here on business." When he looked up, his expression changed instantly, regarding us like inmates and not law-abiding citizens.

Okay, maybe *law-abiding* was pushing it, but still.

"You have guests, I see," he growled, not at all pleased.

"Clients," Mina hurried to tell him.

The word stabbed at my heart. I didn't want to be a client. I wanted to be more.

"Clients?"

Mina nodded firmly. "Clients. Can I invite you in for a drink?"

He shook his head. "No time, sadly. I'm here in response to reports of a fire."

"Fire?" Mina pasted on a fake smile.

Boy, was she a bad liar. Good thing Mr. Law and Order was more focused on glaring at us.

Bene's fingers dug into my shoulder as he tugged me aside. I resisted, then realized moving upwind wasn't such a bad idea. Especially as a dragon shifter at the scene of suspected arson.

"Yes, a fire. In the woods. You didn't notice?" the officer asked.

"Oh. *That* fire." She gulped, then played it down. "I did. My clients were kind enough to go out and check it."

"They did, did they?" Officer Baywatch grumbled.

Roux nodded. "I'm no expert, but it looked like a lightning strike to me. The fire was already out when we got there."

"Lightning, huh?" The policeman eyed him suspiciously.

A good thing Roux, unlike Mina, could lie through his teeth like the rest of us. And that he stood upwind, hiding his scent from the wolf's.

"Like I said, I'm no expert..." Roux shrugged.

"And what do you do, Mr...?"

"Anand. I'm a logistics contractor," he supplied smoothly.

The police officer looked around skeptically. "Logistics. Moving goods in and out of Auberre?"

I nearly laughed out loud. Auberre was so small, and its population so old, that there wasn't much movement of *any* kind in town.

Roux flashed a friendly smile. "Not here, no. We're here for a retreat. You know — working to anticipate trends in a rapidly changing global network, et cetera, et cetera."

He managed to hit exactly the right tone to sell our cover story — a story that Gordon, that conniving bastard, had come up with.

The line he'd had me memorize was, *We move high-value goods through risky areas*, and I'd practiced it dozens of times. Now, more than ever, it didn't sit well with me.

"A retreat. I see," Baywatch murmured, looking over the rest of us.

Speaking of which... Bene whispered, nudging me backward.

"And this fire was — where exactly?" Officer Baywatch demanded.

Mina pointed. "Over there. Would you like to see?"

"Yes, please."

My dragon nearly burst out of my skin when he and Mina stepped toward the forest.

"Oh no, you don't," Bene murmured, clamping down over my arm when I moved to follow them.

Roux cut in, hissing at Bene. "I'll go. Take him inside before he torches another few acres." Then he strode after

Mina and the cop, slipping his hands into his pockets in a way no self-respecting mercenary ever would. Which was the point, I supposed.

"Come along, Romeo." Bene shoved me toward the front door. "Let's get you some breakfast."

"Not hungry," I growled.

"Well then, let's get me some breakfast. We'll find some meat for you to tenderize or something."

"Heathens," Henrik sighed, bringing up the rear.

"Says the one who sucks blood," Bene muttered.

I went inside because I had no choice. But I stayed glued to the front window for the eternity that dragged by before Mina reappeared from the woods. She smiled and shook hands with the cop — the shithead. No kisses this time, though the guy definitely wasn't happy with that.

At least that gave me a glimmer of hope about Mina.

Then I caught myself. I didn't want hope. I didn't want her. In fact, it made perfect sense for her to hook up with him. A teacher and a policeman. She could work in the local school. He could keep this sleepy little town safe from guys like me. They could have two-point-three children and live happily ever after.

It made sense, but I just couldn't stomach it.

The cop glanced at Roux, then pulled Mina aside and whispered. She whispered back while Roux casually admired the roofline of the château.

Finally, Mina nodded, though neither she nor the cop looked satisfied. He gave the château one last, suspicious look-over before sliding into his patrol car — a pathetic, boxy Citroën that was more *Mr. Mom* than *Miami Vice*, I noticed with some satisfaction. Then he drove off slowly, considerate enough not to leave tire marks in Mina's gravel driveway.

Goody-Fucking-Two-Shoes. I scowled.

Roux waved, keeping his distance, but the cop only had eyes for Mina.

Finally, he disappeared down the tree-lined driveway. Good riddance.

When I get my claws on that bastard. . . my dragon snarled.

"Get your claws on this instead." Bene pressed a plate of bacon into my hands.

I ignored him, watching Mina. She crossed her arms and gazed down the driveway for a long time. Longingly? Hopefully? Or was she, like me, happy to see him leave?

Chapter Fourteen

MINA

I stood in the driveway for a long time, replaying what Clement had said.

Look, I don't like this.

Ha. That made two of us.

Any of this, I mean, he'd said, waving to the house. *Those men. At least one of them is a shifter. Maybe the others too.*

Yes, I knew that. And I knew it was iffy. But, honestly. Did he think I needed him to point out the obvious?

He meant well, but it grated somehow.

And damn, Mina. What are you doing, keeping a vampire in the house?

Keeping him, like a pet? Not exactly.

I'd explained about needing the money — desperately — but Clem had just shaken his head.

Nothing is worth keeping a vampire around. Nothing.

In principle, I agreed. But principles wouldn't feed me, and they sure wouldn't fix the roof.

I'll come by again, Clem swore. *Often.*

To him, it was probably a gallant gesture. To me, it was a giant red flag. I was not a damsel in need of rescuing. I was a damsel harboring four mercenaries, and the less my police officer friend knew about them, the better.

You will not, I'd insisted a little too quickly. He eyed me suspiciously, and I rushed to cover up my slip. *These are my clients — paying clients — and I cannot afford for them to feel harassed.*

Poor Clement had looked up at me with an expression that asked, *What happened to you? When did you change?*

Funny, I was tempted to ask him the same thing.

Then I caught myself. It was sweet of him to look out for me, and my fault for being too stressed to appreciate his concern. And, really, in a few weeks — okay, months — my clients would be on their way, and Clem and I could pick up where we'd left off. We could spend more time together — non-judgmental time — and enjoy a wholesome, friends-to-lovers, small-town romance. We could settle down. Have kids. Enjoy long summer walks and quiet winter evenings...

I did my best to keep the list going, but it petered out quickly. So quickly, I found myself wondering. Did I not want those things any more?

A moment of intense introspection told me I absolutely did. Yes to settling down with a good man. Yes to kids. The whole nine yards.

So, what was my problem?

I glanced toward the house, and my heart thumped, telling me exactly what — or who — the problem was.

Which was ridiculous. Clem was perfect for me, while Marius practically had *regrettable mistake* tattooed into the underside of his wings — a message I was sure to see the day he broke my heart and flew out of my life, if I was foolish enough to let him in in the first place.

So, no. Marius was an infatuation. An addiction. It was only his dragon aura that drew me in.

Clem was a good citizen. A safe bet. A sweet, reliable man.

Or so I tried telling myself. I could conjure all the right words, but not the sentiment.

I gazed down the empty driveway for a long, quiet minute, then headed inside. I had business to attend to, and a real-life intruder to track down. Now was not the time for such foolishness.

I stepped inside the grand entrance hall and headed toward the kitchen, hearing the guys there. But my steps slowed, and I stopped, searching for an excuse to avoid him — er, them. I hadn't gotten a wink of sleep last night, and the morning hadn't been a big improvement. Didn't I deserve a little mental break?

A good plan, except for one thing. Marius stepped out of the kitchen, spotting me. He froze, taking up most of the doorway, casting a long shadow into the hall.

My eyes met his, and *zing!* There it was again. That fire. That live current zipping through my veins.

My heart warmed, because his eyes held joy, hope, and desire. My head urged me to run, because, well...joy, hope, and desire.

Running won.

I spun around and hurried to the spiral staircase, not ready to face him. Footsteps followed. Big, heavy, dragon-shifter-size steps that quickly caught up with me.

I stopped and glared, though he got the first word in.

"Where are you going?"

I stuck my hands on my hips, grateful that the stairs allowed me to look down at him.

"I need a minute," I said.

"Now? We need to talk."

We, as in him and me, or *we,* as in all of us?

"We can talk later." I turned and stormed up another few stairs.

Again, he clomped after me. Again, I spun, practically shouting this time. "What is it with you?"

He blinked. "What is it with *you*?"

I made a show of scratching my chin. "Let me see. Oh, yes. I was stalked last night. I didn't get a wink of sleep. Then Clement shows up..."

"He is an ass," Marius muttered in agreement, though I'd said no such thing.

"He is not an ass. He was just checking on me."

Marius snorted. "Oh, he was *checking* you, all right."

I huffed. "Even if he did, what's it to you?"

Marius crossed his arms firmly. "Nothing."

Ha. Nothing, my ass. The hair around his jaw bristled, and a squall whirled in his eyes.

I stared, then blurted in surprise. "You don't like another man looking at me?"

He scowled and stuck his hands in his pockets. "No, I don't. He wants you, you know."

Yes, I did. And I was flattered to have a man like Clem interested in me. Flattered and, frankly, a little thrilled. But the thrill had faded quickly, and I'd found myself craving more distance from him.

But back to Marius, dammit.

"And this is your business because...?" I demanded.

He clicked his jaw, and I knew I had him. It was none of his business.

"Marius?" Bene called from downstairs.

We both froze as if caught in a secret act — which this was absolutely, positively not. Then Marius hustled me up another few steps, safely out of sight. I complied, feeling like an accomplice to a crime I didn't commit. A willing accomplice, because something shifted in me as we went.

I stopped, as did Marius — a scant step below me, putting him awfully close.

Nice and close, something inside me purred.

He glanced down, and we both held our breaths, avoiding detection.

Which made no sense. What was I hiding, and who was I hiding it from?

Myself, I quickly realized. I was trying to hide that I liked — no, loved — having Marius close. That my heart revved and butterflies fluttered through my soul.

"Seriously," I whispered, desperate to know. "What's it to you?"

His glowing eyes said, *You are everything to me.*

I shook my head, confused. "You don't even like me. You hate me."

Didn't he?

He stared. "I don't hate you, Mina."

"You do. You avoid me. You barely notice me. Every time I speak, you look away."

His lips parted, but he didn't utter a word.

I rushed to fill the awkward silence. "Look. I'm a grown woman. If I want to get involved with someone, I'll get involved. My decision."

"Involved?" he growled.

I nodded crisply. "Involved. My choice. Who I want. Who I touch. Who I kiss..."

And oops. My voice had slipped from indignant to sultry in the space of a few words. Where had that come from?

You have a lot more of your ancestors in you than you think, my dear, my grandmother used to say.

I gulped. Like the hot-blooded, lusting animal part?

"Kiss? That asshole?" Marius growled.

"You prefer that I kiss you?"

And, double oops. Where the hell had that come from?

From instincts I didn't know I had and that I'd somehow unleashed, apparently, because I found myself inching closer to him.

"I could kiss you, you know. I'm capable of deciding that too."

"I bet you are," he murmured.

Was he mocking me? Daring me? I couldn't tell. But his lips were temptingly close.

I didn't actually say, *You doubt me? Well, how about this?* But I might as well have, because a second later, my lips landed on his.

A little gasp rose in my throat, but it faded into a sigh, and I lost myself in that kiss. *Literally* lost myself, like I'd stumbled through a mirror or a magical wardrobe into a whole new world. A world ruled by touch, where sight, sound, and smell all stood by on mute.

His lips were pillow-soft and perfectly shaped. So perfectly, our lips rocked together with no effort at all. They rocked so well that I began to explore up...down...left...right... A good thing for the stubble around his mouth, which acted as a guardrail. Every time I grazed it, I bounced back to the centerline of the kiss.

But I did need to breathe at some point, and when I did, I dragged my cheek against his. Such poor, neglected stubble. Why should his lips get all the fun?

Apparently, there was a little-known nerve that connected one's cheeks to their core, because every long, lusty scrape made me want more. I dove back into the kiss, exploring deeper that time.

Then a delayed alarm flashed in my mind, and I drew away with a gasp.

"Oh God. Sorry." My hands flew to my face.

Marius blinked, still lost in that other world. "Sorry?"

"I didn't ask. I just…just…"

Attacked your lips fit best, but I couldn't bring myself to say it.

He frowned. "Ask what?"

"If it was okay with you. You know, if you wanted it. I mean, um…"

"So, ask," he growled.

I fluttered my hands. "No, it's okay. I mean—"

He caught my hands. "Go ahead. Ask," he ordered, all gruff.

I hemmed and hawed before my primal side won out.

"Would you be all right with me kissing yo—"

"Yes," he blurted.

And, *boom!* My lips slammed over his, and off we went to Narnia again.

Thick, muscled arms wound around my shoulders, reeling me in. My chest pressed against his. My lips opened, inviting him in.

In the haze of my mind, I sensed him easing from the lower step to mine, boxing me in. Bit by bit, he pressed my body against the cool stone wall, though I barely noticed, thanks to the flames racing through my veins. He slid a hand around my waist, anchoring me securely in place. A good thing too, now that I had a hurricane roaring through my ears.

Marius swiped his lips against mine, gently tugged my lower lip, then scraped his coarse cheek over my skin. All hard, then all soft, venturing close to the edge of *too much* but still not enough.

Will never, ever get enough, the back of my mind cried.

Ding-ding! A sound rattled through the stairwell, and we snapped apart. Only an inch, but it felt like a chasm after being so close. I gasped for air, trying to place the sound.

Ding-ding!

I slumped. The bell. The goddamn servants' bell.

"Bene..." Marius growled.

I knew I would regret showing the lion shifter how that system worked.

"You did mention a meeting," I sighed.

"It can wait," he said, smoothing my hair back, then puckering up.

I chuckled. "What is that for?"

"Giving you permission to kiss me again."

"So, you really don't hate me, huh?"

He shook his head. "Of course I don't hate you. I only hate that I can't stop thinking about you. That I can't stop wanting you."

My mouth hung open.

He stroked my cheek gently. "So, about that kiss..."

"Well, if you insist..."

I meant to press slowly into another kiss, but it got away from me, and soon, we were panting...touching...needing...

We were playing with fire, and I knew it. But that was the thing about fire. Once you got a blaze going, it took on a life of its own.

When Marius slid a hand down my leg, I raised it eagerly. When I slid my hands down his ass, he surged forward. I started calculating the distance to my bedroom.

But the bell rang again, more insistently this time.

"Dammit..." Marius growled.

I forced my foot back to the floor and caressed his cheek.

"We should go," I said, though I didn't budge.

He arched an eyebrow. "In a rush?"

"No, but the longer I stand here, the more I want to kiss you."

He snorted. "The longer I stand here, I more I *need* to kiss you."

A chorus of angels hit high notes in my soul. The big, bad dragon shifter needed me. Me!

Somehow, I kept myself together and played coy. "Would that be so bad?"

He shook his head. "It would be too good."

And damn the man for saying all the right things. I half hoped he would be too rough, too demanding, or plagued by bad breath. Then I could stop lusting after him all day and get on with my life.

The bell rang again, and I cursed. Then I sucked in a deep breath, patted his chest — a big, broad chest, like a platter, if platters came in solid steel — and eased up one step.

Marius closed his eyes. His nostrils flared, savoring my scent. Then he loosened his grip, slowly pulling his hands away from my waist.

I missed his warmth immediately, but my senses were gradually emerging from their fog, and I knew we'd gone too far.

Not far enough, my libido grumbled.

I ran my hands over my hair, then my rumpled clothes.

"You need to...um..." I motioned to his shirt.

He arched an eyebrow. "Hide the evidence?"

I gave him a look, then straightened his shirt myself, sneaking in a few last touches.

"So...um..." I started, then stopped. "Maybe we shouldn't read too much into this."

A lie, because my heart was already racing away with deep analyses and plans.

His lips curled in a cocky grin. "You mean, you pawing me?"

I rolled my eyes. "I did not *paw* you."

"You did."

"I did not!"

"You did. Without permission, even." His eyes sparkled.

"Ha. Don't tell me you feel violated."

Not violated enough, his glowing eyes said.

"You owe me now," he decided.

"I do not!"

He grinned, like baiting me was oh-so fun. A small but beautiful *life is good* smile. A smile I wanted a million more of.

A lifetime, something in me whispered.

"Well, I apologize," I offered, not all too sincerely. "I got a little carried away..."

A little? his dancing eyes said.

"But as I said, no need to read into this too much."

Wouldn't dream of it, his cocky, bad-boy grin said.

I went on quickly. "Oh, and thank you for your help last night."

He waited, locking his arms across his chest like a pair of thick swords.

I caved in. "And that night I was hurt. I'm grateful for your help then too."

Taking care of me was more like it, but that made me sound weak.

I gulped, then touched his arm. "That was you, wasn't it?"

His eyes hit the floor. "Maybe."

Definitely.

"I know it was you, and it was very...touching."

"Touching?" he grumbled, not at all pleased.

I hid a grin. "I promise I won't tell anyone you have a soft side."

"No soft side here, lady." He smacked his own torso.

Ha. Like I hadn't noticed.

I shook my head and touched his chest, near his heart. "I meant here."

He caught my hand to steer it away, but stopped, wrapping his fingers around mine. The glow in his eyes rekindled, and the haze of that other world started creeping in again.

Ding! Ding! The bell rang again.

With a sigh, I motioned down the stairs.

"Come on. We have a vampire to catch."

Chapter Fifteen

MARIUS

I was going to kill Bene — if I could resist the burning urge
to drag Mina back into the stairwell and kiss her senseless. It
was more like her kissing me senseless, though. And in case I
needed any proof of that...I wobbled along, following her on
unsteady feet.

We found Bene at the stovetop in the kitchen, frying away.
Onion peels and a messy carton of cracked eggshells sat on the
counter beside him, and the smell of that with bacon was so
good, I reconsidered my plan of killing him.

Breakfast won. Besides, I could always kill him later.

Not noticing us, he turned and reached for the bell. Mina
flew into a leap worthy of a World Cup goalie and slapped her
hand over it.

"About the bell..."

Bene grinned. "It's very practical."

Mina put on a stern, teacher look. "Practical *and* off-limits
to anyone except Madame Picard and me."

"But Roux said to call a meeting," Bene protested.

Mina shooed him back to the stove, composed herself, and
pulled the cord with an authoritative look that said, *This is
the* right *way to do it.*

Like there's a difference, Bene's eye roll said. He gave the
food another stir, then gestured. "So, what did he want?"

Mina's eyes flew to me, then hit the floor.

"That cop, I mean," Bene clarified.

Every tense muscle in her body relaxed, and I nearly chuckled. She thought Bene meant what I wanted?

My eyes burned, a sure indication that they were glowing with desire.

You, Mina. I want you. And you want me too, don't you?

I didn't voice those thoughts, but she must have gotten the gist, because her cheeks turned crimson. A look I loved, except, oops — Henrik did too. His head snapped around, and his pupils dilated.

I stepped between them, sending him a mental warning.

Don't even think about it, asshole.

Henrik licked his lips. *Think about what?*

Fire burned my throat, and who knew what might have happened if Roux hadn't sliced the air between us.

"Don't even start, you two," he warned.

Luckily, Mina hadn't noticed, more focused on Bene.

"Did the cop buy the story about lightning?" he asked.

"I doubt it. He figured out what you are."

Roux whipped around. "What do you mean?"

"He knows there's at least one shifter and a vampire among my clients."

"Do you know what *he* is?" Roux asked carefully.

Mina huffed. "Of course. A wolf shifter. I've known Clement since I was a kid."

There was knowing, and there was *knowing*. Which applied to Mina and that policeman?

Either way, I wanted to kill him. Too bad civilized dragons didn't do such things.

My beast side rumbled. *Civilized? Since when?*

Since Mina. At least, I was trying.

"And you are...what exactly?" Bene tried, oh-so casually.

Roux, Henrik, and I leaned in. That was the million-dollar question. What powers did my destined mate — er, Gordon's goddaughter — have, if any?

"Your host," she snipped, handing him a pepper shaker.

Which only made the mystery that much more irresistible, like the rest of her.

Bene grinned, letting it go. "Well, hopefully the cop doesn't make any trouble for us."

"Simple solution if he does." Henrik let the points of his fangs extend.

And boy, did Mina jump all over that one. She whirled and stuck a finger in Henrik's face.

"Don't you dare," she growled. "Don't you dare touch him."

And, fuck. That wasn't just out of principle. She cared about the guy. What did that mean for me? For us?

There is no us, I tried telling myself.

No, but there will be, my dragon hummed confidently.

Mina went on fiercely. "If there's trouble around here, Clement is not the one causing it. You guys are — whether or not you intend it."

"You mean, like that punch Roux caught you with?" Henrik reminded the tiger shifter.

Roux bared his teeth.

"All right, everyone. Give the cook a little elbow room, please." Bene brandished the spatula.

"You're the one who rang the bell," I grumbled.

"Yes. About that..." Mina started.

"Oh, look," Bene cut in, dodging the subject. "Brunch is ready. Everyone grab a plate and meet me in the dining room."

You had to give it to the lion shifter. He knew how to clear a room quickly.

Twenty minutes later, we were scraping our plates clean and leaning back in our chairs.

"You should fire Claudette and hire Bene," I half joked.

Mina grimaced. "I might have to, now that she's left town."

Pity, Henrik's frown said.

Mina sighed, then flapped a hand. "More importantly...the intruder."

"Fucking Szabo..." I muttered.

"Are you sure it's him?" she asked.

I looked at Roux. He liked to pretend he was in charge here, right? Let him handle the tricky stuff.

"No, but he's our most likely suspect," he admitted.

"Because...?" Mina rolled her hand impatiently.

"Because he hates us?" Bene offered, then held up the coffeepot. "Seconds, anyone?"

Mina, Roux, and I held out our mugs.

"Now, as hard as it is to imagine anyone hating any of you..." Mina let her gaze sink into Henrik. "What if that's the case? Who could possibly hate you? And why?"

Bene chuckled into his coffee. "Very diplomatic."

"I try," she mumbled.

"Szabo is a vampire," Roux started. "He was slated to... er, work for Gordon, like the rest of us."

Mina pursed her lips and looked at Bene. "Translation, please."

"We all fucked up. Gordon offered a way to clear our records."

"Records that say...?" Mina asked, alarmed.

"Um... Embezzlement, unauthorized conversion, attempted murder..." Roux's eyes jumped from Bene to Henrik and me as he spoke.

I glared. "The guy owed me money."

Not the whole truth, but part of me wanted to test Mina. To see if she could really accept me in spite of my past.

Her jaw dropped.

"Don't forget insubordination," Henrik growled at Roux.

"Random examples," Bene said with a winning smile.

"I bet," Mina said dryly.

"Being accused of a crime doesn't mean you committed it," Roux muttered.

"True — or the 'victim' might be the real criminal," Bene added. "Like Marius's guy."

"Not *my* guy," I growled.

Bene chuckled. "I mean the guy Marius nearly killed. He ran an illegal fight ring and shanghaied people off the streets whenever he needed 'extras.' Picture the Roman Colosseum at its bloodiest, if not as big. Am I right, Marius?"

I clenched my jaw and gave a curt nod. So much for testing Mina.

"He also ran a sex trafficking ring. Our man here put an end to that too." Bene patted me on the back.

I showed him my teeth. *Too much information, asshole.*

You want her to think you're a lowlife? Bene spoke into my mind.

No, I wanted to keep her expectations realistic. I was no saint, and she needed to be clear about that.

"Too bad the guy's cronies stepped in before Marius killed him," Bene finished.

Truly too bad, because I'd made a dangerous enemy. Gordon had promised to deal with him, but I wasn't holding my breath on that.

"As for Roux's court-martial..." Bene went on.

"For asking questions when no one else would," Roux snarled, revealing a raw wound.

"Questions like...?" Mina ventured quietly.

"Like, why describe *civilian casualties* as *collateral damage*?" he rumbled. "Questions like, how much is acceptable, and who is qualified to make that call?"

Ah, Roux. A man too principled for his own good.

"Then there's Henrik and his unauthorized conversion..." Bene went on.

Mina paled. "You mean, changing someone into a vampire?"

Henrik shrugged. "She begged me to."

"Too bad the coven didn't see it that way," Bene observed.

"Says the convicted embezzler," Henrik snarled, like that crime was on par with his.

Bene scowled. "Yeah, if embezzling means sleeping with a mob boss's daughter." He looked at Mina and quickly added, "Not like she was underage or anything. It was just that Daddy didn't approve."

"Better than getting your balls cut off," Henrik observed dryly.

Bene winced. "The plea bargain was definitely worth it. My balls are worth an embezzlement charge."

Mina looked like she wanted to slap her hands over her ears. "How does any of this involve Gordon? And how does working for him help you?"

Roux ran a hand through his hair. "Gordon has clout and connections. He can pull strings. Get records changed. Make problems go away."

"Isn't there a group that's supposed to preside over supernatural crimes?" Mina snapped her fingers, thinking. "What are they called? The Guardians of Europe?"

We all exchanged surprised looks. Mina knew a lot more than we'd assumed.

"They try," Roux said. "But some crimes slip through. And in some cases, it's not in the parties' interests to go to the Guardians."

"You mean, like Marius's guy," Mina murmured, thinking aloud.

"Not *my* guy," I huffed.

She tapped her lips, clearly digesting — and sickened by — the news. "What about Szabo? Who is he? What does he want?"

Roux drew invisible lines on the table, and I watched, afraid his fingernails would extend to claws.

"Szabo was supposed to join us, but we went to Gordon with some...er...concerns."

I grimaced, but Roux had been right. We had to do it.

"Concerns?" Mina's voice went up.

"Concerns." Roux nodded firmly. "The rest of us were committed to...well, getting things cleared up. Moving on."

I worked my jaw back and forth, wishing things were different.

"But not Szabo," Roux said. "We didn't think he'd be able to toe the line — any line — and we told Gordon as much. So, he cut Szabo."

Roux finished there, though his throat bob revealed there was more to the story.

To Mina's credit, she didn't ask. She just said, "So, Szabo lost his chance to clear his record, and he resents you for that."

"Resents is one word," Bene sighed.

"Hates," I grunted.

"Despises," Roux added.

"Out for revenge on," Henrik finished, pretending it was all the same to him, which it absolutely, positively wasn't. I didn't know the details, but I knew he and Szabo had once been friends — to the extent that vampires were capable of friendship. What had ended it, I had no clue, and even I wasn't dumb enough to broach a topic that irked Henrik so badly. Even now, points of red shone in his eyes and reflected on the surface of his coffee.

Mina rubbed her face, then straightened with an effort. "Great. I mean, good to know." She grimaced. "Maybe."

Bene patted her arm. "Sorry."

"Well, I'm grateful that you chased him away. But how do we make sure he stays away?"

Killing him was my first idea. My second one, also. I kept it to myself, figuring Mina wouldn't like to hear that.

Our glum silence must have given us away, because Mina slumped back in her chair. "Great. Another vampire out to get me."

"I'm not out to get you," Henrik said defensively.

"Oh good," she mumbled dryly. "Just one vampire out to get me."

"He's after us, not you," Roux pointed out.

"But if I happen to get in the way..." She slid a finger across her throat.

Bad move, because Henrik's eyes lit up again.

Bene pushed the last of the bacon over to him. More meat meant longer intervals a vampire could go without sucking blood. But sooner or later, he would need to sate the impulse or risk going crazy — a little like Szabo.

The ideal case was a willing donor — better yet, donors. Those were usually reckless young things, male or female, who didn't shy away from kink — the gateway drug, so to speak, to letting a vampire suck their blood.

Gross, my dragon wrinkled its nose.

Definitely not my thing, but there were plenty of willing and able blood donors out there, most of whom had their memories wiped by the vampire afterward. All they recalled was hitting incredible highs through some combination of drugs, sex, and alcohol. As long as the vampire didn't overbinge, everyone would go home happy and reasonably healthy — give or take a few pints of blood.

I made a mental note to ask Roux if he'd been keeping tabs on Henrik's diet. For now...I kicked Henrik under the table. He could try his luck with any woman he wanted. Just not *my* woman.

He glared back, then stabbed his fork into the bacon.

"Maybe we shouldn't jump to conclusions," Bene tried.

"We absolutely should, at least when it comes to Szabo," Roux said wearily.

"So, where do we start?" Mina asked.

A woman of action. No wonder I liked her.

Love her, my dragon corrected me.

Like. Love. Lust. I'd lost track of the difference. Hell, I doubted I'd ever known it.

I scratched my chest. Didn't Mina deserve someone better?

So, be better, my dragon rumbled. *That's what we're here for, right?*

I stared into my coffee. Frankly, my only goal had been *marginally* better. Just enough to stay on the right side of shifter laws and politics. But Mina deserved way, *way* better, and I wasn't sure I was up to that. Was it even worth trying?

I waited for the usual answer — *no* — to pop glumly into the back of my mind. But, huh. Nothing. Nada. Zero.

Of course it's worth it! my dragon roared.

I gripped the armrests of my chair, fighting the urge to shift, roar, and claim my mate.

A phone beeped. Mina, Bene, and Roux all pulled out their devices, but only Roux's rang.

"Hello?" he answered, then froze. "Oh. Hello, Gordon."

Everyone went silent.

"I see... Yes... You have a job for us..."

Now? I mouthed.

The more Roux listened, the more deeply his brow folded.

"Where?" he interjected. Then his eyebrows jumped. "Mallorca?"

I did a double take, then calculated how long it would take to reach that Mediterranean island. A two-hour drive to Paris, then a short flight. Unless Gordon could get us a private jet from Dijon...

Don't want to go to Mallorca, my dragon pouted. *I want to stay with Mina.*

My eyes locked on hers, and her expression said she was thinking the same thing.

Maybe I could talk my way out of the trip. Maybe I could stay and protect Mina.

And other things, my dragon hummed.

My body heated, and her eyes sparkled.

"When?" Roux asked, then gulped at the reply. "*This weekend?*"

We all stared at one another, and Bene mouthed, *This weekend?*

"What's today?" Henrik whispered.

"Thursday," Mina said.

My gut clenched. Did Gordon's weekend start on Friday or Saturday?

Roux checked his watch. "I'll have to look into tickets—"

Gordon must have cut him off, because he nodded slowly. "Oh, good. Everything is arranged, then."

Not good. Even Bene looked concerned.

"Can I put you on speaker?" Roux asked.

Normally, my dragon side jumped at any hint of action — especially after a week cooped up in France's answer to the outback. But this time, my gut clenched, and all I could think of was Mina.

"Mina?" Roux furrowed his brow. His eyes met hers. "No, she's not here. Just us four."

Mina's lips parted, and her hands tightened on the armrests of her chair. She started to stand, but—

"Roger. For our ears only," Roux said to Gordon, still watching her. "Not a word to Mina."

She looked at me, swallowed hard, then lowered herself again.

"Okay, I'm putting you on speaker..." Roux said, giving her one last chance to decide.

I could see her warring with herself. But, hell. She had every right to know about what games her loving godfather was playing behind her back.

"Can you hear me?" Gordon's gravelly voice boomed over the line.

"Loud and clear," Bene said.

"Henrik here," the vampire murmured.

"Marius," I chimed in, watching Mina.

Roux let a beat go by, then spoke up. "That's it. The four of us. Go ahead."

Mina bit her lip and stared nervously at the phone.

"All right," Gordon announced. "This is the plan..."

Chapter Sixteen

MINA

Long after Roux signed off, I stared silently at his phone. He and the others jumped right into organizing the practicalities of their assignment, but I barely paid attention. My head was still spinning with what I'd heard.

Mallorca. . . private estate. . . infiltrate and extract. . .

Gordon's words made it all sound fairly harmless. But it wasn't. At all.

Because *infiltrate* meant *break in. Extract* meant *steal.*

Worse still was *By any means necessary, as long as you leave no loose ends.*

Gordon — my sweet, loving godfather — had just given his mercenaries license to kill. Even before he'd gotten to that part, the plan reeked of sketchy morals and jail time.

I must have mumbled that aloud, because Bene shook his head. "Nah. Jail is for human crimes."

I stared. "You mean, this Baumann guy he mentioned isn't human?"

"Nope," Bene said in his usual upbeat tone. "Ronald Baumann is a wolf shifter. A nasty one."

Unlike Clement, I couldn't help thinking.

What would he say if he knew about me getting involved in all this?

"What's the penalty for a crime among supernaturals?" I asked.

Bene shrugged. "That's only relevant if you're caught."

"You mean, the way you were caught at whatever it is that you did? The crime that made you need Gordon?"

He grimaced. "I prefer *incident*."

"And you're really ready to risk another *incident*?" I stared at the rest of them. "You're seriously ready to do this?"

Roux shrugged. "We have to."

"Do you?" I shot back.

Silence filled the air, heavy as cigar smoke.

How you get it all done is your business. Gordon had said. *The less I know, the better. I just want it done. Understood?*

Every one of them had echoed that line. *Understood.*

Well, I didn't understand, dammit! None of it. What had happened to the kind, considerate Gordon I knew? And my clients... I'd started seeing them as — well, not friends, but tolerable, basically decent neighbors. (Okay, not Henrik. But the others.) Had I been wrong about them?

"If anything goes wrong, you're the ones in trouble, not Gordon," I pointed out.

Bene shrugged. "That's the way this works."

I gaped.

Roux switched to his most reasonable tone. "Look, we recognize that there are some gray areas..."

"Gray? This is closer to midnight, dammit. Stealing is wrong. Just wrong."

"What if I told you Ronald Baumann is a murderer and arms dealer?" Marius offered.

I frowned. That shouldn't play into the equation, but somehow, it did.

"And what if I told you the target was stolen, and we're just there to return it?" Bene threw in.

I narrowed my eyes. "Is it?"

He looked at his feet. "No. Well, not that I know of."

Roux shook his head impatiently. "Look, you don't have to be part of this. We let you listen in on the call as a courtesy, but we don't expect you to participate — other than keeping what you heard to yourself."

He meant me spilling the beans to Clem, didn't he? I crossed my arms indignantly. How dare he question my morals?

On the other hand, my morals were pretty messed up. As wrong as this mission was, I already knew I wouldn't call it in.

"Of course I'll keep it to myself." I stood, took two steps toward the door, then spun around. "But one thing — once you're gone, you're gone. I don't want you coming back."

They all stared at me, and it took everything I had to hold my ground. Because all of a sudden, we were back to Day One, when they were just a bunch of strangers — powerful, scary strangers — and I was no one to them.

But when my eyes locked on Marius's, I wavered. His lips twitched, reminding me of our stolen kiss — er, kisses, plural.

Was he a mercenary and criminal or my guardian and protector — the sweet, gentle soul who'd held me all night long?

My knees started to wobble. My lips too.

"Understood," Roux said in a clipped, emotionless tone.

The other three whipped around and stared at him.

"Wait a minute," Bene protested. "I like it here."

Even Henrik looked unsettled. And Marius... He looked at me through eyes filled with pain...hope...desire...

Roux's phone pinged with the details Gordon had promised to send through.

I forced myself to step toward the door. This was all for the best. It was the reality check I needed. It had been a mistake to start to trust my housemates — er, clients — and downright stupid to think of Marius as anything but a very attractive, very dangerous man.

"Okay, here's the file," Roux said to the others.

Their phones pinged with the files he forwarded, punctuating the sound of my footsteps.

"The first document is a file on Baumann..." Roux explained. "The second is a picture of the target."

I moved toward the threshold, though my body protested every step. Then I cursed and headed back for my plate. It had taken me a week to train the guys to clean up after themselves. I couldn't set a bad example now.

In the periphery of my vision, I saw Marius cock his head at his phone.

"Huh."

I frowned, picturing gold ingots. Precious jewels. A briefcase of nuclear codes.

"Oh." Bene's eyebrows shot up as he checked his screen. "That's what we need to extract?"

Roux nodded.

"Well, that's different," the lion shifter murmured.

Henrik didn't seem interested, but when Bene angled the phone toward him, his eyes widened.

"Oh." He drew out the word into several syllables, clearly impressed.

Okay, my curiosity was officially piqued.

Mercenaries and criminals, I reminded myself. *Guaranteed jail time.*

Grabbing my plate and mug, I turned back toward the door.

Bene squinted at his screen. "A painting. With squiggly trees. Doesn't look too valuable to me."

"What is that? A Picasso?" Marius rumbled.

"Not Picasso, you fool. Van Gogh," Henrik said.

I stopped in my tracks. A real Van Gogh or *like* a Van Gogh?

Bene shrugged. "Hell, I could paint in better focus than this."

A comment I'd heard in a dozen museums in front of real masterpieces.

"Okay, okay." I gave in. "What is it?"

Bene covered his screen. "Thought you weren't interested."

I wasn't. Was I?

"You don't want to see it," Marius assured me.

I reminded myself that I didn't. Except, suddenly, I did.

Roux held his phone against his chest. "Sorry. If you're not involved, you don't need to know. Nothing personal."

The more he refused, the more I wanted to see the damn thing. Just to satisfy my curiosity.

I motioned to Bene. "You've insulted my coffee machine for a whole week now. You owe me."

He shot Roux an apologetic look and turned his phone toward me.

I stared, then sat down. Hard.

And, yikes. If Marius hadn't stuck a chair under me, lightning-fast, I would have been ass-down on the floor.

"What is it?" Marius asked from what seemed like a hundred miles away.

I stared at the picture, then him, then back at the picture.

My heart thumped ponderously. By their own admission, these men were mercenaries — but they had been decent enough to me. Even kind at times (except Henrik, obviously). Shouldn't I at least inform them what their target was? What it represented?

Marius touched my arm, and I swallowed. Hard. Then I turned to Bene and motioned for his phone. "I need a closer look, please."

Roux shook his head firmly. "Sorry, Mina. You already know more than you should."

"Maybe you know less than you should," I shot back.

He frowned, then shrugged. "We've been hired to extract goods. Whether that's a painting or a pumpkin, it's not our business."

"That's not any painting."

"No? Then what is it?" Roux demanded.

I pursed my lips, then whispered as if someone might be eavesdropping. "Van Gogh. The *Painter on the Road to Tarascon.*"

"Road to where?"

"Tarascon," I murmured, staring at the phone.

Bene studied the image again. "Is it super valuable or something?"

I shook my head. "No. Yes. I mean, that's not the point. This painting has been missing since World War II."

"Well, I guess someone found it," Bene muttered, unimpressed.

I shook my head. "It's called *Raubkunst.* War plunder — if it's the real deal."

Roux shook his head. "What it is isn't our business."

"Well, maybe it should be," I snipped. "Maybe you should think."

He glared, but I glared back. When that got me nowhere, I did my best to explain.

"Throughout the war, Nazis confiscated, stole, or 'bought' thousands of masterpieces at extortionary prices. Some were recovered. Others were destroyed. Some just disappeared." I pointed at the image on the phone. "Like that one. It was hidden in a salt mine in Germany with a lot of other art."

"Were you an art major or something?" Bene asked in the same disapproving tone I might use to ask if he was a mercenary.

"Yes."

His mouth formed a surprised O. "I thought you were a teacher."

"I am. I started out as an art teacher, but the school district scaled back the program, and I had to switch to classroom teaching." Reducing a valuable art program was another crime as far as I was concerned, but I forced myself to get back to the point. "A fire broke out in that salt mine in the last days of the war, and that Van Gogh was reported lost with everything else."

"But it wasn't," Marius murmured, catching on.

"There have been rumors about it being part of a private collection ever since. An *illegal* private collection," I said.

"What happens if it's found?" Bene asked.

"It's supposed to be returned to its rightful owner or their descendants. Best case, it goes to a museum for the public to enjoy."

"Supposed to be, huh?" Bene said dubiously.

Roux jutted his chin at Bene to put away his phone. "Well, thanks for informing us. But since we have some planning to do..." He tilted his head toward the door.

My mind spun. Leaving now was the prudent thing to do. But my heart thumped wildly, and not because of a Van Gogh, or even a long-lost Van Gogh.

I knew about that painting — and others like it — because I knew someone who'd worked tirelessly to track plundered artworks. Someone who had died while hot on the trail of *The Painter on the Road to Tarascon.*

My father.

A familiar old ache settled into my chest — especially at the irony. My father used to joke that the enemies he'd made in search of missing art would get him someday, but he'd died in an ordinary accident on an extraordinarily slippery road.

I bit my lip. What if fate was giving me a chance to finish what he'd started? What if I could right one small wrong in a complex, unfair world?

A list of crimes I could be convicted of paraded through my mind. Trespassing. Stealing. Art trafficking across international borders.

Steer clear. Stay away, I told myself.

The kitchen door was only a few steps away. All I had to do was amble over there, erase the past few minutes from my mind, and continue living a quiet, happy, and crime-free life.

I glanced at Marius and amended that to *quiet, lonely, and crime-free.*

His eyes bored into mine, warning me away...from their mission, or from him?

"Mina..." Roux said more gently. "I mean it. You don't want to be part of this."

After one last look at Marius, I found myself jumping to my feet and calling over my shoulder.

"Meet me in the drawing room in two minutes."

"Meet you...?" Roux's question faded under the thump of my footsteps. I raced upstairs and into the library, past the box I'd found in the stable and over to the shelf I needed.

I crouched, running a finger along the spines of the big books near the bottom. Diamond-shaped stained-glass windows lined the front wall of the library, casting colored blocks over the books.

And, *bingo!* I grabbed the book I needed and ran to the drawing room exactly as the men filed in.

Thumping the book on a table, I flipped through the worn pages, many marked by scraps of paper with notes in my father's tight, slanted script. Eventually, I found the page I wanted and pointed.

"Van Gogh's *The Painter on the Road to Tarascon*."

Everyone leaned in.

Destroyed in a blaze, 1945, the caption said, but the sticky note my father had added beside it listed several plausible leads.

"Mina..." Roux warned.

Ignoring him gave me childish pleasure. I gestured for Bene's phone. He hesitated, looking at Roux, who finally relented with a huff.

I zoomed into the painting on Bene's phone, comparing it to the one in the book.

"Hard to tell, but it's definitely a contender," I said more to myself than them.

"It hardly matters if it's real or a forgery," Henrik said. "If Gordon wants it, we get it."

"It matters to me," I said so fiercely, he backed away.

Marius gently closed the book and handed Bene's phone back. "You really don't want to be part of this, Mina."

"I have to be."

Roux shook his head. "No, you don't. Think about it."

I shook my head vehemently. "I have thought about it. I'm in, Roux."

"Thanks for the offer, but no. Not an option."

It was Henrik, of all people, who sided with me.

"Maybe it is an option," he mused, stroking his chin.

"No, it isn't," Roux insisted.

"We let Mina in on this in exchange for her letting us finish out our contract here," the vampire said.

Roux opened his mouth to protest, then shut it again.

"Too dangerous," Marius growled.

Bene tilted his head from side to side. "Maybe, but do you want to be the one to explain to Gordon why she's kicking us out?"

Marius frowned but didn't waver. "Still too dangerous."

"I agree," Roux chimed in.

I scowled at them both, but Henrik beat me to it.

"Oh, I think she's capable of making up her own mind."

I stared at him, every suspicion aroused.

When he grinned, the sharp points of his fangs interrupted the smooth line of his lips.

"Besides, she could be useful."

My enthusiasm waned. Useful to a vampire? In what way?

"As a distraction, I mean," he elaborated.

"He has a point there," Bene mused.

"How?" Roux frowned.

"Getting in," Bene said. "Every infiltration operation has two options, right? Going in through the front door or the back door." He pointed to me. "With her, we can do both."

I crossed my arms. "That better not be some kind of dirty sex talk."

Bene's eyes lit up, and he tsked. "Naughty, naughty. Not meant that way, but I like how you think."

I put my face in my hands. Another day of these imbeciles and I would break.

"Just ignore him," Henrik murmured. "That's what the rest of us do."

"Gee, thanks," Bene protested.

"Bene!" Roux snapped. "Get to the point."

"Well, this Baumann guy is throwing a party, right?"

Roux nodded curtly. "So?"

Bene pointed to me. "So, we put her in a nice dress, do up her hair—"

"Hey," I grumbled. I was a person, not a Barbie doll.

Bene went on, unperturbed. "And she waltzes through the front door with the rest of the guests. I mean, with one of us as her gentleman companion." He grinned and smacked his chest. "I nominate me."

"Forget it," Marius snarled.

But Bene did not forget it. "I can totally pull off a tux. Can you?"

Frankly, my mouth watered a little at the prospect of any of them in a tux. Especially Marius, who was sure to give the outfit a sinfully good, *dark and dangerous* look. Probably not the best way to sneak into a party unnoticed, though.

"The rest of you losers go in through the back with the catering team, and bam!" Bene smacked his hands together. "We make off with the painting."

"That easy, huh?" Roux muttered.

"No, but it's not a bad start." Henrik cut in.

Bene grinned from ear to ear. "See? Even the vampire agrees."

Not exactly comforting. Still, my mind was made up, for better or worse.

The corner of my eye twitched with a foreboding of *worse*. But, hell. I would be surrounded by three tough shifters and a vampire. They would protect me, right?

Marius's eyes blazed, swearing he would.

Worst case, I could count on Gordon's help. He wasn't supposed to know I was there, but in a life-and-death situation, he would help first and berate me later. I hated to count on his help, but the painting made the risk worth it.

Roux considered for another minute, then sighed. "Okay. Here's the deal. We let you in, and you let us stay. Not a word to Gordon about anything. Deal?"

"Deal." I nodded firmly, letting the word echo through the room.

Chapter Seventeen

MARIUS

"Not a good idea," I barked, first at Mina, then at Roux. "Do you know how dangerous this could be?"

Roux opened his mouth, but Mina stuck up a hand. "Don't even start."

"Dammit, Bene. . ." I growled as I followed Mina out of the room.

"How is this my fault? I was just brainstorming."

"Brain-farting is more like it," Henrik — the only one of us who found any of this amusing — quipped.

Chairs scraped the floor, shouts broke out, and Mina came stomping back in.

"Oh no, you don't. Not anywhere near my grandmother's china, dammit!"

Bene and Henrik paused, though they kept their hands on each other's throats. Bene looked around.

"China?"

She pointed to a single teacup and saucer on a sideboard. "China."

I was starting to suspect she'd placed pieces of her grandmother's vast collection in strategic locations to have an excuse for sending us outside to fight.

"Take it outside, dammit," she boomed loud enough to make the china shake. Then she spun around and marched away.

I fell into step behind her. Well, I tried. But she quickly opened a gap on me, flying down the hallway in huge, angry strides that said *Leave me the fuck alone.*

And boy, did she mean it, because she kept that up all the way down the hallway and up the far stairs.

Spiral stairs, my dragon hummed happily. *Perfect place to kiss.*

A perfect place to chew me out was more like it, given her pissy mood. But fool that I was, I rushed after her anyway.

"Hey!" I ducked when she ambushed me at the top with a wild, angry look.

"Stop following me!"

"I will when you start listening." And, crap. The words came out half snarled.

Not the way to woo our mate, my dragon snipped.

She might be my mate, but this was not about wooing her. This was about keeping her safe.

"How about *you* listen?" she growled. "I make up my own mind. I decide what I will and will not do."

I opened my mouth to argue — to tell her she didn't get it, that she underestimated the danger — but she jabbed a finger into my chest hard enough to make me take a step back.

Unfortunately, there wasn't much stair left to step onto.

"So when I say—" she started.

I lurched, flailed, and grabbed for the doorway but got Mina instead.

Her eyes went wide as we toppled over. I pictured us crashing from wall to wall, around and around, all the way down to the ground floor.

Clenching every muscle in my body, I dragged us to one side while Mina grabbed the edge of the doorway. My back smacked into the curved stone wall, and Mina smacked into my front.

Oof. I winced.

On the bright side, we hadn't tumbled down the stairwell.

Also on the bright side, my hands landed on her hips, and she stayed nice and close.

"Whoa. Are you hurt?" Mina asked an inch away from my lips.

"Yes," I gritted, touching my ribs. "See what happens when you don't listen?"

"See what happens when you recklessly chase me up a damn staircase?"

"Reckless?"

"Reckless." Her face was so close, our noses almost brushed.

There was a long, charged beat. Her chest heaved against mine and her eyes blazed, glowing like the blue heart of a fire.

She'd make a great dragon, my inner beast whispered.

She would, and I could make her one if she accepted me as her mate.

Dangerous fantasies filled my mind. Fantasies I'd never entertained before but desperately wanted now.

Now and forever, my dragon agreed.

Mina glanced over her shoulder. "Good thing I caught you before you fell."

I scoffed. "I caught *you.*"

"Sure. Right. That explains why I'm on top."

And, *whoosh.* Her word choice woke the wrong part of my brain — the part with a hotline to my cock.

"No, you're there thanks to these." I brought her hand to my stomach. "I believe they're called abs."

She snorted but didn't remove her hand. She kept it right where it was, nice and warm and teasing.

"So refreshing to find a guy who's not full of himself."

I shrugged. "How else should I put it?"

"You could try *agile as a cat.*"

I grimaced. "Agile as a dragon."

She chuckled. "Making you jealous, am I?"

"You want Bene? You can have him. Or Roux, for all I care." I said, lying through my teeth. If she so much as looked at either of them, I would kill them — in or outside the house, grandma's china be damned.

Her eyes made another orbit. "I don't want Bene. Or Roux."

Silence ensued — heavy silence, punctuated only by our panting breaths — making me hyperaware of her warm hand, resting comfortably on my ribs. Ribs that felt a lot better now, though the ache hadn't disappeared. It had just migrated south, where my cock swelled against my jeans.

"Who do you want, then?" I whispered.

She moved her lips, and I braced myself for her retort.

Wrong way to brace myself, as it turned out. Because a split second later, she covered my mouth in a deep, bruising kiss.

A-plus answer, my dragon hummed.

I kissed back just as hard in a furious, messy clash.

Destiny, my dragon crooned, though my brain was running on two cylinders, at best. Not a good time to analyze whether this was destiny, pure chance, or plain old lust.

Destiny, an earthy voice grumbled in my mind.

Her hands fisted, crushed, and released my shirt — only to repeat the cycle all over again. I inhaled her rose-and-lilac scent while doing a little fisting and crushing of my own.

When I pushed my hips against hers, she gasped against my mouth. I caught that sound and swallowed it, deepening the kiss until her fingers dug into my shoulders.

I broke away. "You want me to stop?"

"Absolutely not," she panted, diving straight into another kiss.

My inner dragon roared in approval, and my last shreds of control tumbled away in the hurricane Mina unleashed.

We'd been tiptoeing around each other long enough. Pretending we didn't have chemistry, when the truth was, we had enough to blow the roof off a research facility.

The stone wall at my back was cool, but her body was a wall of heat, pressing against my chest. My stomach. My hips...

We broke off for air and ended up staring into each other's eyes.

"You still mad?" I murmured, my lips moving against hers.

"Furious," she whispered.

I chuckled, a low, rumbly sound that made her shiver. Sliding her arms behind my neck, she pulled me into a deep, hungry kiss. I leaned forward greedily. Too greedily, because we teetered on the edge of the stairs again.

She clutched at me. "Oh! Watch out."

Nice of her to think I was capable of such a thing, given the haze that had taken over my mind. Especially now, with her scent curling around me, spiced with sweet frustration.

"Hang on," I ordered. Without waiting for an answer, I hustled her up the stairs and into the safety of the upper hallway.

Relative safety, I decided when we crashed into a bookshelf. Paperbacks rained down, bumping off my shoulders and onto the floor. Better that than grandma's china, though.

"Sorry," I murmured.

"You will be if you stop now," Mina growled, spearing her fingers through my hair.

Good thing I had no such plan. Hell, everything about this was improv and instinct. I was operating by the seat of my pants.

Speaking of which... my dragon hinted.

I lifted her, prompting a muffled squeak, though she didn't break the kiss. I carried her down the hall, hunting for the nearest flat surface. She wrapped her legs around my waist, making me groan with need.

The east wing of the house was a mirror of the west wing, and her bedroom called to me like a beacon. But this was a fucking château, not a house, and that hallway stretched endlessly. One by one, portraits of her ancestors blurred by, and I felt the disapproving gaze of each.

Young people these days, I practically heard them scold.

Like they'd never careened down these hallways in a lust-blinded rush.

We passed four... five... six portraits and a haughty, Greek-style bust. Another four portraits separated us from the El Dorado of her room in the distance.

I groaned. What I wouldn't do to trade this château for a bungalow.

"Tired already?" Mina teased, hanging on to me like a baby baboon.

I shook my head. "It's not the *weight.* It's the *wait.*"

She chuckled, angling her head to one side. "Well, there is the floor. The wall..."

"The hallway, carrying every sound to the assholes downstairs. . ."

She groaned, burying her face in my neck. God, that felt good.

But, shit. Wrong thing to say, because a moment later, she gulped and loosened her legs.

"Put me down," she ordered.

My heart stopped. My cock groaned. A thousand emotions — want, need, shattered hopes — hammered in my head as I dipped and loosened my grip on her side.

"On second thought. . ." She clamped her legs back around me, and I held her tight.

Her face was so close, my eyes nearly crossed. She studied me, looking through my eyes and into my soul.

Can I trust you? Will you hurt me? Will this change things?

My heart cracked at the questions I sensed zipping through her mind — and at a world that forced women to consider such things more than men did.

It hurt, too, because I'd had those questions aimed my way so many times. *Can I trust you? Will you hurt me?*

Yes, dammit. I could be trusted. And, no — of course, I wouldn't hurt her. Yet the same unspoken interrogation came up every fucking time. Renegade dragons like me drew women like moths to a flame. But once a woman ventured close — if she ever worked up the nerve to — fear set in, delivering a cold, hard slap to my soul.

If she didn't trust me, how could I trust her? Had she been teasing me all along, when I hadn't been teasing at all?

But my heart ached for Mina as much as my body did, so I hung on.

"Made up your mind yet?" I finally asked, doing my best to hide desperately thin hopes.

Her eyes softened, and she cupped my face gently.

"Yes." Her lips brushed against mine, then pressed in harder. "Yes. . ." she murmured, turning the whisper into a plea. "Yes. . ."

Time and space blurred, and the next thing I knew, we were falling into her bed. Desperately touching, tasting, stripping each other bare. *Consuming* each other.

"Oh..." Her breath hitched when I left her mouth to migrate south. I lashed my tongue against her breast, then nipped the straining bud.

She groaned, guiding me from left to right.

Eventually, I slipped away, zigzagging the edge of my jaw down her smooth skin. Lower and lower until—

She gasped, then groaned as the first, tender touches of my tongue turned to deep, hungry licks.

A damn good thing we'd closed the door, because the sounds we made...

My dragon preened. *We...*

The haziest, furthest corner of my soul registered that. Not me, not she. *We.*

Every time I moved, Mina moved too, bucking, surging, heaving. Every time I gasped for air, she did too. We were that in tune, that perfect together. More perfect than I'd felt with anyone.

Listening, my dragon hummed. *The key is to listen.*

As in me listening to her — the opposite of what I'd demanded back at the stairs. What, where, how did she like it best? I tuned in to the quaver in her voice, the tension in her body, the tenor of each shaky breath.

My tongue and fingers brought her higher and higher until—

She gasped, shuddered, then arched sharply against me. "Yes!"

Her cry hung in the air, and her body tensed for a good minute. Then she went limp, except for her heaving chest. I snuggled in beside her, holding her close.

"Oh. My. God," she whispered between breaths.

My cheeks stretched in a huge grin despite the ache in my groin.

"Good?" I asked as casually as I could.

"Very...er...very..." She waved vaguely, searching for words. "Very good."

I propped myself on an elbow and smoothed back the strand of hair stuck on a corner of her mouth.

"Just good?"

She stuck a finger against the middle of my chest. "Don't let this go to your head." Then her eyes took on a sly sheen, and she slipped a hand around my stiff shaft. "Plus, I'm saving *amazing* for later."

"Later?" What started as a growl turned into a choked stutter.

"Maybe sooner than later." She grinned, running her hand up, then down as she rolled onto her back.

My brain didn't play any part in how quickly my body followed her cue. It just happened, and a short time later—

I slid into her hot, tight sheath, and my dragon's roar thundered through my mind. *Mine. Mine. Mine!*

Chapter Eighteen

MINA

I tipped my head back, suppressing a howl when Marius pushed in. He huffed into my neck, straining for control, then pulled back and hammered in again.

I clamped my legs around him, hungry — no, starving — for more.

He stopped suddenly, and my gut clenched.

"Fuck."

Yes, please.

But, darn. That wasn't what he meant.

I moved my hands from his perfect, muscled ass to his shoulders, waiting.

"No condom. Problem?" he asked, barely stringing the syllables together.

Flustered dragon made for a cute — and rare — look, and I barely hid a smile.

"No problem," I assured him in equally simple caveman talk. Let his mind focus on what mattered — like picking up where he'd left off.

I was on the pill and blessed with a shifter's hardy immune system — a huge perk, despite missing out on so many other abilities my ancestors had enjoyed.

He didn't actually say, *Whew*, but his body practically screamed it.

I smoothed my hands over the lumps of his shoulders, then gulped. I wasn't just in bed with any man. I was in bed with a dragon shifter. He could roast me, tear me to pieces, or kill me with his bare hands — the very hands gliding over my body right now.

A ripple of anticipation went through me, and I nudged his ass.

"Definitely no problem. Now, where were we?"

He grinned, making my breath catch. "Bossy, aren't we?"

"You love it," I muttered, grinding my hips against his.

His smile turned into a needy hiss, and a moment later, I was moaning again. Only seconds in, and this was already the best sex of my life, exceeding the previous high point — the flaming orgasm he'd given me a minute earlier. And if I looked further back in time... well, the performance of other men seemed laughably amateur in comparison.

"No... second... thoughts?" he teased, punctuating each word with a deep, hard thrust.

No thoughts at all, actually. My mind was blissfully blank, except for yowling for more.

I must have mumbled something along those lines, because he laughed — so hard, it rippled through every corner of his body. Yes, even *that* corner, cueing me into another deep, long moan.

He grew serious again. Focusing. Thrusting harder and deeper.

I closed my eyes, then opened them, desperate not to miss a single sensation. But I might as well have been trying to catch every raindrop in a summer storm, because impressions cascaded aplenty, and I could only capture so many. The shooting stars in his midnight eyes. The sweat glistening over his skin. The searing grind inside.

"Oh..." I gasped, losing the battle to hide my delight.

A battle Marius was fighting too, judging by the way he kept his jaw clenched.

Up to then, I'd kept a tight grip of his shoulders, hips, or ass, trying to maintain a shred a control. But now, I was consumed by the burning urge to let go. One last scrap held on, though, stubbornly asking questions.

Could I trust him?

Yes — with my life, I sensed.

Would he hurt me?

My heart, maybe, if — when? — this all came to a crashing end. But I would have to share the guilt for that.

And as for hurting my body... Waves of ecstasy pulsed through my veins, crossing that question off the list.

I released his shoulders and stretched my arms over my head. I even closed my eyes, trusting myself to him and to fate.

"Yes..." I whispered as our bodies rocked together.

The bed creaked, and the sheets tangled around my feet.

Blood pounded in my ears. Lust swirled through my veins. Cries dammed my throat. Then Marius hammered in one last time, and that dam shattered.

My vision blurred, and my whole body sang. And sang and sang, because the high lasted a long time — long enough for me to circle the château a couple of times in dragon form, if I were capable of such a thing.

At that moment, I really believed I could fly like a dragon. I believed I could roar and soar with my mate. I believed all kinds of crazy things, and they didn't seem at all crazy.

Just as I was about to sag, Marius exploded inside me, and I shuddered with another orgasm. Marius gasped and went perfectly still, a statue chiseled with muscles, veins, and an expression between *victorious warrior* and *shaken to the core*. Then he sucked in a ragged breath and slumped, pressing me into the mattress.

I locked my arms around his back. I locked my lips, too, trapping off-limits words a guy like Marius would not want to hear. Four-letter L-words that had no business popping into my mind, even at a time like this.

We lay tangled together for a long time, too lazy — or too wrecked — to move. Eventually, Marius wiped us both off with the sheet, prompting me to make a mental note about moving up laundry day at the château. Then he snuggled in, absent-mindedly tracing circles on my shoulder.

I should have said something or cracked a joke to lighten the mood. Instead, I buried my face in the warm curve of his neck, inhaled, and clung to him.

At some point, nature called, and the only thing that scared me more than marching to and from the bed naked was the thought that Marius might not be there when I returned.

But his eyes followed me both ways like a hawk — or a dragon. A dragon standing guard over a priceless treasure. I gulped at the thought — and at the way he tucked me right back beside him. He pressed a kiss to my temple so gently, I thought I imagined it.

My chest squeezed.

Dangerous. So damn dangerous. Not just the man, but the direction of my thoughts.

If it had been night, we might have drifted off to sleep and dealt with the aftermath… well, after. But sunlight streamed through the windows, laying bare the truth of what we'd just done. Laying bare lots of things, in fact. Big things. My eyes kept drifting down, and I kept yanking them back up.

Finally, I rolled to my side to face him. His eyes — more *mysterious lake* than *stormy seas* for a change — met mine, then dipped to my chest and slowly, casually soaked in the view.

An uninhibited dragon. Why was I not surprised?

Fair was fair, so I decided to peek too. Down his broad chest, across his abs, all the way to his—

I ripped my gaze away just in time to catch him stifle a grin.

"I don't know about you, but sex in broad daylight is kind of like… like stealing in broad daylight," I said. "I feel like I ought to feel doubly guilty."

He snorted. "Why feel guilty at all?"

I opened my mouth, but no words came. Why feel guilty, indeed?

I finally settled on, "Let's just say it's new to me."

He traced another tiny circle into my shoulder. "*Good* new, I hope."

I nodded, then caved in and corrected the understatement of the year. "*Very* good new."

"Good enough to try again sometime?"

"I would say *definitely*, but I think *it depends* might be a safer bet."

His brow furrowed. "Depends on what?"

"Neither of us ruining this with whatever we say next."

His chuckle was a little dry. "Well, then I probably shouldn't bring up—"

I cut him off with a vehement shake of my head. My decision to help with the heist in Mallorca? "You definitely shouldn't bring that up. Not if you want to get laid again."

He arched an eyebrow. "Do *you* want to get laid again?"

Hell yes. But it was only — I glanced over, then gaped at the clock — er, *already* ten in the morning, and we had a long day ahead of us. Maybe even a flight to Mallorca.

My hand went from the neutral territory of his shoulder to the riskier terrain of his hip. "Well, yes. I'm only human, you know."

Are you, though? his eyes asked, though he didn't actually speak.

Good, because that was a long story, and frankly, our time was better invested in sex.

I did, however, cave in enough to give him the short version.

"My father's side of the family — the American side — is a mix of fox and bear shifters."

Marius considered that. "That doesn't explain how you evaded Henrik that night he stalked you from the attic."

Ah, the shadow-walking. Hard to explain — especially since I hadn't completely mastered it.

"Old family secret," I said. "Not mine to share, sorry."

He pursed his lips but didn't press me on it.

"That comes from your mother's side of the family, I take it?" he asked.

I nodded. "A mix of shifters and witches from here in Burgundy. But so mixed, and so far back, that we don't have any truly special abilities."

He snorted. "You mean, except for evading vampires?"

I flashed a thin smile. "Occasionally."

We lay quietly for a while, thinking, touching, nuzzling.

"My turn for a question," I eventually whispered.

"Uh-oh," he murmured, only half joking.

I traced a line of muscle in his forearm, working up the courage to ask.

"That charge of attempted murder. Any regrets?" I quietly asked.

"Only that I didn't succeed in killing him."

So, points for honesty, if not lawfulness. But if that man was as bad as Bene said, well... Could I blame Marius?

I digested that for a while, then decided to try my luck with another question.

"What will you do when you finish working for Gordon?"

His eyes wandered over the ceiling, then the walls.

"Not sure," he said.

I nodded, uncertain what I wanted his answer to be, let alone how I might reply.

Stay, a voice in the back of my mind pleaded. *Forever.*

A minute ticked by, far more comfortably than I expected.

"Did you paint those?" Marius murmured sometime later, indicating the row of framed art on the wall.

I shook my head. "Only that one." I pointed to an oil painting of the garden fountain in better days. "There are dozens more in storage. As a kid, I came here every summer and spent most of my time sketching and painting." Then I cleared my throat. "That one, that one, and that one are my father's." I pointed to watercolors of the local landscape. "He loved it here. My grandmother used to joke that he was more her child than my mother was."

A mourning dove sang in the distance, almost in tribute, and a lump formed in my throat.

Marius held me a little tighter. "Those notes in the book you showed us... Were they his?"

I nodded, tempted to tell him everything. But I lost my nerve and pointed to a different artwork instead.

"That sketch of a horse by the window is a Toulouse-Lautrec."

Marius did a double take at it. So, whew. Change of subject achieved.

"A real one or a forgery?"

I laughed. "Real. But it's just a sketch, and it has some water damage, so it's not super valuable." I sighed, thinking of the blank walls of the lower hallway. "Apparently, my great-great grandparents had quite an art collection, but that's all that's left of it. Everything was sold over the years to pay for upkeep."

I looked at a crack in the plaster ceiling, then thought about loose roof tiles. Was I fighting a losing battle?

"Hey." Marius stroked my cheek.

I swallowed hard and looked at him.

"You'll find a way," he murmured.

I bit my lip. Who knew the cover boy for *Bikes, Booze &* *Tattoos* magazine would turn out to be such a sweetheart?

I took a deep breath, then faked a smile. "Yeah. As soon as I get back from Mallorca."

His lips quirked, but then his mood grew somber. "About that. What are my chances of convincing you to stay here?"

I patted his chest. "Close to zero. But given that I'm in a fairly...er, agreeable mood..."

He cracked a grin. "Agreeable, huh?"

I nodded. Two mind-blowing orgasms would do that to a girl.

"...I would listen to what you had to say," I finished. "That doesn't mean I'll change my mind, though."

His eyes drifted over my body as he thought that over.

"What makes you so interested in the Van Gogh?"

My eyes drifted to the cluster of framed photos on the dresser. The one in the middle showed my family at the last Christmas we'd shared with my father, although we hadn't known it at the time.

When Marius followed my gaze, I jerked my eyes to the window.

How much to tell him? Why make a secret of it at all?

Because memories of my father were too precious to share with just anyone, and even a man I trusted enough to sleep with didn't automatically meet that bar.

"Let's just say, I have a passion for art," I said.

"Passion enough to risk your life?" His voice was flat. Dead flat, one might say.

"Maybe not that passionate," I admitted a little weakly.

"So why not leave it to the experts?"

I made a face. "Sorry, but I doubt you guys are experts in post-Impressionist art."

"No, but we're experts in other things."

I did my best not to imagine what that entailed.

"And expert enough to know you have no place on this mission," he added — gently, to his credit. Or maybe he was just buttering me up for more sex.

"Right. The *mission*." I made quote marks in the air. "A mission that doesn't ensure that the painting — if it's genuine — ends up in the right hands. It will just change hands, from one private collection to another."

He shrugged. "You don't know that."

I made a show of tapping my lips. "Let's see. The person who wants this painting *and* knows where it is doesn't contact the current owner or the special commission responsible for such things — and believe me, there are several that would be delighted to unearth a long-lost Van Gogh — such a person doesn't exactly scream *generous philanthropist*, does he — or she?"

He raised then dropped a shoulder. "I wouldn't know. Not a lot of generous philanthropists in my line of work."

I frowned at the photos on my dresser. Gordon appeared in the one taken at my college graduation, one arm around my shoulders and one around my sister's. My mother was out of frame, behind the camera. My gratefully debt-free mother, and us, her debt-free children, thanks to Gordon's generosity.

For the tenth time that morning, I prayed Marius and the others were wrong about him. And for the tenth time that morning, I seriously doubted it.

But how could we have missed the dark side of his business dealings in all our years of close contact?

"Let's pretend for a minute that going after that painting doesn't come with any risks," Marius said. "You come with us, we get the painting, and you have a close look. It turns out to be the real deal..."

I nodded along, loving that version of events.

"...and we hand it over to Gordon, who hands it over to his client."

I frowned.

He touched my chin gently, and I met his eyes. "Still no happy end. Not for you anyway. Could you live with that?"

"How can *you* live with it? Doing deals like that, I mean?"

His eyes clouded over. "Better not to ask about my morals, Mina. You'll only be disappointed at what you find."

"Would I?"

Of course you would, his stormy eyes promised. Stubbornly, almost.

Maybe. But something made me think there might be a rainbow hidden behind that tempest. Something to believe in. To trust. Maybe even to love.

Naive? Probably.

Definitely, the back of my mind warned. But I still couldn't help believing in him.

"Anyway, it's likely to be a forgery." I forced myself to hit a lighter tone.

"Do you know enough to spot a fake?"

"I'm a...a very expert amateur," I said truthfully.

My father had an entire dossier on lost artworks of World War II and the forgeries that had surfaced since, and I'd been over the details countless times. I'd used that dossier for everything from a tenth-grade art project, to my college thesis, to designing an interdisciplinary unit for my school district. At least half of the forgeries my father catalogued had been easy to spot, even for me. I'd also interned at a Boston auction house, and everyone there, including the most highly regarded veterans, declared I had a sixth sense for discerning genuine art from forgeries. So maybe a little ancestral magic had trickled down to me after all.

"Let's say we quickly decide it's a fake," I said. "Then I'll know not to care about it, right?"

"And if it is real?" Marius challenged. "You realize you can't tell Gordon, right? He can't know you know. And if we fail in this job..." He trailed off, then shook his head. "We can't fail, Mina. That painting might be worth a lot, but what about us?"

So far, he'd been pretty cavalier about... well, everything. His past, his present, his future. Bene had done most of the talking when it came to how much was riding on their bargain with Gordon. But for the first time, Marius communicated that too. Not in words, but in the scratch in his voice, the anxious flicker in his eyes.

They could not afford to fail. Period.

So, shouldn't I help them — and find a way to save that painting?

"I'll think of something," I bluffed.

He chuckled dryly. "That's what scares me."

I bit my lip. It scared me too. Bringing that painting into the public eye would be the ultimate way to honor my father. But what was one painting compared to the lives of four good men?

I caught myself there. What made them good? What proof did I have? Was I just being fooled by Bene's charm, Roux's sincerity, and Marius's bad-boy appeal?

(I left Henrik out of the equation. No need to skew the curve with him.)

No, I decided. They were good at heart. I could sense it.

"Listen, if you want to succeed—" I started.

"We have to succeed," he cut in.

"If you want to succeed, I can help. Bene said as much."

Marius grimaced. "You need to take everything he says with a grain of salt."

I ran my hand over his shoulder. "Is he wrong? About me improving your odds of success, I mean?"

Marius considered for a long time before answering.

"No. He's not wrong."

"Then it's in your own interest for me to join in."

He huffed. "No, it isn't. Not when I'd worry about you every step of the way."

"Hey! Do I seem so incapable?"

He snorted. "Of lying? Of sneaking around? Of anything illegal? You're hopeless."

"Gee, thanks." I pouted.

He caressed my shoulder. "That was a compliment."

I sighed. It was. What was wrong with me?

Marius went back to drawing circles on my shoulder. Gently, making it hard to keep up the pout. And, er...making *him* hard, as a stray glance told me.

"If anything happened to you..." he murmured.

My heart leaped. He cared. He really did!

"You're not going to get all sappy on me, are you?" I teased quietly.

He huffed. "Sappy, no. But I might change the subject."

He skimmed his hand down my ribs and across my stomach, leaving fire in his wake.

I drew in a sharp breath and snuck in another quick peek.

All systems go, from the look of it. I licked my lips.

"You just planning to look?" His grin was pure sin.

"I'm considering my options." I did my best to sound prim. Then I looked at the clock, eliciting a deep, husky laugh.

"You got enough time to pencil me in?"

"You want sex? You'd better be nice."

"Yes, ma'am," he said, turning on his inner Boy Scout.

A very big, very sexy Boy Scout who moonlighted as a dragon.

I pictured huge teeth and wings, bursts of fire... Bad idea, because that only turned me on more.

"What about you?" I turned the question around. "Are you planning to just look?"

He shook his head solemnly, but his eyes danced over my bare body. "No, ma'am. Planning to make you forget how to breathe."

I opened my mouth, only to discover he'd already proven true to his word. I was already breathless, dammit. And when he snuck a hand over my ribs, every thought scattered like ash on the wind.

Chapter Nineteen

MARIUS

The pilot's voice came over the intercom. "Ladies and gentlemen, please fasten your seat belts for landing."

The flight attendant came through the cabin of the private jet, checking that we'd complied. Bene flashed a grin and motioned proudly to his groin — er, lap.

The flight attendant winked at him, and I rolled my eyes.

What? Bene protested, throwing the words into my mind. *She's gorgeous — and single.*

I shrugged. Would she look as good without the makeup? With her hair a mess? With her brow sweaty and a hammer in her hand?

My eyes slid to Mina in the seat across and ahead of mine.

Wow. Someone has it bad, Bene teased.

Great fucking timing, Roux grumbled.

He was right. Getting involved with Mina on the eve of a major assignment was a terrible idea. But it wasn't an idea. It was instinct. Maybe even destiny.

Unfortunately, we'd also been loud enough to alert the rest of the guys to what was going on. Even if that hadn't been the case, the scent of sex would have been impossible to miss, no matter how hard I'd scrubbed Mina in the shower afterward.

My dragon grinned at the memory of how *afterward* turned into the run-up to yet another round of ravenously hungry sex.

I shifted in my seat, getting hard just thinking about it.

I like thinking about it, my dragon protested.

So did I. I replayed it again and again. The sight of Mina's bare body... Of her lips moving in incoherent syllables... Of

165

her sleepy, satisfied smile when we'd lain together afterward. Maybe best of all, the bone-deep peace I felt just from holding her.

I thought she had better taste, Henrik grumbled, then chuckled to himself. *Although I'm sure her taste is exquisite in another way.*

Try, and I'll kill you, I growled.

Children, children, Bene chided. *Behave. And remember, the only way our sorry asses will get anywhere is teamwork.*

Teamwork. With a fucking vampire. In whose world was that a good idea?

Gordon's, my dragon snarled.

A sentiment I snatched back when Mina frowned and looked around. Ever since we'd slept together, I had the sneaking suspicion she could read my mind — if not specific thoughts, then at least the general drift.

Which meant I had to be careful with my thoughts. My emotions. My impossible fantasies.

I can't believe you slept with her, Roux grumbled for the hundredth time.

I can't believe he got her before I did, Bene said in his usual carefree way. *But, hey. Bonus points for moving fast.*

I growled out loud. Sleeping with Mina wasn't about scoring. It was about...about...

The L-word snuck into my mind, but I shoved it away.

I wasn't the one who had the bright idea of bringing her along on this mission, I growled at Bene.

I wasn't the one who okayed it, Bene deflected.

You're right. I was, Roux barked. *Because she's our best shot at getting in unnoticed. But only if Romeo here doesn't fuck things up.* He shot me a dark look.

I'm as invested in this as you, I reminded him.

Maybe too invested, Roux grumbled.

Well, all he has to do is keep his hands off her for the next forty-eight hours, Henrik observed snidely. *And keep his mind on the job.*

I grimaced, knowing full well I could do one but not both. I had kept my hands off Mina since our tryst — but that took all my focus and willpower. So, keeping my mind on work. . . tricky.

Maybe we ought to give them a couple of hours together, Bene suggested. *You know, let them get it out of their systems.*

Great idea! my dragon cheered, totally on board with that plan.

I was too, except it was doomed to fail. I would never get Mina out of my system. I didn't want to.

I had to, though, and I knew it. She probably knew it too. But we would face that after this mission.

Mina gazed out her window at the bright lights of Palma de Mallorca. My side of the plane showed moonlight rippling over a dark sea. Which better reflected the future? Were there any truths to be found down there at all?

The pilot lined up with the runway, and my eyes picked out a red wind sock.

Wind from the nose and slightly to port, I noted unconsciously.

The tail of the jet wobbled slightly to the right before the pilot corrected and bumped down into a landing.

Bene looked at me, and I shrugged. "Seven out of ten."

Mina looked over, confused. Then her eyes went wide, as if to say, *Oh, right. You can fly too.*

My chest puffed out a little. Damn right, I could. No jet fuel needed either.

"Ladies and gentlemen, welcome to Palma de Mallorca, where local time is 10:35 p.m. Please remain seated until we have reached our final position," the captain announced.

Minutes later, we stood and filed out. Mina ran her hand over her leather seat and glanced around the cabin before following Roux outside.

First time in a private jet, I figured. Not mine, but the luxury was rare enough.

A limo awaited us on the tarmac, where stewards were already loading our gear into the trunk.

Bene grinned. "Gotta hand it to the boss. He works in style."

Mina stiffened, because that boss was her godfather. A true *Godfather*-style figure, too, though she'd only just discovered that. Or was she still holding out hope that it was one big misunderstanding?

I wouldn't hold my breath.

The night air was cool, but still several degrees warmer than in Burgundy, and thick with Mediterranean scents, along with the cries of sea gulls.

All those sights, smells, and sounds hit me, so fresh and invigorating after the dull air of the jet. Then the limo doors shut, reminding me we were prisoners in Gordon's gilded cage.

"First time in Mallorca?" Bene asked Mina, who sat pensively, taking in every streetlamp, every stone building.

She nodded, craning her head to catch a glimpse of the floodlit cathedral. "You?"

"Nah. Been here lots of times."

To the party mile, probably — a world away from the hilly interior the limo headed for. Soon, the long vehicle was straining around the tight turns of a mountain road. Startled drivers in the oncoming lane stared through the windshields of their tiny, two-door Opel Corsas or Seat Ibizas, the vehicles of choice on this island outpost of Spain.

"Note to self," Bene quipped to Roux. "The limo is great, but we'll need a couple of Land Rovers for tomorrow."

Roux nodded wearily. "They're already on the list."

Bene chuckled. "I love jobs with big budgets."

I made a face. What was to love?

Mina's scent swirled around me. Her face reflected in the window, so melancholy and anxious that I ached to reach out and stroke her cheek.

Nearly an hour later, the limo swung off the main road, crawled over a mile of gravel, then bumped down a cobblestone driveway.

The moment the driver stopped, I leaped out and sucked in a lungful of fresh air.

"Home sweet home," Bene murmured, stretching his arms high.

If Roux hadn't nudged him along, he would probably have folded over into one of those butt-up, head-down poses cats and yoga practitioners loved.

A distinguished older guy met us at the arched entrance. "*Buenos noches.*"

"*Bienvenidos a Finca ses Roques.*" His wife — or so I assumed — motioned us into the courtyard of the complex.

"*Buenos noches,*" Bene echoed, leading the way.

"Wow. Nice," Mina murmured, taking in the exposed stone walls and ancient beams of the complex.

Once upon a time, the place had been a farm. Now, like so many other *fincas* on the island, it had been converted into a luxury getaway. Where goats had once milled around, blue lights illuminated a pool. Glass covered an entire wall of what had been a barn. Leather furniture lined the brightly lit room inside, and a steel stairway led to what were probably sumptuous suites. I spotted at least five smaller outbuildings, one of which served as a luxury kitchen.

The chef had left out finger food and drinks, and we dug in. The caretakers pointed out the basics, then retired to their private quarters at the far end of the property. Mina watched them go, and I couldn't help probing for her thoughts.

Despondent thoughts, I discovered, as she looked around the spectacular but soulless place. Her mouth bent into a frown, and I guessed at the questions pooling in her mind. Did the old couple descend from those who had once scraped out a living on this farm? Had they had any say in how the place had been transformed, or was that all in the hands of a faceless corporation?

Her mood seemed overly sentimental until I thought of big, sprawling Château Nocturne. Was Mina's property doomed to a similar fate, or would she find a way to maintain it in a way that honored the spirit of the place?

A balcony door on the upper story of the barn opened, jolting us out of our thoughts.

"Oh! You're here!" a woman called, beside herself in excitement.

Henrik barely waved, but she squeaked and rushed downstairs.

"Ah, the lovely Delphine." Bene grinned as a woman burst out of the door and ran toward Henrik in a sea of billowing red silk.

"Henrik!" The faux redhead threw herself into a huge, openmouthed kiss.

Mina's eyebrows jumped up.

Roux grimaced with an expression that asked what kind of woman would prostitute herself to a vampire.

Easy. A woman without better options. Was that so hard to understand?

Maybe for a guy like Roux.

Fucking snob, my dragon grumbled.

If anyone was predestined to be a snob, it would be Mina, who'd inherited an entire fucking château. But she mustered a genuine smile and looked at Delphine with zero judgment in her eyes.

"Delphine, meet Mina. Mina, meet Delphine," Bene said, as if Delphine had eyes for anyone but Henrik.

"Nice to meet you," Mina murmured, looking at the happy couple, then at the ground.

So, whew. Not a snob.

My dragon huffed. *Snobs don't plaster their own walls or retile their bathrooms.* I knew, because I'd seen her do both.

Delphine gave a short, blind wave, but she was too busy exploring Henrik's mouth to utter a sound — until she tipped her head back and moaned. Henrik's fangs extended, and her body rippled in anticipation.

"Ugh, guys? Is there somewhere private you can take the show?" Bene tried.

Delphine giggled and dragged Henrik toward the converted barn.

Roux stuck out a hand. "Hey! We're having a meeting."

"Not for an hour, we're not," Henrik called over his shoulder.

We watched them go without a word. Moments later, a lusty cry broke out from upstairs, making Mina wince.

Bene turned away and sighed. "I call the room farthest from them."

"I call the second farthest," Mina chimed in, looking a little pale.

"Dammit..." Roux ran his hands through his hair.

"Like herding cats, huh?" Bene laughed, giving him a playful smack on the shoulder. "Get it? Cats?"

"Cat," Roux grumbled, making a point of the singular. "I have to herd you, a surly vampire, a maverick dragon, and...and..." He motioned at Mina.

I dare you, her wary expression said.

"Our gracious hostess?" Bene supplied.

Roux nodded wearily. "Our gracious hostess."

Mina winced at the next lusty cry that came from the barn, and even Bene looked a little grim.

"Just remember, Dorothy," he murmured. "We're not in Kansas any more. This here is a whole new world. A dangerous one."

Mina's eyes drifted to the balcony as low moans carried out into the night. "Yes, I got that much."

The cries from the barn grew louder and more frenzied, and Bene grimaced.

"I hate to say it, but I don't think we'll get much done tonight. Can we adjourn until tomorrow morning?"

Roux frowned but gave in. "Seven sharp."

"Nine," Bene countered.

"Seven," Roux growled.

Mina pointed silently to the balcony of Henrik and Delphine's room.

Roux smacked the table in frustration. "All right, already. Eight."

We grabbed our things and followed a snaking path marked by dim garden lights. On the far side of the property — out of earshot of the barn, thank goodness — Bene pointed at a row of cottages.

"Oh, damn. Only three. Someone will have to share." He waggled his eyebrows at Mina.

"You and Roux do make a cute couple," she said dryly.

"A commander always gets his own quarters." Roux speed walked into the closest building and slammed the door.

Click went the lock, and Bene sighed. "He really, really needs to get laid." Then he brightened and looked at Mina. "Speaking of which..."

She crossed her arms, daring him to continue.

"Okay, okay. For real, now. We have two options. Option one, you and me." Bene indicated himself and Mina. "Or option two, you and him," he finished, pointing to her and me.

"Or boys in one, girls in another," Mina pointed out.

Bene chuckled. "Like I said, you and him."

I growled under my breath.

That put us at an impasse. Crickets chirped. An owl hooted. Mina scuffed the ground. I watched her, desperately trying to restrain my hopes and desires.

Finally, she closed her eyes. "I'm too tired to argue. And too tired for anything else," she added firmly. "So, you two can duke it out. I'll be asleep — on the couch — in that one." With that, she headed to the middle cottage.

"On the couch?" Bene waved around. "In a place like this?"

"Goodnight," she murmured in that flat, *end of argument* tone she did so well.

Bene tilted his head as she opened the door and disappeared inside.

I smacked his shoulder, and he jerked upright. "What?"

He'd been admiring her ass, and I knew it.

"Maybe," he chuckled, reading my mind.

I rolled my right hand into a fist and waved it in front of his face.

He backed away. "Like the boss said...goodnight." He headed for the last cottage, leaving me alone.

I stood there deciding which feline I was going to kill first, and how.

Then Mina cracked open the door of the middle cottage, looked around, and flashed a *This is ridiculous* look.

I pointed silently at Bene's cottage. *His fault.*

She searched the heavens, presumably for patience. Then she crooked a finger, beckoning me closer.

"Nothing personal, but considering we're on a job..." she started when I joined her at the threshold. Then she petered out and put her face in her hands. "God, you guys have corrupted me already. I sound like a hardened criminal."

Ha. Not by a long shot.

"I get it," I said gruffly.

And honestly, I did. It made perfect sense...in my head. In my heart, however—

I dropped my bags before my dragon made me think, say, or do something stupid, and did an about-face. "No problem. I'll take the couch — after I have a look around."

Mina followed me outside. "A look around? Now?"

I yanked off my shirt and tossed it at her, then bent to unlace my boots.

"Now," I growled.

The sooner I shifted and put some space between us, the better my chances of resisting the urge to throw her over my shoulder and take her to bed.

I threw my boots beside the entrance, undid my pants, and hooked my thumbs into the waistband.

Mina's eyes went wide. "What are you—?"

"Catch," I muttered, dropping my pants, then tossing them to her.

She caught them, more with her face than her hands. Not very nice of me, but if I didn't shift and fly away, I might just hustle her to the bed, the couch, or that rug in front of the fireplace.

Rug, my dragon voted.

We're flying, I hissed to my dragon.

Maybe after? the beast tried.

I ignored the comment, a tactic I'd picked up from Mina.

The cottages clustered around a small, open yard — too small for a sane dragon to shift and take off in. A desperately horny dragon, on the other hand...

I ran three steps, shifting as I went. Then I spread my arms — already turning into wings — bounded to a knee-high boulder, and leaped.

Whoosh! Wind stung my eyes as I strained to fly while pushing away the last vestiges of my human body.

I gritted my teeth, pumped my wings a few times, then held them still. I barely cleared Bene's cottage, but clear it, I did. The moment open air tickled my belly, I exhaled. Then I coiled my tail and let it crack like a whip over his roof, making the walls shake.

Fucking dragons, he cursed.

Nighty-night, I rumbled before shooting up toward the stars, hotdogging in a spiral in case Mina was watching.

Of course she's watching, my dragon chuckled smugly, releasing a long, sparkly plume of fire.

Show-off, Bene muttered into my mind.

Isn't it past your bedtime? I shot back.

Steadying out, I set off to reconnoiter. Partly because that was the smart thing to do, partly to try to keep Mina off my mind.

Operative word: *try.*

Actual result? Epic fail, because all I saw, smelled, and heard was Mina. I pictured her flying at my side, marveling at it all with me. The patchwork blanket of fields and olive groves... The dry, undulating hills... The gentle sea breeze, carrying a faint message to my ears.

A whisper that said, *Destiny.*

Chapter Twenty

MINA

I stood on the threshold for a long time, gazing up. Clutching the doorframe, because, wow. I'd seen a few dragons in my time, but there were dragons, and there were *dragons*, like there were cars and *cars*. Every previous sighting in my memory was the Ford Fiesta type. Marius had the lightning speed of a Lamborghini and the power of a Land Rover.

Or a tank, I corrected myself as another burst of fire lit the night.

I imagined the view from up there. The olive groves. The dry, undulating hills. The terra-cotta roofs, the distant cliffs. . .

More than ever, I felt tiny. Insignificant. Incapable.

I dragged a foot across the gravel path, then stepped inside. Marius was a dragon. I was nothing special. Whatever sparks flew around us were sure to fade out soon — for him, if not for me.

Fifteen minutes later, I was in my knee-length sleep shirt and on the couch, trying to convince myself to sleep.

Still trying an hour later, when heavy thumps shook the ground. The bushes rustled from the sudden burst of wind, and the crickets went still. Gravel crunched — *large* areas of gravel trampled by huge, clawed feet. The sound approached my door, growing fainter as Marius transformed and strode along on two human feet, slowly retracting his mighty wings. At least, that was the picture my ears painted.

The door creaked open, and moonlight sliced into the room.

Click. Darkness fell as the door closed, and I heard his soft breaths.

A shiver went through my body. The good kind.

Er — bad kind. Very, very bad.

He stood by the door for a while. Letting his eyes adjust? Locating his clothes? Looking at me?

Look at me, my body begged.

Soft steps sounded, and my skin prickled. I followed the sound as he detoured around the couch to reach the bedroom. Then he stopped.

I held my breath.

"Mina," he whispered.

I kept perfectly still.

He backtracked, coming closer.

"Mina," he said, barely a step away.

My heart raced, though I did my best to fake a bored, sleepy tone. "Mmm?"

"Want to trade? For the bed, I mean."

If he wasn't in it? No, thanks.

I rolled away, pulling the blanket over my head. "I'm fine. Good night."

The moment the words slipped out, I berated myself. Was I nuts?

Throughout the day, I'd rationalized it all. We'd slept together, and it had been great. But we had a dangerous mission to focus on, with a potentially priceless artwork on the line. It was no time to mess around. We both had to rest so we could operate at peak level tomorrow.

But my libido seemed to have nixed that plan. Out with sleep. In with another kind of peak performance.

Now! Right now! my hormones raged.

"Last chance," Marius murmured in a low, raspy voice.

So, yeah. I wasn't the only one whose body had torn up the script. But if I exercised supreme discipline, Marius would too, and we could both get to sleep.

I kept up my bluff. "Good night."

He waited, unconvinced, then sighed and moved toward the bedroom. I cursed myself with each of his soft steps.

Sleep. Rest. Regenerate. Prepare for secret mission, I told myself, trying to get into a James Bond frame of mind.

Bad analogy, because James Bond didn't rest or regenerate. He danced between silk sheets with nubile young women for half the night.

Nubile young women who usually ended up dead at the hands of the vengeful villain, but hey. I decided to ignore that part. Besides, I wasn't nubile, and I wasn't beautiful. Also, I had at least half a brain, unlike most of the Bond girls.

A brain chanting for me to give up this charade and get it on with my dragon *tout de suite.*

I peeked at the glowing clock and set a five-minute goal. Five minutes to settle down and erase dirty thoughts from my mind.

Two minutes and sixteen seconds later, I groaned and threw back the sheet.

"Marius," I whispered, inching toward the bedroom.

No answer. I frowned.

"Marius," I hissed.

The sheets rustled slightly, and he grumbled, "I said, last chance. You missed yours."

I stuck my hands on my hips. Seriously?

He kept it up for five of the longest seconds of my life, then chuckled and raised the sheet.

"Get in here, woman. Naked, preferably."

I yanked off my sleep shirt and dove into the bed. Into his arms. Into his hungry kiss.

He tasted of fresh, seaside air with the slightest hint of ash. Smacking my lips, I found myself not in the least turned off. Quite the opposite, in fact.

Marius arched a dark eyebrow, striking a *Take it or leave it* look, but I could sense his heart race.

"A little ashy, but otherwise, not bad," I bluffed, touching down for another kiss.

He snorted. "Not bad?"

I grinned into the kiss. "Only the good kind of bad."

"You speak in riddles, woman," the man who was the very definition of *bad* complained.

I ran a hand down his side, inching toward his hip. "Are you saying I should stick to another kind of communication?"

His eyes glowed in the dark. "Works for me."

"All right, then. Lie back," I ordered, guiding him with firm hands.

"You're still talking."

"Patience. I'm about to put my lips to a better use."

His eyes sparkled. "Oh yes?"

"Yes," I promised and made good on that by diving into a deep, hungry kiss.

Those were the last coherent words either of us uttered for a long, long time. I leaned in, doing my best to pin down his body, and he slowly relaxed into the mattress with an amused expression.

Amused irked me, though. He considered himself such a master of control?

I set about proving him wrong, working my way inch by inch down that magnificent body. My lips journeyed from his mouth to his chin, then his neck. They paused at the swell of his chest to kiss, then circle his nipples.

He sucked in a breath, and I hid a *You ain't seen nothing yet* grin.

I slid lower, bumping my way over his abs while scouting ahead with my hands. Another sharp inhale told me I was on the right path. Seconds later, I licked my lips and sealed them over my goal.

He croaked, and every muscle in that fine-tuned body tensed.

I stopped, tilting my head in a tease. "Oh. Did you say something?"

He shook his head at the ceiling and rasped out an exasperated, "No." Then he muttered, "Little minx."

"Little?" I feigned offense.

He wrapped his hands gently around my head and guided me back down. "I won't utter another word. Just don't stop. Please."

I grinned, imprinting the moment into my memory. A dragon, begging. For me.

There was only one thing to do — make him beg more.

Which he did, profusely, though silently, if you didn't count hisses, moans, and clutching the sheets. But just when I was sure he was on the verge of coming — hard — he nudged me away, panting.

"Wait. Turn. Here. . ." he growled, back in caveman mode, and claimed the top.

I wrapped my legs around him, swept up on the same crashing wave of desire. When he drove deep into me, it was my turn to beg, moan, and hiss. And if I cried out a few times. . . Well, how could I not, given the amazing things he did to me?

The man wasn't just a master of *hard* or *deep*. He got full marks for angle, pace, and attention to detail too. Not to mention multitasking, because he put his mouth and hands to equally good use, turning me into a sweaty, incoherent mess.

"Mina," he croaked, then exploded inside.

I dug my fingers into his back, coming half a second after him. And coming and coming in the longest, hardest, highest orgasm of my life. Maybe the longest, hardest, and highest of his too, because when we finally collapsed into the sheets, his expression was all wonder. Wonder with a hint of worry that I could totally relate to. It was one thing to satisfy your body's cravings with a good, hard screw. But losing that much control — *wanting* to lose it — was a whole different thing.

His eyes swirled, two inky, shining universes, and he cupped my face, stroking my cheek with his thumb.

I opened my mouth half a dozen times, forming words, only to hold them back. What was there to say? What was I ready to admit?

Finally, I gulped and tugged on the sheet. "Just to clean up," I whispered, terrified to spoil the mood.

Marius helped, and soon after, we kicked the sheet away, opting for just the blanket. All I really felt, though, were his arms looped firmly around me.

I regarded him silently from a few inches away.

"Careful," he whispered, gently touching my lips. "Don't. . ."

I waited, then squeezed his arm. "Don't what?"

His jaw tightened. "Don't make it mean something."

"Might be too late," I whispered, half hoping he wouldn't hear.

His eyes flared, telling me he had — and that part of him agreed. But his left eye twitched, and I sensed another part of him wrestling with the notion.

I braced myself, sure he would give me the cold shoulder and shatter my foolish heart. But he drew a deep breath, then leaned in with a long, lingering kiss. His chest lifted and fell in a sigh, and he nudged me into the curve of his chest and held me there.

My lips moved again, but he was right. There was nothing to say. That didn't mean my mind ceased to think. Of him. Of us. Of what the next day — and beyond — might bring.

"Good night, Mina," he murmured.

I wrapped my hands around his and closed my eyes. "Good night."

Chapter Twenty-One

MARIUS

"Hell of a way to focus on a mission," Roux grumbled over breakfast the next morning.

I bared my teeth at him. Yes, I'd spent the night with Mina, doing more than just resting. Surprisingly, though, we'd both managed to get some sleep. A deeper, sounder sleep than I'd found in years.

Doesn't take a genius to know what that means, my dragon side muttered. *She's our destiny.*

Bene wandered into the dining room, mumbling, "Good morning." Then his eyes went wide, and he leaned over to sniff me. "Glad someone had a good night."

"Someone other than me," Roux muttered.

Bene shrugged and yawned so wide, his lion fangs showed. "Maybe it will mellow him."

I glowered. Dragons did not mellow, dammit.

"Just what we need going into a mission." Roux hacked at a breakfast sausage with his fork and knife. "And here I was thinking Henrik was going to be our goddamn liability..."

Bene stuck out an arm, blocking me from the coffeepot, as if he expected me to hurl it at Roux. A damn good idea. But maybe great sex had mellowed me, because that hadn't even entered my mind.

I pointed at the clock.

"You said, meet at eight. It's ten to. How's that for focus, asshole?"

Roux didn't look impressed, but Bene nodded cheerily. "Top marks, baby. Especially since you had to leave a warm bed. Or did Mina kick you out?" When I glared, he stuck up his hands, grinning. "Hey, I wouldn't leave her."

A low, dangerous snarl built in my throat. He wouldn't be with Mina in the first place.

Light footsteps sounded behind us, and we whirled.

Mina stepped up, braiding her hair on the go. "Leave who?"

"Uh, I was just saying, it will be hard to leave *here*." Bene motioned at our surroundings and the sumptuous breakfast spread. "Beautiful, huh?"

Mina shot him a dubious look but went on braiding.

It had taken every ounce of resolve I had to leave her in the shower a short time earlier, and now... My cock ached as I soaked in the sight of her. Five foot nine inches of sass, intellect, and determination. Five foot nine inches that had been wrapped around me, moaning in ecstasy, not too long ago. Not to mention when she'd gone down on me and—

Mina's cheeks flushed, and her gaze bounced off mine.

We'd both sworn to focus on business once we stepped outside the cottage, but apparently, her mind was just as stuck back there as mine.

"Sugar with your coffee?" Bene asked Mina.

I nearly huffed. She drank her coffee black. Hadn't he noticed?

"No, thanks. I prefer it black," she said at exactly the same moment.

So, there. I strode over and shouldered between them, loading my plate.

Bene moved aside, chuckling. *All yours, man. All yours.* Then he took his plate over to sit beside Roux and announced, "So, we're all here. Well, everyone except a certain blood-sucking—" Footsteps sounded, and Bene looked up. "Speak of the devil."

Literally, I thought as Henrik appeared at the edge of the patio.

"Good morning," the vampire said in a tone that was merely icy, rather than his usual glacial, *Fuck with me and*

I'll kill you/Don't fuck with me and I still might kill you undertone.

"Now don't you look positively ruddy," Roux observed dryly.

Mina stopped midway through filling her plate, then scraped the Spanish omelet back into the platter. I couldn't blame her for losing her appetite.

I glanced at the upstairs window, hoping Henrik hadn't completely drained poor Delphine. But vampires only looked that flushed after a heavy feeding, so the chances were fifty-fifty.

I started to stand, intent on checking on her, but Roux grabbed my arm. "Where the hell are you going?"

I opened my mouth to reply, but Henrik beat me to it.

"It's eight. Are we meeting, or shall I find another form of entertainment?" He glared, moving quickly to the deepest shade of the patio, right up against the cold stone walls of the building. Like all mature vampires (if mature was the right word), he could tolerate, but preferred to avoid, direct sunlight.

Roux sighed and kicked out the chair opposite him — the one in the shade. "We're meeting. We need to work out the details for today."

Henrik sat without so much as a glance at the breakfast bar. So, he was definitely sated. Bad for Delphine, good for the population of Mallorca. Still, I wasn't about to leave Mina alone around him, so I stayed put.

"Don't worry. I got it all figured out," Bene said through a mouthful of food.

Henrik turned away with a disgusted expression. Which was pretty rich, considering his dining preferences.

"You do, do you?" Roux muttered.

"Yep. Ronald Baumann's party starts at seven, right? I figure we spend the day reconnoitering. At seven-thirty, I march through the front door with Mina and—"

I cut him off with a growl. "I march through the front door with Mina."

Roux pointed firmly at Henrik. "No, *he* marches through the front door with Mina."

The vampire looked just as surprised as I was — and a hell of a lot more pleased. Mina, on the other hand...

"Do I get a say in any of this?"

"No," Roux said, steamrolling along. "We need someone who looks rich and snobby enough to collect art. That's Henrik."

"Thank you?" the vampire grumbled.

Mina gnashed her teeth, but even I had to agree the tiger had a point. Still, I wasn't ready to give up.

"Why not me?"

"Because you'll give us away. Seething fury just won't fit in." Bene patted my shoulder. "But next time we have to infiltrate a fight club, you're in, man."

I balled my hands into fists.

"Delphine and I will arrive at the party first, posing as a couple," Roux said, then looked at Henrik, choosing his words carefully. "That's assuming Delphine will be...er, up to it this evening?"

Henrik flashed his fangs. "Of course she'll be up to it."

Mina looked between Roux and Henrik, aghast. "Does Delphine get any say in this?"

"No," they both said coolly.

Henrik shrugged. "Don't trouble yourself. Delphine knows her role, and she'll be paid handsomely."

His tone sickened me. This wasn't my first time witnessing Henrik's "arrangement" with Delphine, but it was the first time I'd considered the imbalance there. What kind of bastard did that make me?

"You're with the caterers," Roux told Bene, then turned to me. "And you're with the local security staff, if Gordon can pull some strings and get you in with them."

"If?" I asked.

Roux tapped his phone. "He's already on it. Worst-case, we'll get you in as a parking valet."

I bared my teeth. Parking valet?

Bene laughed. "Look at it this way. You'll get to drive some really cool cars for a few seconds each."

I growled at Roux. "I'm with security — or else."

Roux rolled his eyes and went on. "Gordon got his hands on the plans of Baumann's estate." He tapped a few keys on his phone, and our devices pinged with the message. "We need to work out how to secure the target, what extraction route to take, contingency plans..."

He went on for a while, and we listened attentively — a sign that everyone appreciated the risks. If things went south, Gordon wouldn't rush to our rescue, and Baumann had a reputation for shooting to kill.

I looked at Mina, desperate to keep her out of this. But something about that painting had lit a spark in her — a spark bright enough for her to ignore all the warning signs flashing *Danger! Danger!*

It was just a painting, dammit.

Or was it? I hadn't put it all together yet, but there was definitely more there, considering her love of art, the notes in the art book she'd shown us, the references to her father...

Roux fielded a few questions, then assigned tasks. "Bene and Marius — time to reconnoiter. I want everything you can get on Baumann's estate and on Dobrov, the art dealer. Henrik, do whatever it takes to flesh out your cover story. You'll need IDs, credit cards, cash, accounts that look real...the usual."

Mina's jaw dropped, and my gut did too. It wasn't just her rosy view of her godfather that was being pulverized. It was her view of us, what we did, and how we did it.

Even worse, her view of *me*.

But that was for the best, right? The sooner she realized she was better off without me... Well, the better off she would be.

"I'll stay here to iron out loose ends and coordinate," Roux finished.

Mina frowned. "What about me?"

What about you? Roux's furrowed brow asked.

Mina's eyes glowed in anger. And not just a little glimmer — a full-on blaze. Her supernatural ancestry was much closer to the surface than I'd realized. Maybe closer than she realized too.

Roux flapped a hand. "You're going shopping with Delphine."

"Shopping?"

Everyone winced at her shrill tone.

"Shopping." Roux handed over a credit card — as if he hadn't already offended her. "You need to look the part for tonight."

Some women might jump at their chance for a *Pretty Woman*-style shopping spree. But Roux would have been better off handing Mina a discount card to a home improvement center.

Bene patted her hand. "Hey, I'm on catering. We all have to make our sacrifices."

Mina pinned him with a cold, hard glare, then snatched the credit card out of Roux's hand.

"Fine. But I'm doing it for the art, not for the client."

Don't blame us. Blame Gordon, I burned to say. But Mina must have been making me into a better man, because it occurred to me that whatever Gordon was guilty of, I was guilty too, simply for getting myself into this mess.

So, get yourself out, my dragon grumbled.

Easier said than done, especially if the goal was to win over Mina.

A challenge I considered all day while carrying out my assignment. That meant scoping out Baumann's estate from aloft, then joining Bene at the airport to tail the art dealer after his jet touched down on Mallorca.

I borrowed a page from Mina's playbook, however, in thinking for myself while I did all that. Who was Gordon's client, the person behind all this? Why did he — or she — want that particular painting? Or was the painting secondary to some second, hidden agenda, like satisfying a vendetta against Baumann or Dobrov? Worse, was the entire operation some kind of setup?

Many questions, no answers. But one thing was for sure. I was more invested in this mission than I'd been in anything for a long, long time. Which was kind of ironic since the only thing at stake was art, not military secrets or millions of dollars.

Art and Mina, my dragon insisted.

The day passed quickly, with multiple trips between Baumann's estate, Dobrov's hotel, and all potential routing options. Before I knew it, my phone pinged with Roux's reminder to return to our base for a final operations briefing.

I snorted at the text, but Bene just shrugged. "You can take the man out of the military, but you can't take the military out of the man."

"That, or he was born uptight," I muttered.

"That too," Bene chuckled.

At that point, we were at the St. Regis Mardavall Resort, where Lukas Dobrov, the art dealer, had checked in to one of the Royal Penthouse Suites. The drive to our home base at Ses Roques took forty minutes — thirty with Bene's hell-for-leather driving, but still — and I longed to fly instead.

I had the window rolled down, and the wind whispered, *Destiny.*

I nearly rolled it back up, but I closed my eyes instead, considering the possibilities.

Eventually, the tires crunched over gravel, signaling our arrival.

"Home sweet home," Bene announced.

The image that popped into my mind was the château, but when I opened my eyes, I was disappointed to find the *finca* on Mallorca.

"Back to business, Romeo," Bene chuckled, tapping my arm.

What did he think I'd been doing all day? Buying roses?

We found Roux surrounded by documents, maps, and grainy surveillance photos, some of which we'd taken only a short time ago. I had to hand it to the guy — he didn't just step into a job, he tackled it like a goddamn linebacker.

Henrik stood in the innermost corner of the room, sipping red wine. At least, I hoped that was what he was sipping. He and Roux were dressed to the nines, as appropriate for their roles at the party.

Roux greeted us with a nod and motioned to our rooms. "Get changed. The minute Mina and Delphine return, we'll deploy. Bene and Marius first, then Delphine and me, followed by Henrik and Mina."

I clenched my teeth. Henrik might not have a problem with another guy posing as his girl's date, but I definitely did. Especially when the poser was a vampire.

"Oh, and good news." Roux tossed me a clip-on ID. "Gordon got you on to the security detail. Just the local team, of course, not Baumann's private squad, but still an in."

I caught it one-handed, checked the photo, and snorted.

"How much security are we expecting?" Bene asked.

"Minimal," Roux replied. "Think of the art dealer as a pop-up boutique operator. He won't have time to rig the place with cameras, motion detectors, or any of the other usual safeguards. And he'll only have a handful of guards since Baumann will want him to keep a low profile."

"I guess he gets a commission?" I asked.

Roux shrugged. "That, or first dibs on the best pieces or just bragging rights among the millionaires he schmoozes with." He checked his watch again. "Time for you two to get moving."

"Five euros says I beat you," Bene dared me on the way to his cottage.

A deal I took and easily won, with twenty-two minutes to his thirty for a shower, shave, and wardrobe change.

"Well, as security, you don't have to look good," he said, touching his perfectly coiffed, golden hair.

"And catering does?" I snickered.

Roux looked up, then shook his head at Bene. "Marius is right. You can't look so...so..."

Bene flashed his best Hollywood grin. "Good? Dare I say, hot, even?"

"Memorable," Roux grunted. "You can't stand out in a crowd."

Bene's grin widened. "Not my fault I'm outstanding. I was born this way."

"Born with extra-volume conditioner and aftershave?" Henrik wrinkled his nose. "What is that? Dolce&Gabbana?"

Bene looked offended. "Jean Paul Gaultier. Enough to cover my scent from other shifters."

The rest of us had taken similar precautions, but you never knew. A shifter with a really good nose might still ferret us out.

Roux pointed back at the cottage. "Whatever that is, change it. Now. And not just the aftershave. The hair too."

"How?"

Roux shook his hands in exasperation. "I don't know. Just change it. Look more like a bozo."

"Comb it back like Henrik does," I offered, earning a lethal look from the vampire.

Bene sighed and returned ten minutes later, looking marginally less striking and smelling incrementally less seductive.

"Better? Or should I say, worse?" he asked sullenly.

Roux rubbed both hands over his face in exasperation.

A vehicle pulled into the driveway, and we all turned.

"Oh, the girls are back," Bene said, spotting the limo.

Women, I nearly growled.

My inner dragon perked its ears, cheering, *Mina! Mina!*

The driver parked and opened the rear door, offering his hand to the first passenger.

Delphine exited, looking surprisingly... Well, *classy*, despite the fire-engine-red dress. Amazing what toning down on makeup and jewelry could do.

Bene whistled. "Delphine, you look stunning. Not that I'm surprised."

Delphine grinned at him, but she positively glowed at Henrik and turned in a slow circle for him. "Do you like it?"

"Nice," he said in his usual detached way.

Limited as his attention was, Delphine basked in it.

I wondered if Mina could talk some sense into the poor girl. Surely, Delphine could do better than Henrik?

I caught myself there. As surely as Mina could do better than me?

A light, arched foot in sand-colored heels slid out next, and my breath caught. A good thing too — otherwise I might have growled when the driver leaned in to offer Mina a hand. And when she emerged—

My mouth hung open, and my mind went blank.

"Damn, Mina. You look really good," Bene breathed.

Heavenly was more like it. The gold-and-cream dress shone in bright contrast to Mina's cocoa-colored hair, which bounced over her shoulders in long, elegant locks. Tiny studs shone from her earlobes, matching the sequins of the dress.

"Giorgio Armani," Delphine gushed, flouncing her dress beside Mina. "Mine too."

Giorgio knew what he was doing, showing just a hint of Mina's cleavage and a hell of a lot of her long, toned legs.

Mina put an arm around Delphine, and they grinned at each other like a couple of sisters. Kind of a contradiction, because Mina was educated. Poised. Classy, in a word. Delphine was a hooker Henrik had found on a street corner in Marseilles. Nothing personal — truly — but that was just the way the world was.

But Mina didn't seem to see it that way. So, hmm. Maybe I ought to... What was that called? Broaden my perspective.

Mina gave Delphine a hearty hug. "Yours looks better."

I begged to differ, but I kept my mouth shut.

The effect wasn't even spoiled when Mina tottered over the gravel. Clearly, she had more practice in work boots than heels.

"If I break an ankle in these things, I'm blaming Roux," she grumbled.

He frowned. "How is everything always my fault?"

Bene thumped him on the back. "Because you're in charge, champ."

Roux ran a hand through his hair, but Delphine fixed it on her way to glueing herself to Henrik's side. "Remember, you have to look the part. Both of you."

That was my only consolation. I didn't get to go into this mission as Mina's date, but I didn't have to wear a tux either.

Still, the flesh-toned parts of Mina's dress made me look twice, and I didn't relish her flashing that much skin — or pseudo-skin — to anyone, least of all a vampire.

"Dammit, this thing is giving me a wedgie," Mina groused, plucking at the back of her dress.

Bene waggled his eyebrows. "Want me to help?"

"Not a chance, buster."

She glanced at me next, then looked away just as quickly. Still, my groin ached.

"All right, already. Time to review and make sure everyone's got the last details." Roux set his hands on the paper-strewn table and began his final briefing.

It was hard to focus, but when I reminded myself Mina's life could be on the line... Well, I was all ears.

Chapter Twenty-Two

MINA

"Not the time for second thoughts," Henrik hissed, looming over the limo door. Beyond him, party lights sparkled and guests chatted.

I clutched my ridiculously overpriced purse, harboring not just second but third, fourth, and fifth thoughts. Not that I had much choice now.

I did my best to slide, not trip, out of the limo — one that had picked us up at a pricey hotel, not our base at the *finca*, in order to better cover our trail. Henrik reached down, helping me out with his cold, clammy vampire hand.

My skin crawled, but I forced myself to wind my arm through his.

For Dad, I told myself. *For art lovers everywhere.*

I teetered on my heels, grimacing. Plan B — making a run for it — was definitely out.

I pasted on a smile, lifted the hem of my dress, and followed Henrik up the stairs of the imposing villa.

Prudence told me to focus on the marble stairs, because *death by high heels* was a distinct possibility. But the villa was practically a palace, all glass planes and sleek lines, and I couldn't help gaping at the stunning clifftop views. The setting sun cast glittering orange and red lines over the Mediterranean. The clear, clean notes of a string quartet drifted skyward, welcoming guests to the party.

It ought to have been beautiful, but all I felt was foreboding.

Henrik mumbled out of the corner of his mouth, "Focus. It's showtime."

Showtime was right, with everyone dressed like they'd come straight from the Oscars — including whoever had arrived in the helicopter standing on a pad at the far end of the property.

Dressed to kill, I reminded myself. According to Roux, the guest list included arms dealers, mafia bosses, and crooked politicians.

"Welcome, welcome," the man at the top of the stairs greeted the couple ahead of us.

Ronald Baumann, I presumed. Roux's photos were a little dated, but otherwise on the money.

Hugh Grant's evil stunt double, Bene had quipped, and he was right. The features were a one-for-one match, minus the goofy charm.

The woman ahead of me curtsied, and I panicked. Was I expected to curtsy too? How the hell did one curtsy anyway, especially in heels? It was all I could do to keep my center of gravity over the damn things when I was upright.

Henrik flashed a little fang and tightened his grip on my arm. "Don't worry. I've got you, darling."

I stuck an elbow in his ribs. "And I have wooden stakes up both sleeves, *darling.*"

The couple proceeded into the house, and the host turned to us with a smile.

"Ronald Baumann," he said, shaking Henrik's hand.

"Henrik van Hoerde," my "date" replied smoothly, then motioned to me. "Miss Maria Orlemann."

Baumann's eyes lit as he looked me over the way one studied a nude statue in a museum — pretending not to be interested but leering on the inside. That included a long, hard look at the scarf around my neck — a last-minute addition by my stylist, Delphine.

You're posing as a vampire's date, she'd explained, all matter-of-fact. *And vampires' dates get marks on their necks. So...*

My skin crawled.

We couldn't be sure Baumann would peg Henrik as a vampire at all, especially since he'd doused himself with expensive cologne. But I had to look the part in case Henrik's cover was blown.

Baumann took my hand — literally *took* it before I even offered — and grazed his lips over my knuckles.

"Isn't she lovely," he murmured to Henrik.

My fake smile threatened to slip, but I managed to keep it glued in place, mainly because the alternative — kneeing him in the balls — wouldn't get us any closer to our objective.

Also, I would topple down the stairs if I tried kneeing any-one while perched on suicidal heels.

I caught the barest whiff of a canine scent in Baumann.

Wolf shifter, Bene had said. *An especially nasty one too.*

Baumann's eyes traveled back up my body, and when his eyes met mine—

Boom! I was hit by an out-of-nowhere, *brushed-by-moonlight* moment that opened a door on his soul. And, yikes. If I had any misgivings about this mission, they vanished, be-cause all I saw were evil and greed.

Briefly, I wondered which of my ancestors that power stemmed from and what else they could do. Mostly, though, I clutched Henrik's arm. Even a vampire was better than Bau-mann.

"Enjoy the party," our host said, turning to his next guests.

And just like that, we were in. But boy, was I nervous.

"Now what?" I whispered to Henrik. "How do we get an invitation to wherever the art is?"

Henrik smirked. "Patience, *ma belle.* Patience."

He looked around, oozing old-world mannerisms and...well, *charm* would be an overstatement, but there was a certain appeal in his aloof bearing. Women were already eyeing him like he might be titled nobility. *Duke* this, *Prince* that, or even *Your Highness.* And hell, he might be.

"Champagne for you, señor? Señora?"

I nearly cheered at the familiar voice. Bene!

Henrik was about as comforting to have around as an arms dealer, but having Bene around helped. Marius would be even better, but Bene was a good start.

The lion shifter's eyes danced, but he kept his expression neutral, reminding me to do the same.

"Or would you prefer sparkling water?" He held out a tray, jerked his eyes to the right, and dropped his voice. "Dobrov is the short guy in blue at three o'clock. He arrived with three big crates, which are in the library." He jerked hiis eyes the other way. "Down that hallway, third room on the right. Two guards."

Henrik nodded crisply, taking two champagne flutes and handing me one.

I frowned, staring into it. "What if I wanted water?"

Henrik shrugged, raised his glass, and sipped.

I held my glass in front of his face and gave it a little shake. "I won't throw this at you now, but who knows?" I smiled sweetly. "I might get my chance back at the château."

Bene chuckled. "Watch your back, buddy."

Henrik motioned with his champagne. "Shoo, kitty. Shoo."

Bene waltzed off, unperturbed. Henrik took another sip and glanced around, haughty as ever.

I stood at his side, waiting. And waiting and waiting...

Finally, I nudged Henrik. "What now?"

Another disinterested sip. "Patience."

Not my strong suit. I looked around and piqued my senses. Most of the guests were human, with a few scattered supernaturals, each of whom kept a low profile. A wolf shifter here, a vampire there...

My heart pounded. If only I had more of my ancestors' powers! But even if I did, I was never going to outfight, outfly, or outmagic anyone. I could only maximize what I had, like brains, cunning, and art knowledge. Not exactly Marvel-comic superpowers, but hey. I wasn't about to give up now.

I scanned the room for a better look at Dobrov, but I spotted Marius first. A rainbow arced over my soul, and my heart leaped. If I hadn't exercised supreme self-discipline, I might have jumped up and down.

He stood against a wall between a catering table and a ceiling-high palm, looking all the world like a secret service agent in his dark suit. When our eyes met, a mix of heat and ice shot through my veins. Heat, because Marius was Marius, and my body reacted that way every time. Ice, because his look was that cool and detached.

Henrik chuckled, and I glanced at him, annoyed.

And, oops. In the next split second, I learned Lesson One about undercover work with a vampire. Never, ever turn to face him without your guard firmly up — as in up in the stratosphere. Otherwise, you might get dragged into a smothering kiss.

Make that a *superglue* kiss, because it took several seconds of struggling to break loose. I raised my hand to punch him, but he grabbed it.

"Now, now, darling," Henrik chuckled. "Remember, you have to look the part."

The air pressure in the room spiked, and a growl sounded in my mind.

I turned, spotting Marius, and boy, did he look furious.

I will kill him, I swore I heard him snarl.

Yeah, well. Get in line, I grumbled, then shoved Henrik. "Stop provoking him."

His eyes glittered. "Most fun I've had this century."

By some miracle, I hadn't spilled my drink, and I held it up in a mock toast. "Until the day — very, very soon — when you get roasted by dragon fire or staked in the heart. Cheers."

He had the nerve to laugh and touch his glass to mine a second time. "Cheers, *ma belle.*" But something over my shoulder caught his eye, and he frowned.

Following his gaze, I found Roux and Delphine across the room. The tiger was positively striking in his tux. Delphine looked every bit as stunning in her red dress — but wounded to the core.

Henrik looked at her a moment longer, then turned away. A small but infinitely cruel gesture that angered me as much as the kiss.

"You're a bastard, you know that?" I couldn't help hissing. "The way you treat her..." His blank look made me huff. "Unbelievable."

He frowned. "You mean Delphine?"

"Yes, I mean Delphine!"

He waved his glass. "Look around. See the caterers? The musicians? They're all staff. That's what Delphine is. She's been hired to do a job, just like them."

"Not at all like them," I muttered.

His eyes flashed and not in a good way. "Delphine is here for a paycheck, and she'll get it — a very handsome one."

"What if a paycheck isn't all she's after?"

He frowned, genuinely confused. "What else would she be after?"

Boy, he really didn't get it, did he?

"When we arrived last night, Delphine ran into your arms. That wasn't an act," I growled.

Henrik's brow furrowed.

"Every time she looks at you, her eyes light up — and not with dollar signs. All that time we were out shopping, it was, 'Do you think Henrik would like' this or that? She couldn't wait to show you her dress."

"She showed everyone her dress."

I shook my head. "She showed it to you. And all you could say was 'nice.'" I mimicked his deep, bored voice.

In truth, the last thing I wanted was for those two to hook up. But Delphine was truly sweet, and she'd endured some hard knocks. Over the course of the day, the cruelty of her line of work had slowly dawned on me. Men desired her — desperately — but God forbid she made a guest appearance in a client's "real life." She was smart, funny, and interesting, but all men saw were tits, ass — and blood, in Henrik's case.

"I pay the baker for my baguettes, but I thank him too. Sincerely," I ranted.

"You want me to thank her?" Henrik blinked, uncomprehending.

It took everything I had not to shove him. "I want you to *appreciate* her. To *see* her."

"I see her," he insisted.

"You see her the way you see furniture. You barely even notice she's there."

His face hardened. "It's better that way."

"For you or for her?"

His eyes flashed, and for the first time that evening, I wasn't just annoyed. I was afraid.

"For everyone involved." He tossed back the rest of his drink, set it down with a thump, and straightened his tie. "If the lecture is over, I'd like to get back to work."

He strode off, leaving me gaping. Then I caught myself and followed him, tightening the scarf around my neck.

I glanced around, but if anyone had noticed, they looked away politely. All except one strikingly curvy woman over by the wall, who didn't bother hiding her amusement. She didn't bother hiding her interest in Henrik either.

Yes, he looked good — not to mention rich and aristocratic. But, yuck. The guy was a self-absorbed, coldhearted vampire.

She was a dark-haired Spanish beauty, all curves from her lips to her hips, like Catherine Zeta-Jones or Russell Crowe's hot, doomed wife in *Gladiator*. And, yikes — even from this distance, I could sniff her perfume — a label Delphine had pointed out to me during our shopping spree.

Carolina Herrera "Good Girl," she'd said. *They call it "cat-nip for men."*

I wanted to huff and tell the woman, *He's all yours, honey. I'm just his fake date for the evening.*

But I couldn't. Anyway, what did I know? She might be just as self-absorbed and coldhearted as Henrik. Maybe they were a perfect match.

For the next ten minutes, I remained as close to Henrik as I could stand, quiet and sullen. I figured I could get away with it, because a self-absorbed man's date had the right to grow disgusted with him from time to time.

Still, I had to admit, Henrik knew how to schmooze. I didn't catch on at first, wondering why he devoted his attention — such as it was — to the people around Lukas Dobrov rather than targeting the art dealer directly. But that's what he did, dropping offhand remarks about apartments in London, Paris, and Dubai, as well as racehorses, vineyards, and disgruntled employees. Even I was buying into the bored billionaire act until he mentioned a château that sounded a hell of a lot like mine.

He glanced my way, and the twitch at the corner of his mouth was a smirk aimed at me.

And bit by bit, he reeled Dobrov in.

A mention of golf courses — courses Henrik implied he owned, not just played on — and Dobrov's head turned. A comment about Scotch whisky aged for sixty years in sherry casks made the art dealer step closer. And when someone mentioned the decor in Baumann's lushly appointed villa, Henrik heaved a sigh of deep suffering.

"I've been looking for a good decorator for months."

Over by the wall, Marius rolled his eyes.

But, hell. It worked, because Dobrov hurried over to introduce himself to Henrik with a long, hearty handshake. I barely merited a glance, despite a dress that made every other man in the place leer — especially at the skin-toned part covering my chest. But to Dobrov and Henrik, I was just there, like the rug under their feet.

I balled my hands into fists and fantasized about telling Dobrov about *my* château, my vineyard, and my racehorse.

Okay, no racehorse and lots of leaks in the château, but the wine from the vineyard was mighty fine, if I did say so myself.

"I couldn't help overhearing you," the slick, diminutive man said. "I dabble in decorating myself."

I bit back a snort. Dabbled or dealt — as in precious, lost art?

Henrik stifled a yawn and turned away. Which had the same effect as ignoring Delphine: the more Henrik shunned, the more desperately she — or Dobrov — sought him out.

The man stuck to Henrik like a burr to a sheep, nodding and smiling at anything Henrik said. Behind him, I spotted the curvy woman with her big lips, big boobs, and plunging neckline. Her gaze caught on someone across the room, and her eyes lit up with mischief.

I watched her sashay away, and good riddance. Let her seduce some other man tonight.

Dobrov gradually maneuvered himself in front of Henrik, and when the conversation paused, he jumped at his chance.

"What really sets Ronald apart is his taste in art," Dobrov said, picking up where he'd left off minutes earlier.

Henrik let his eyes slowly drift over the walls, where monochrome works of modern art hung in minimalist frames.

"Not to my taste."

"Oh no. Not this," Dobrov said quickly. "I mean, not *just* this. Ronald has decorated different sections of the house in different styles."

"You don't say," Henrik murmured, signaling for another drink.

Bene ambled by and presented his tray with a flourish. Clearly not his first catering gig.

I snagged a water, while Dobrov snatched two flutes and offered Henrik one. The vampire accepted without a word of thanks to either man.

"What are you looking for? Maybe I can help," Dobrov tried.

Oh, I bet he could.

Henrik gestured vaguely. "Something less. . . contemporary, I suppose."

I nearly snorted. Yes, by about 150 years, give or take. Or were decades mere dog years in a vampire's world view?

Dobrov lit up like a kid on Christmas. "I've helped Ronald acquire a few good pieces over the years. I was about to present a selection of exclusive pieces to a few friends. Would you like to have a look?"

Henrik frowned at his watch as if he had somewhere better to be. Then he sighed. "I suppose I could. What do you think, darling?" He locked his hand over mine.

It took everything I had not to yank away. "Of course, *darling.*"

My pulse rose as we followed Dobrov down the hallway Bene had indicated, with three other guests joining us along the way. I glanced back at Marius for reassurance and—

—nearly stumbled over my own feet. Miss Curves and Plunging Neckline was practically hanging off his arm. Whispering in his ear. Chuckling.

When she ran her hand over his chest in an easy, intimate gesture, my heart stopped. This wasn't her first time touching Marius. She knew him. Intimately.

Bile rose in my throat.

"Who's that?" I asked Henrik

He turned to look with the same dull, *what do I care* expression, then blanched.

"Celeste." His tone dropped dangerously.

"And she knows Marius?"

He snorted. "Oh, she knows him, all right."

Then it hit me. Celeste — Marius's ex.

"Will she cause trouble?" I asked, though I already knew.

"That woman is nothing but trouble," Henrik sniffed.

At last — something we agreed on.

Over by the far wall, Roux looked equally shaken.

"Does she know you? All of you, I mean?" I asked.

Henrik grimaced. "Yes. She works for Gordon too."

I grimaced. "What crime did she commit?"

Henrik scowled. "She doesn't have to work for Gordon. She chooses to."

My gut roiled. It was bad enough to discover that Gordon dealt with arms dealers, vampires with ambiguous morals, and other criminals. But somehow, Celeste made it even worse. I didn't know much about her, but one thing was clear. The woman was a crocodile creeping through murky waters, waiting to prey on unsuspecting souls.

"Come along, come along," Dobrov called.

Henrik shot a last look at Celeste, then tugged me along.

"Come along, darling."

Conspiracy theories flashed through my mind. What if Henrik was in cahoots with Celeste? What if they were plotting some kind of double-cross?

Marius looked more thunderous than ever, and his eyes telegraphed urgent messages. *Stop. Don't. Danger!*

Two burly security types stepped into the hallway, blocking my view of him.

Henrik shot me an icy look that echoed what he'd said before. *Not the time for second thoughts.*

I sucked in a breath, though my throat was dry and tight.

For Dad, I reminded myself, following Dobrov, Henrik, and the others into the library.

The moment I stepped inside, guards thumped the heavy oak doors shut behind me.

Chapter Twenty-Three

MARIUS

Watching Mina with Henrik was torture, especially with that bastard playing up every touch and gesture.

Like that kiss, my dragon snarled.

It had taken everything I had not to roar, shift, and pummel the guy. Mina looked furious too, and I'd been rooting for her to punch him. Even if it had blown our cover, it would have been worth it.

Grab her, my dragon growled. *Get her out of here. To hell with Gordon and his fucking client.*

But Mina wanted that painting badly, and I needed to finish my six months with Gordon if I was ever going to move on to a new life. A better life.

A life with Mina, my dragon breathed.

Thin-ice territory, for sure, but that fantasy was getting harder and harder to ignore.

I scanned the room. Baumann's party was in full swing, with guests filling the vast living room and a terrace big enough to play tennis on. The glass doors in between had been pushed back, creating one huge, indoor/outdoor area.

In terms of party vibes, it was amazing. In terms of security, it was a nightmare.

Which played into our hands, of course — multiple exits, no clear perimeter, the cover of noise and darkness, people coming and going...

The hair on the back of my neck prickled, and I turned at the sound of heels clicking over the marble floor.

"Well, well. If it isn't Marius," a woman murmured.

205

I froze. Celeste? Here? Now? How?

She chuckled. "Aw, how sweet. So happy to see me, you're tongue-tied."

I couldn't tell if she was joking. That was the thing with Celeste. You could never tell anything, and you could never, ever let your guard down.

"Imagine seeing you here," she clucked cheerfully.

I steeled my shoulders. "Pretend you didn't."

She chuckled. "Trying to go incognito?"

I shook my head. "Trying not to draw attention."

"And yet here I am, drawing all your attention," she practically purred. "Go on. Try to resist. You know you can't."

The thing was, I could. A huge — and welcome — surprise. Not even a monk could resist a succubus when she turned up her charms.

Which Celeste did, ratcheting them all up to the highest level. I could sense her seductive haze creep in around me, along with tendrils of heat that tried to spark something within me — but nothing like the irresistible inferno of our previous encounters. Why?

My dragon snorted. *Do you have to ask?*

My eyes slid to Mina, and I found myself thanking destiny, for a change. To have brought me Mina — and armor me against Celeste... Maybe destiny's intentions weren't all bad.

Celeste followed my eyes and scoffed. "Now, don't tell me that little mouse has caught your eye." She leaned in, sniffed, then cackled. "Oh, she's caught more than your eye, hasn't she?"

Shit, shit, shit. Not good.

Her eyes narrowed, and she studied Mina more intently. "She's not that bitch Gordon was so worried about the night Szabo visited your humble abode, is she?"

A long row of red flags popped up in my mind. So many, I barely knew where to begin.

"Szabo? What do you know about Szabo?"

The minute I asked, I regretted it, because my tone gave me away.

Celeste's eyes sparked with interest. "Well, someone has to keep an eye on you four after all. You, most especially. Just to keep you out of trouble, of course."

I jutted my jaw. Gordon had seen fit to have someone check up on us — only to call Mina, worried, a short time later? It didn't make sense.

Something in Celeste's smug expression finally made it click. Gordon didn't have a reason to check on us, but Celeste did — at least in her warped, twisted world. I was one of dozens, maybe hundreds, of men who'd fallen for her, but I was also the first — and only — to break free of her spell. Not only that, but I'd warned Bene and Roux away from her too.

Hell hath no fury like a woman scorned, the saying went, and that went double for a sex-craving succubus. Had she sent Szabo to check on us — and nearly gotten Mina killed?

A growl built in my throat, but Celeste just tut-tutted. "My, my. Isn't someone all worked up about one lowly human?"

She's neither human nor lowly, I wanted to snarl. But I kept my mouth shut for a change.

"And, oh, the poor girl. Szabo gave her a real scare, didn't he?" Celeste snipped, watching Mina closely. "It must be so hard, her life. You know — inheriting her own château and all."

Clearly, Celeste hadn't snooped too closely. If she had, she would have known what a money pit that place was.

And how hard Mina is working to save it, my dragon added fiercely.

"Not only that, but she has to put up with Gordon paying her to keep a whole crew of strapping young men for company." Celeste's voice dripped with sarcasm, then turned cruel. "Has she fucked all four of her guests or just you?" My growl only made her chuckle. "Ah, I see. Only you." Then she snorted under her breath. "Amateur."

My blood boiled, and I berated myself for the hundredth time. How had I ever allowed myself to get involved with Celeste? But my guard had been down, and magic as strong as hers was hard to resist.

Still, it made me sick. As sick as her sudden interest in Mina.

"What is our little mouse up to now?" Celeste clucked as Dobrov led Mina and Henrik toward the library. Baumann's private security guards hadn't let the extra hands — like me — anywhere near the room, but I'd seen the crates carried in earlier.

Getting Mina and Henrik access had been the plan all along, but now, alarms clanged in my mind. Letting Mina out of sight, especially around Henrik, was bad enough. Letting her enter a locked room with Henrik and a shady art dealer was even worse. And now, Celeste had appeared. Was she here to report to Gordon, or was she pursuing another goal?

Mina glanced back at me, and our eyes met.

Stop. Forget it. Something is fishy here, I tried pleading.

Her lips quivered, but she set her shoulders and stubbornly disappeared down the hall.

"Now, now. Where might those two be going, I wonder?" Celeste chuckled mischievously.

I stepped sideways, blocking her view. "I'm trying to work here. Shouldn't you be doing the same?"

She laughed, tiptoeing her fingers down my chest. Once upon a time, that had turned me on. Now my skin crawled.

"Poor Marius. What's happened to you? You used to be so much more daring."

No, I used to be much stupider. I kept that to myself, though.

Celeste eased away with a dramatic sigh. "I suppose you're right. Back to work I go. See you later?"

I clenched my teeth. God, I hoped not.

When she sashayed away, I made a point of slowly scanning the rest of the room — any part that didn't have her in it — though my mind spun the entire time. Celeste worked for Gordon, which put her on our side. Technically. But Celeste had only really ever played for one side — her own — and she was capable of anything. Especially jealousy.

Hell hath no fury... my dragon reminded me.

When Celeste wanted a man, she wanted him. Even men she'd chewed up and spat out remained on her radar. They were supposed to pine after her for the rest of their days, all lonely, pathetic, and miserable.

I hadn't fallen quite that low, but I hadn't been far either. Until Mina.

My eyes started sliding toward the library, until I caught myself and yanked them away. As a security guy, I shouldn't show any interest in Mina — or Celeste, for that matter.

I forced a blank expression. But inside, I seethed — and fretted — as time dragged on.

At one point, a laugh rang out over the hubbub of the party. Looking over, I found Celeste hanging on Baumann's arm.

Laughing. Flirting. Calculating how to manipulate the situation to her benefit, my dragon grumbled.

And Baumann was eating it up. Clearly, he was one of those men who only considered his own power and ambitions. He might recognize potential threats from other men, but women were mere objects, and definitely not rivals.

He ought to have been on guard, though, and not just against Celeste's seductive charms. Every move she made, every word she uttered, was calculated. But what was her goal?

I checked my watch for the tenth time. Still no sight of Mina or Henrik, and not a peep from Roux. I tugged on my collar and stared at the hallway Mina had disappeared down. What was taking so long, dammit?

Chapter Twenty-Four

MINA

Stepping into the library, we traded the breezy, bustling reception rooms for a quiet, stuffy space. I glanced around nervously. Other than a narrow rear hallway leading to a toilet and an office, there was nowhere to run. Not even a window, at least not in this room.

Not here to run, I reminded myself. *It's time to find that painting.*

First, though, I had to check that our intel was correct — right down to the dumbwaiter in the corner of the adjoining office. A peek down the connecting hallway told me, *Bingo.*

I looked away quickly.

Dobrov made a sweeping gesture. "Apologies. I've only unpacked the smaller pieces so far..."

I stared. Was that an Olmec mask? And that jade carving...

"Qing dynasty," Dobrov said as one of his prospective buyers inspected it.

"Lovely," the man murmured, while another reached into a crate and pulled out a long, thin object.

"Now, be careful, Rodrigo," Dobrov joked as the man carefully unwrapped it.

The man whistled. "Is this what I think it is?"

Dobrov nodded smugly. "Sixteenth-century Ottoman scimitar with jeweled scabbard."

It was amazing and probably worth a fortune if it was the real deal. Hell, even a modern replica would cost a pretty penny.

Henrik turned back to the door. "Not what I'm looking for."

Maybe not, but I sure was mesmerized.

Dobrov darted in front of Henrik and motioned to the left. "Allow me to direct you this way. Might a Monet be of interest?"

I nearly gave myself whiplash. Monet?

Henrik followed him reluctantly, like a man too polite to turn down an invitation to a friend's kid's third-grade musical recital. Except Henrik wasn't polite, and he didn't have friends. Not from what I'd witnessed anyway.

"Closer to your taste?" Dobrov asked.

Henrik cocked his head, not too inspired. "Perhaps."

My eyes just about popped out of my head. The painting propped against the wall on a table there looked a hell of a lot like *Thaw*, one of the artworks on my father's list of lost masterpieces.

"And the provenance?" Henrik asked, barely looking at the painting.

I was all ears. Without provenance — proof of an artwork's origin and legitimate transfer from owner to owner over the years — an artwork couldn't be considered genuine.

Like that Monet, I quickly decided. The signature looked good, but it was over in the left corner instead of Monet's preferred right, and the brushstrokes were a little too blurred to have stemmed from Monet's hand. Probably a forgery — to my eye, at least.

Dobrov pointed to the signature, then pulled an envelope from behind the frame. "You'll find a full record here."

I masked my skepticism, because records could be forged too.

The other paintings propped on the table were a hideous still life by Kirchner and a bleak landscape that screamed *Edvard Munch had a bad day.*

Henrik beelined straight to that one.

"I see love, hope, and possibility," I murmured, testing him.

He sighed happily. "I see darkness, death, and despair."

Aha. Just the theme for his apartment in Paris, then — if he actually had one.

I caught myself wondering. If Henrik were actually shopping for art with his own money, would I tell him that overly bright red pigment in the Munch made me peg it as another forgery?

Nah. Which only proved how far my morals were sliding.

I motioned to the crate beside the table, where more paintings were stacked sideways like framed posters at Walmart. Downright sacrilegious — if they were real. Another reason to doubt them?

"May I?" I asked Dobrov.

The art dealer turned to me, though his eyes went to my cleavage, not my face. "Go ahead, sweetheart. Especially if you convince your date to buy one."

I gritted my teeth. God, I hated being eye candy.

Placing my purse on the table, I started flipping through the paintings.

"Lukas? I'd like to hear more about this piece, please," one of the other guests called.

Dobrov scurried away, and Henrik sidestepped, blocking their view of me.

"Anything?" he whispered.

Everything might have been the best answer, given the works in that crate. A Canaletto. A colorful, abstract Paul Klee. A glowing, sixteenth-century portrait by Caravaggio, if the label was to be believed.

By my amateur estimation, about half the works appeared genuine, although their provenance or owners were probably shady. Why else would the work of a great master be traded in a backroom deal like this? A very posh back room, but still. Either the paintings had been purchased with dirty money, or they'd been carted off by one or another army in World War II and written off as collateral damage, when they'd actually landed in private collections.

Briefly, I thought of Clement. What would he think of my being here? And, shit. Hadn't he worked for a task force that brought down crime syndicates in Marseilles? Had my host,

Ronald Baumann, or Dobrov come up in any of his cases?
Had Gordon?

Dammit. I ordered myself to focus on the paintings. *Concentrate.*

The other half of the works in the crate appeared to be forgeries, like the Monet. Very good forgeries, but still. Some were so good, I almost preferred them to the real thing — like the delightful unicorn I came across "by Franz Marc." My favorite artist had painted lots of horses in all colors of the rainbow, but never, ever a unicorn. A damn shame.

That painting was big enough to jut above the others. The next was smaller. I turned to it and inhaled sharply.

Henrik coughed into his hand. *Watch it.*

Easier said than done, especially when stumbling across a long-lost Van Gogh.

I blew out my cheeks. What my father would have given to be in my position now.

"You're here to assess, not admire," Henrik hissed.

Right. Assess. Was that *The Painter on the Road to Tarascon* the real thing?

Veteran art critics assessed paintings by the details, but also by intuition, often on the basis of an initial, split-second impression.

I wasn't a veteran, but damn if my intuition wasn't screaming, *This is the real thing!*

I leaned in, trying to be scientific. Brushstrokes...paint...the canvas... All matched other works by Van Gogh. The composition also matched the original, as captured in a 1930s photograph. My sister and I used to argue about two leaves on the left side of the image. Were they falling or just not clearly connected to the tree? Either way, the leaves in this painting were exactly as I remembered them, right down to the way they'd been dabbed onto the canvas.

Then I turned to the back, and there it was — the final piece of evidence. A stamp in Gothic script that said *Kaiser-Friedrich Museum.*

My heart skipped several beats. Museum stamps could be forged too, but everything pointed to this being the real thing.

Beside me, Henrik went perfectly still. So, huh. Maybe the vampire did have a heart after all. At least for great artworks.

But when I glanced up at him, he was staring across the room — to the extent that vampires stared at anything that wasn't warm-blooded. His breaths were short, like mine, and his eyes flickered red in a moment of shock and discovery.

I followed his gaze. What was so interesting about that cigar-shaped box over to one side?

When I elbowed him, he jerked around, looking downright guilty.

Which he surely was — guilty of a hundred heinous crimes, or so I assumed. But I wouldn't have put *noticing an innocuous box* among them.

Unless that box wasn't so innocuous.

"What?" he growled, flushing a little.

And a *little* was a lot on a vampire. I'd only ever seen him look that lively at the prospect of fresh blood. I glanced at the box again. What was in there? And, yikes. Did I want to know?

Pandora's box, my imagination said. *Open it, and the world will be inundated with strife, disease, and greed.*

I sighed, thinking of recent headlines. Make that *even more* strife, disease, and greed.

Then again, *hope* had also come fluttering out of Pandora's box. But I doubted that was what excited Henrik.

"It's real," I whispered, trying to draw his focus back to the Van Gogh. "I'm ninety-nine percent certain."

He rubbed his cheek to cover the furtive looks he shot at the box.

"Good. Fine." He straightened his already-perfect tie, then checked his watch. "Seven minutes to go."

We spent the next five minutes at a second crate of abstract painters — Rothko, Mondrian, Klein, to name a jaw-dropping few. Then we wandered over to the other guests, who were still admiring the jeweled sword. I checked my watch, counting down the seconds.

"Find anything?" Dobrov asked.

Henrik shrugged. "Possibly."

Definitely, I thought, glancing at the box he was so interested in. Now that we were closer, I could see the lid was inlaid with ivory and exotic wood.

The lights flickered.

"Oh!" I yelped, grabbing Dobrov's arm. "What was that?"

Actually, I knew exactly what that was — Roux cutting the power.

The lights cut entirely, plunging us into utter darkness. I screamed for good measure.

The lights flicked on again, but everyone looked spooked — everyone but Henrik, who squinted uncomfortably in the sudden burst of light.

"Ladies and gentlemen, we need to ask you to vacate. Just for a few minutes," one of the security guards said. The other had already opened the door and was heading out, one hand pressed to his earpiece.

"Of course." Dobrov ushered us out, taking up the rear. I dawdled, staying half a step ahead of him as the chitter-chatter and cries of a nervous crowd grew at the far end of the hallway.

The lights flickered again, and I drew a mental map of the room. Then the lights died a second time, plunging the entire villa into utter darkness.

More cries and screams broke out, but mine wasn't among them. I was too busy sidestepping Dobrov and navigating my way back to the crate with the Van Gogh.

All my life, I'd wished for real supernatural powers. Now, I was grateful for the few that had trickled down to me, like unusually sharp senses. I couldn't see well, but a sixth sense outlined every piece of furniture, every crate I had to maneuver around.

"Keep moving, everyone. Keep moving," the security guard called urgently.

Oh, I would keep moving, all right. I ran my hand along a table, then took three measured steps through the darkness and reached out. Nothing. My heart pounded as I reached farther. Then, whew. My hand tapped the edge of another table.

I felt along it, located my purse, and pulled out a tiny, laser-point flashlight. I held it with my teeth without turning it on, then bent down, feeling along the frames in the crate.

There. My hands found the biggest, then flipped to the smaller painting beside it. Only then did I click on the flashlight.

Bingo. The Van Gogh. *Dad's* Van Gogh, as I'd started to think of it.

I turned off the light, removed the painting, and crept across the room. This would be the hard part.

"Anyone left back there?" someone yelled.

I crouched and held still, thinking, *No one in here but us art thieves.*

My heart hammered, and I piqued my senses, locating the silhouette of someone in the doorway. They waited, listening. Looking.

I took a deep breath and prepared to activate my emergency backup plan. The one I hadn't told the guys about.

Shadow-walking. Being there, but not there, like that night Henrik had stalked me from the attic.

If I'd had more practice — or better nerves — I might have tried shadow-walking into this room in the first place. No invitation from Dobrov needed. But I'd only pulled off that trick a handful of times at home, never in an unfamiliar environment.

So, shadow-walking was strictly a backup option. Like now, with the security guy squinting into the darkness right at me.

He turned away and shut the door behind him.

Whew. Good news, but where the hell was Henrik? He was supposed to help me, dammit.

Well, fine. I started feeling my way forward, then stopped and grabbed a second painting — *Thaw* by a Monet wannabe. Yes, it was a forgery, but it was a good one, and a sudden brainwave told me it could be useful.

I felt my way forward, then grabbed in panic for whatever I'd just knocked over.

Clang! A goblet hit the floor and rolled against my foot.

I froze, looking toward the doorway.

After a few heart-stopping moments, I exhaled, placed the goblet carefully on the table, and continued slowly across the room. Too slowly?

I glanced at the door, then hurried the rest of the way toward the dumbwaiter in the adjoining office. All I had to do was place the paintings there and knock three times. Bene would lower the contraption to the ground floor and stash it in a vehicle he and Marius had parked on an adjoining property earlier. If a problem arose, the backup plan was for him to hide the paintings amid catering supplies.

I reached the threshold of the adjoining office and—

The lights went on.

I jerked back, cursing. Roux had promised to give us four or five minutes. That had barely been three.

Footsteps sounded in the hallway, and my stomach dropped.

I looked at the paintings, then the dumbwaiter. Not enough time to reach it. I shoved both paintings onto a row of books in one of the library shelves and hurried back to where I'd left my purse. Too hurried, because I knocked over the dreary Munch in the process. It toppled over, and I grabbed for it.

Which was why I was clutching a flashlight in one hand and a painting in the other when the security guard dashed back into the room.

"Hold it right there!" he yelled, pulling a gun.

I stuck both hands up, flashlight in one, painting in the other. "Don't shoot!"

Someone ran up behind him. Running at full speed, in fact, then tackling him. They both went flying, and the gun skidded across the floor.

I jumped back, clutching the painting to my chest as they tussled. One thumped the other's head against the floor, and he went limp. The assailant rose to his full height and turned to me.

I shrank back, then nearly jumped in glee. "Marius!"

He reached for my arm. "Are you all right?"

Butterflies fluttered in my belly, because what girl didn't appreciate her lover coming to the rescue when she really needed it?

It might have been a beautiful moment (apart from the unconscious security guy), had it not been for the four men who ran into the room next, brandishing guns and shouting, "Freeze!"

A good time to shadow-walk to freedom — if I were an expert in that trick. But I wasn't.

I stuck up my hands, holding the Munch for all to see, including the people who rushed in behind the gunmen.

"What the—?" Dobrov started.

"I told you she was up to no good," a woman snipped.

"Unbelievable," someone else agreed grimly.

Marius snarled, and I touched his arm. Spraying the room with dragon fire was not a good option. Not that a better one occurred to me.

The gunmen moved aside, and Baumann strutted forward.

"What exactly is going on here?" The points of his canines flashed.

"I just came back for my purse," I tried.

The woman sneered. "With a flashlight in one hand and a painting in the other?"

Okay, not a good look.

"It fell over. I just caught it."

Ironically, that part was 100 percent truthful.

But the woman just snorted. What a bitch.

Double bitch, I decided a moment later, recognizing Celeste, Marius's ex.

He growled, taking a step toward her.

The barrels of four guns swung in his direction, and the man he'd tackled stirred, groaning.

"How dare you?" Dobrov lectured me bitterly.

Which was pretty rich, coming from a guy who made a living from illicit art deals.

"Stealing — a Munch, no less!" he concluded.

An ugly, forged Munch? You've got to be kidding, I nearly blurted. I might be stupid enough to join a band of men I barely knew in a mission to steal a long-lost Van Gogh, but a fake Munch? My pride was definitely wounded.

One of the gunmen listened to his earpiece, then nodded to Baumann. "They got the guy."

Shit. Did he mean Roux or Bene? And where the hell was—

"Henrik," Marius snarled as the vampire appeared behind the others.

For the first — and probably last — time in my life, I was happy to see the vampire. If anyone could sweet-talk us out of this mess, it was Henrik.

But all he did was shake his head and mutter, "Unbelievable." Putting his hand over his heart, he turned to Baumann. "I take full responsibility. I have my people run background checks on all my escorts, but clearly, they missed something."

So many parts of that statement were offensive, I didn't know where to begin.

"Escort?" I finally sputtered.

Useless hussy, his glare said. Rolling his eyes, he turned to Baumann. "They all convince themselves it's love, don't they?"

Baumann patted his shoulder, like he'd suffered the same problem. "It happens. Don't blame yourself."

That meant blaming *me*, which they did with cool calculation.

"I can assure you, she'll be dealt with." Henrik stepped toward me.

I shrank back, too frightened to say, *What about dealing with you, you traitor?*

Marius moved to block Henrik. Much as I appreciated it, I didn't like being sandwiched between an angry dragon and a backstabbing vampire. Unless Henrik was faking it in an attempt to salvage this operation.

But that would require loyalty and a sense of teamwork. So, no. I really doubted it.

A slow-motion reel of my life flashed before my eyes, and a tragic soundtrack played in my mind as I thought of Clement. He had never sparked emotions in me as powerfully as Marius, but boy, would he have been the safer bet. We could have lived quietly (if not happily) ever after in the French countryside with two children, a dog, and a humble home purchased with whatever I could salvage from the château. The building itself would slowly crumble, and if my grandchildren ever asked why I gave up on generations of family history, I would admit I hadn't had the heart to try.

Bitterness pooled in my stomach. Was that really what I wished for?

I straightened my shoulders. No, it wasn't. And I would not give up, dammit. Not even now, when things looked bleaker than Munch's dreary landscape.

I tightened my grip around the painting, calculating who to swing it at first and which direction to escape in. Henrik made a good target, distracted as he was. His eyes kept darting to the inlaid box. Had he double-crossed us for that?

I raised the Munch, ready to smack him, then the nearest guard.

But Marius came to his senses and backed off, growling into my mind to do the same.

I like your thinking, but no. We'll wait for a better chance later.

I blinked, surprised by how clearly his thoughts reached me.

Fated mates, I remembered my grandmother sighing. *You can hear every word. It has its pluses and minuses.*

"Obviously, they were in this together," Celeste announced.

I bared my teeth, though she was spot on the money. Marius and I were in this together — but so was Henrik, dammit. How was he getting out of this so easily?

The room grew suffocating, and a hint of red shone in Henrik's eyes.

"Truly a piece of work," Henrik grumbled, meaning me. "She had me fooled. And now she's gone and disrupted this lovely evening."

Fucking vampire, Marius cursed into my mind. *He's enthralling them.*

"Don't be so hard on yourself," Baumann reassured him. "My men will take care of this issue."

I glared. A clogged toilet was an *issue*. This was my life he was toying with, dammit!

"But there's no reason to ruin a wonderful party," Baumann concluded smugly.

Celeste cozied up to him, shooting Marius a triumphant look.

"You're too gracious," Henrik assured him. "All I can ask is that you leave her for me to deal with later."

Baumann snickered. "Oh, I'm sure you will."

I gulped, trying not to imagine Henrik leaning over me. Biting. Sucking. Draining me to the last drop, then disposing of my lifeless body. Off the cliff, maybe? Down an old well?

They turned and headed back to the party, while the gunmen closed in on Marius and me.

"You bastard," I hissed after Henrik.

If he heard, he didn't let on. He just sauntered away, leaving us to our fates.

Chapter Twenty-Five

MARIUS

I selected a bottle of wine, checked the label, then hurled it. Glass shattered and wine splashed against the stone wall, leaving a blood-colored stain. I reached for another bottle.

Inside, my dragon seethed.

Soon — very soon — I would rip Henrik to pieces. Celeste too, and Baumann. They would regret this, big-time.

For now, however... I chose another bottle and flung it.

"Not helping," Roux muttered.

Yes, Roux, who'd been shoved into this makeshift cell shortly after Mina and me.

"Helps my mood," I grunted. "Fucking Henrik..."

Smash! Bottle number two shattered.

We were locked in an alcove with meter-thick stone walls in the very, very old cellar of the building. The vaulted ceiling was so low, neither Roux nor I could stand straight. It was cold and damp, with tiny stalactites on the ceiling and steel bars separating us from the sole exit.

On the plus side, that same alcove housed the overflow from Baumann's wine collection, so I could vent some of my frustration.

"That was a perfectly good Châteauneuf," Roux muttered.

"You sound like Henrik." I threw a third bottle.

Smash!

Did it make me feel better? No, but it was better than beating up on myself. Why had I allowed Mina to get mixed up in such risky business?

I raised another bottle but stopped when she touched my shoulder.

"I'm ready to kill Henrik too, but those bottles aren't going to do it." The warmth of her touch calmed my inner beast slightly. "Also, the fumes are starting to get to me." She flashed a thin smile. "Get it? Fumes. Fuming mad..."

My lips curled a tiny bit, but Roux groaned. "Very funny. Besides, maybe Henrik isn't a traitor. Maybe he just held back until he could figure out a Plan B."

Mina scoffed. "That would take a sense of responsibility."

"Think about it. He can't afford for this mission to fail any more than we can."

"Maybe he's made a deal with Celeste," I grumbled. "Maybe they're double-crossing us together."

We all fell silent, considering. Mina walked to the bars of our improvised cell and peered out. The space faced a stone wall, so there wasn't much to see unless you looked left or right at an angle, and the sole light was a dim, naked bulb hanging from the ceiling. Occasionally, voices drifted in from the direction of the exit, but all seemed quiet now. More alcoves lay to our right, followed by a dead end.

My mind caught on the words — *dead end* — and immediately erased them.

Mina looked both ways, then turned back to us.

"What about Delphine? Do you think they've caught on to her?" she whispered.

Leave it to Mina to think about someone else when she was the one locked in a cellar.

Roux grimaced. "Probably not, given the fact that she hasn't been thrown in here with us. But there's bound to be security footage of her with me, so it's only a question of time."

"That, or Henrik will turn her in," I muttered.

Mina shook her head sadly. "I can't believe he turned on us. Maybe I shouldn't be surprised, though."

I rolled my fists so tightly, my knuckles cracked. When I got my hands on that vampire...

"So...getting out of here..." Mina gripped the bars of our cell and shook them.

They didn't budge. Not even a rattle.

"I don't suppose you could break them, huh?" she tried.

I loved that she considered that a possibility, but sadly...

I shook my head. "Maybe in dragon form, but there's no space for me to shift in here."

Mina moved her hand between two bars, measuring the gap. "Enough space for a tiger to slip through?"

Roux snorted. "Maybe a cub. Not me."

Mina shook the bars again. "I prefer breaking out to waiting for Baumann or Henrik to come for us."

Me too, but how?

Mina peered at the lock, one of those old-fashioned, skeleton-key setups. One of Baumann's private security guards had locked us in, then exited with the key.

"I hate to say it, but I think Bene is our best hope right now," Roux said.

I huffed. "*Bene*, *best*, and *hope* do not fit in one sentence together. Not even two of the three."

Mina rolled her eyes. "You two are as bad as some of my fifth graders."

I pictured her in a classroom, stern yet caring. My mind clung to that image and stashed it away like treasure. I knew so little about Mina that anything — everything — mattered.

"Well, Bene isn't completely useless. He can follow instructions," Roux tried.

I gave him a look, and he corrected himself.

"Okay, he can *mostly* follow instructions. But having him improvise on his own..." He trailed off grimly.

"Maybe you're underestimating him." Mina crossed her arms fiercely.

Roux sighed. "Always a safer bet with Bene."

"Besides, it's only a question of time before Henrik rats him out too — if he hasn't already," I added.

We bounced ideas back and forth for the next ten minutes. Picking the lock didn't work, nor did heaving at the bars of our cell. That left escaping when someone came for us — the hardest option to plan for. How many men would Baumann send for us? Would Henrik be among them? When would they come, and where would they take us?

We were debating using broken-off bottles as weapons when voices sounded. We rushed to the bars, listening, then fell back when the main door burst open.

I stepped in front of Mina. Whoever that was would have to get through me to get to her, dammit.

Light streamed in, backlighting a tall man who paused in the doorway. He cursed, then glided forward.

"Henrik?" Roux called.

"Henrik," Mina and I growled at the same time.

The vampire beckoned to someone behind him. "Hurry."

I'd been expecting the same cold, hard shell of a man as usual, but Henrik genuinely seemed flustered. Since when did vampires hurry?

He strode closer, but a second person overtook him. The light caught in his fair hair, and—

Mina cheered. "Bene!"

"Heya, Mina." He grinned, then wrinkled his nose at the stench of wine. "Whoa. Have you guys been partying or something?"

She motioned impatiently to the lock. "Key?"

He held up a skeleton key, then bent over to work it into the lock. "You doing okay?"

"Peachy, thank you for asking," she said, glaring at Henrik. "Just full of questions."

Henrik stuck up his hands. "I had to think fast. It was the best I could come up with."

She huffed. "Getting us all locked up was the best you could do?"

"No, taking great personal risk to bring Bene here is," Henrik replied coolly.

Bene glanced up long enough to nod. "It's the truth. He didn't turn you in. It just took us a while to figure out where they'd taken you."

The lock clicked open, and I leaped out, claws bared. But Bene stopped me from throttling Henrik.

"None of that now. He's on our side."

"Is he? Because all I know is that he was on the outside while we were locked up."

"If I'd broken cover too early, none of us would be walking out," Henrik said.

"I don't believe a word, you son of a—" I started, but Roux gripped my shirt.

"Later. We need to move fast. Do you want Mina out of here or don't you?"

Moving fast didn't register, but *getting Mina out* did. I stuffed away my fury and forced myself to focus.

"Out is good," she agreed. "But not without that painting."

Oh no, you don't jumped to the tip of my tongue, but Bene was already leading her to the exit. He peeked both ways, then stepped around three prone bodies.

Mina froze. "Oh my God. You didn't—"

Bene snorted. "Don't worry. Mr. Spirit of the Night here wanted to off them, but he settled for knocking them out instead."

Henrik shot us a haughty look that said, *See? Aren't I such a softy?*

I wasn't fooled, but I saved my two-fisted reply for later.

We regrouped and hurried down the dim hallway with Bene and Henrik in front, Mina and me in the middle, and Roux bringing up the rear. The place was a goddamn labyrinth, but Bene led the way without hesitation. Several twists and turns later, he pushed open an arched doorway, peered out, then motioned us forward.

"The coast is clear."

We tiptoed outside, keeping to the shadows against the side of the building. The bright lights of the villa's service entrance weren't far, but catering vans blocked us from view.

"Okay, everyone. Head that way." Bene pointed. "Roux knows where the vehicle is. I'll give you a ten-minute head start while I find Delphine and get the hell out of here."

Henrik stepped back toward the cellar, and I grabbed him by the collar. "Where the hell are you going?"

He flashed his fangs. "I have to get back to the party. Otherwise, they'll suspect me. You go."

"Not without the painting," Mina insisted.

Bene looked at me. "Will you talk some sense into her?"

I opened my mouth, then closed it. He was right, but anything I said would only infuriate her.

"We're aborting this mission," Roux barked in his best *I'm in charge here* tone.

For once, I didn't question the guy. But Mina dug in her heels.

"I'm not leaving without that painting."

"She's right," Henrik said, surprising the hell out of everyone. "We have to go back."

I frowned. Since when did he care about art?

Roux looked at him, echoing that sentiment.

Henrik took a long time to answer, raising my suspicions.

"Gordon will be pissed if we don't deliver," he finally tried.

Yes, he would, but we could deal with that shitstorm later. I tugged Mina's hand, but she stood her ground, glaring at Henrik.

"You're not risking this for Gordon or the painting." Her words were a statement, not a question.

Henrik's brow furrowed, and his eyes sparked with anger. "You wouldn't understand."

"Try me," she growled.

He didn't, so she went on. "This is about that box, isn't it?"

Roux caught my eye, telegraphing something like, *Box? What box?*

I had no idea, and time was ticking.

"No time now." I tugged more insistently.

Mina yanked her hand away and whirled to face me, angry at first, then pleading. "I know this sounds crazy, but I can't leave without that painting — or at least trying. Please."

I had two choices: to cart Mina away against her will, saving her life but losing her respect forever, or indulging her — and putting her life at risk just so I could maybe, just maybe, have a shot with her someday.

I took a deep breath, then amended the sentiment. Mina was strong, intelligent, and independent. It wasn't my place to make decisions *or* indulge her. Just to support her — or bow out respectfully. And since I sure as hell wasn't going to bow out without her...

"Okay," I said, though it took everything I had. "Just hurry."

Time would tell whether that was the right answer, but the burst of warmth in Mina's eyes promised me it was.

Hell, I hoped so.

Every muscle in my body tensed as she and Henrik moved a few steps away to speak in hushed tones.

"I'll make you a deal," she started.

Crap. Not a good start.

The rest of their exchange was too quiet to hear, which was the point, I figured. Still, it stung to be excluded.

"I don't like this," Roux grumbled.

"What's to like?" Bene checked his watch, then whispered to Mina. "People will notice if Henrik and I aren't back soon."

Mina stuck up a hand in a stop sign and went on whispering.

"Bossy, isn't she?" Bene chuckled. "Like my sixth-grade teacher."

Fifth-grade, I nearly whispered.

Finally, she and Henrik finished, and he stepped toward the cellar with a grim look.

"Keep an eye on Celeste," Roux told him. "Make sure she doesn't give us away."

Henrik grimaced, then nodded. "Understood."

Mina called one more time before he disappeared inside. "Ten minutes. Be ready."

"Ten minutes." Henrik nodded, not entirely pleased.

That made two of us, dammit.

"What's happening in ten minutes?" Bene asked once Henrik left.

We all huddled around Mina, waiting for instructions — even Roux. He might be our leader, but Mina could be a goddamn general when she put her mind to it.

"In ten minutes, we'll be out of here — with the painting," she said, then outlined a plan involving a diversion, a dumbwaiter, and some bodily contortions.

"Sounds a little like the original plan," Bene observed when she was done. "You know, the one you got caught in the middle of?"

"This plan is better. Simpler," she insisted.

"Riskier," Roux cut in.

She shrugged. "When was risk not a part of this?"

I rubbed my chin. She had me there.

The next thing I knew, she was sending Bene and Roux away with final, hushed instructions. They took off, leaving just her and me.

She took my hands in hers. Now more than ever, they felt frail and tiny.

But size and power weren't the only weapons a soldier could wield, and Mina more than made up for that in brains and bravery.

"What's my job?" I asked.

She smiled, then touched my cheek. "You're the best. You know that?"

I snorted, but I couldn't help but puff my chest out a little. No one had ever called me *the best* anything. If anything, I'd heard a lot of the opposite over the years. But coming from Mina...

"Maybe just reckless," I whispered, echoing what she'd once said.

She shook her head. "The best." Then she took a deep breath and went back to general mode. "Your job is creating a diversion."

Fool that I was, I nodded. Mina wanted a diversion? She'd get one. The best goddamn diversion ever.

She leaned in to kiss me — not very general-like, and thank goodness for that. When our lips meshed, peace filled my soul. Which made no sense at a time like this, but whatever. Maybe trusting...hoping...even loving didn't have to make sense.

We drew apart slowly, and Mina checked her watch. "You ready?"

Ready to go to hell and back for her, I realized.

"Ready." I nodded.

Our eyes locked in one last, silent exchange. Then we set off, creeping along the wall. A few steps later, Mina slipped off to the left, while I continued toward the catering area. I glanced back twice. The first time, she was there, but the next, she was gone.

I kept walking, because I had no choice. The plan was in motion, and the clock was ticking.

Chapter Twenty-Six

MINA

Roux held the door to the dumbwaiter open, though his look was skeptical. "You sure about this?"

No, but for lack of a better plan...

I slipped off my heels and started folding myself into the dumbwaiter. "Just watch the door, please."

We were in a storeroom in what had been the original part of the villa, before the superstructure had been updated and expanded. The dumbwaiter was just as old — a vintage wooden model that ran on a pulley system. The minute I transferred my weight into the tiny elevator, it creaked. I froze, then continued more slowly, pulling in one leg, then the other. Roux had knocked out the shelf in the middle of the compartment, but it was still a tight fit.

My mind filled with second thoughts. It was bad enough that I had become a mercenary and thief for the night. Now I was adding *contortionist* to the list. How on earth had I gotten myself into this?

"Just focus," I muttered to myself.

Roux gave me a foul look that said, *I'm always focused. I know no other state.*

I had no doubt, and I told him as much. "I meant me. Anyway, I'm ready. Send me up, please. And listen for my signal."

He didn't look convinced. "Let me hear it again."

I rapped my knuckles on the inner panel — once, twice, then two quicker knocks in succession.

He nodded, though he didn't make a move. He just stood there exuding pessimism.

"Not a word," I warned him.

If his brow furrowed any more deeply, he would injure himself.

"I get that this is important to you..." he started.

"Those are words. Lots of them," I grumbled.

He went on, regardless. "But I'm weighing your wishes up against the pain Marius will inflict on me if you get caught."

"Just send me up, dammit!" I tried to gesture to emphasize the point but only succeeded in banging my elbow.

Roux pushed my right knee in and took up the slack in the rope that raised and lowered the dumbwaiter.

"Okay. Hang on," he said quietly.

My breath caught when the dumbwaiter lurched into motion, and it took everything I had not to shout *Stop! Forget it!*

"Watch your dress. And your knee," he hissed, all annoyed. Like *he* was the one in the damn thing.

I pulled on the fabric, doing what I could in my two-inch range of motion. Roux kept hauling the rope, hand over hand, and the storeroom began to sink beneath me. I looked up, counting the seconds.

Fancy villas, I learned, were nowhere near as fancy from the inside. Open brickwork and wiring slid past, and I clutched my dress even more tightly. The dim light from the storeroom died out the farther I went, making space seem to shrink. The walls gradually closed in on me like an undersized coffin.

It was so dark, I touched my face to check whether my eyes were open. Finally, a sliver of light appeared above and expanded.

Then, *thump!* The dumbwaiter hit its upper limit and swayed. I cringed, praying it wouldn't collapse into the shaft below. Would the fall kill me, or would I lie trapped for hours before dying in misery?

Not dying, I barked at myself. Not tonight anyway.

I listened for a moment, then pushed at the double doors outlined by slivers of dim light.

Nothing.

I pushed harder. Still nothing.

I shimmied around to raise my foot and push harder. Crap. Was the door locked from the office side?

I pushed again, then kicked, then—

With a cry and a crash, I tumbled out onto a carpeted floor. I froze, convinced I would open my eyes to a ring of armed gunmen.

But, whew. Nobody there.

Getting to my hands and knees, I glanced around. Double whew. I'd emerged in the deserted office beside the library. The twin, floor-to-ceiling windows on the north wall were shuttered, but a little light filtered in from the adjacent loading area.

I tiptoed over to the library door and listened. Nothing there, but a scuffle sounded outside the windows, followed by a muffled thump. I froze again, listening.

At first, nothing happened. Then, *whoosh!* Fire roared, illuminating the night and casting flickering shadows over the walls.

Then, *boom!* Something exploded.

I ducked as the windows rattled. Not too far away, glass shattered. The distant sounds of the party stopped, interrupted by cries.

"Hurry!" Roux's muffled warning sounded from the dumbwaiter shaft.

I stared at the windows, then hustled over to the dumbwaiter. "What was that?"

His voice was clearer there — clear enough for me to catch his sigh. "Marius's idea of a diversion."

I stared at the flames outside the windows. The fire was somewhere farther along the building, but still too close for comfort.

"Hurry!" Roux propelled me into motion.

I listened briefly, then eased open the door to the library.

I froze, spotting a figure there. One lone sentry left to guard the room after our heist attempt backfired.

Shit, shit, shit.

He was all the way over by the far door, talking into a headpiece. So, whew. He hadn't noticed me.

I eased back into the office and stood still, my heart pounding.

Now what? The Van Gogh wasn't far, but I couldn't walk in there under the sentry's nose and grab it unnoticed.

Unless...

My breath caught as the boldest — craziest? — plan of my life popped into my mind.

Shadow-walking.

I discarded the thought immediately. Shadow-walking in a sequined dress? Good luck. Also, shadow-walking required maintaining a false image of myself in one location while sneaking over to another. Misdirecting, in other words, the way an amateur magician did. The key was to give your audience a false target to focus on, but I couldn't reveal myself to the sentry.

I slumped against the wall, thinking. Could I get Roux up here to knock the guy out?

No, because Roux wouldn't fit in the dumbwaiter.

And, yikes. The fact that that was my primary reason was really, really disturbing. I was definitely going over to the dark side.

Which left two options. Quitting and shadow-walking.

Quit, ninety-nine percent of my mind barked immediately.

But one percent held out. It could work...theoretically.

"Mina!" Roux's voice carried up the dumbwaiter.

I pushed the doors to the contraption closed, afraid that the sentry might hear. Then I tiptoed back to the door and peeked through the keyhole.

The shelf I'd left the paintings on was barely two steps away. So near, yet so far.

Holding my breath, I eased the door to the library open. The room was dark — too dark for human eyes — except over by the main door, where the sentry stood. But for my eyes...

I could make him out easily. He cracked open the far door to peer down the hallway into the reception area, just like I spied on him from behind. I couldn't hear the communications coming through his earpiece, but I could hear him muttering.

"Fire? There's a goddamn fire now?"

Ha. Yes, thanks to Marius.

"Standing by," he said grimly.

I eyed the shelf where I'd stashed the paintings, then the sentry, who focused on the commotion in the main part of the building. Meanwhile, the fire outside flared, illuminating the windows, and I could sense Roux's mind tapping at mine. *Hurry!*

So I did. I ignored every paranoid cell in my body and started reconstructing the space around me. The soft rug under my feet. The slightly warmer air surrounding my body. The light draft moving from the library to the office...

Then, with a deep breath, I stepped into the library. I kept the image of myself upright behind the doorway, not because the sentry could see it, but because it blocked the glint of fire coming in through the office windows.

"Unit three, over," the sentry said in reply to a summons on his earpiece. Then he turned, scanning the room.

I froze, but his eyes moved right over me.

"Negative. Nothing here," he reported, turning back to the doorway. "But that fire sounds like it's getting closer."

Definitely, and the room was getting warmer. Yikes. How big was that fire?

I inched toward the shelf with the paintings, then reached out cautiously. My fingers tapped over a row of books, then touched wood — the frame of a painting.

"You're evacuating the building?" the sentry said into his earpiece. "What about the art?"

Leave it, I urged him, wishing I could enthrall people the way Henrik did.

"We could leave it, you know," he said.

My jaw dropped. Coincidence, or had I succeeded?

Either way, I had to get moving. I stepped even closer, using both hands to lift the heavy paintings. I bit my lip, sure the light creak would give me away. But someone shouted at the sentry from outside just then, covering the light scratch of wood over leather book bindings.

"Does the boss want this stuff evacuated or not?" the sentry barked to whomever it was.

I held both paintings against my body and hurried back into the office, then pushed the door shut behind me. I panted for a moment. Wow. I'd succeeded in shadow-walking. Okay, in a dark room with a distracted guard, but still. Pretty amazing.

I placed the Van Gogh and the fake Monet in the dumbwaiter and formed a fist to signal to Roux. One trip for the paintings, a second trip for me, and we would be out of here.

"Ready?" Roux hissed.

So, so ready.

"Ready," I called.

The rope moved, and the pulley squeaked as the dumbwaiter started its downward journey. I peered down the shaft, watching it fade into darkness. I heard it thump into place, then a bump and a scrape as Roux extracted the artworks.

"What the...?" he muttered.

"Just send the dumbwaiter back up," I called.

I glanced back at the door to the library, and that was my undoing, because I remembered the inlaid box that had caught Henrik's fancy — and the bargain we'd struck. I'd promised to get the box for him, and he'd sworn not to double-cross us to Baumann. He'd even upped the ante with a second clause, making me swear not to open it, which I'd agreed to in exchange for a favor to be called in sometime in the future.

So, whew. A vampire whisperer, I was not, but I had succeeded in driving a hard bargain. One I hoped the vampire would keep his word on.

My word is my bond, Henrik had assured me.

I had my doubts, but hey. It might turn out to be a useful insurance policy.

The problem was, the box was back in the library, and so was the sentry.

Alarms sounded through the building. A cue to save my skin, or my chance to sneak back in while the guard was distracted?

Save my skin was tempting, but I found myself shadow-walking back into the library instead. Maybe that was a side effect of unlocking a new power, like a genie refusing to squeeze back into the bottle. Maybe it was pure hubris, like a kid racing around town on a freshly issued driver's license. Or worse — maybe Henrik had managed to cast a thrall over me, ensuring that I didn't abandon his treasure.

Either way, I padded into the library a second time, right under the nose of the sentry. But Henrik's box was halfway across the room, not just a step or two into one corner. My heart pounded as I moved quietly toward it. My head pounded too, because maintaining the illusion of a second me, even out of sight in the office, took a hell of a mental effort.

"Unit three, unit three. Position untenable," the uneasy sentry called into his mic.

Boy, I could relate.

I tiptoed all the way over to Henrik's box and gingerly lifted it. It was the size of a cigar box, but surprisingly heavy.

Do not open it, Henrik had growled over and over.

Ha. As if I were even tempted.

I started slinking back quietly, then lost my nerve and rushed toward the office. Somehow, my shadow held, and the sentry didn't notice.

"Quick! Get the paintings and the carvings!" Dobrov barked from somewhere down the far hallway.

I slid around the office door and shut it behind me. I stood there for ten terrifying seconds, listening. Sweating, too, I was that nervous — and because the fire outside was now licking over the windows. The whole room heated and grew stuffy.

I rushed to the dumbwaiter. Roux should have had plenty of time to grab the paintings and send the dumbwaiter back up. But it wasn't moving.

My stomach dropped. Had he grabbed the paintings and left me?

"Roux!" I cried as loudly as I dared.

The dumbwaiter rattled, and Roux called urgently.

"Let go of the rope."

"I'm not holding it," I whisper-yelled back.

Flames crackled, and I jerked around to see them creeping over the roof, toward the library.

"Quick! Get the paintings!" Dobrov barked on the library side of the door.

A crash sounded — part of the roof collapsing? — and another man yelled. "It's too dangerous!"

"Just get them, dammit!" Dobrov ordered.

"Roux..." I called desperately.

He muttered and jiggled the rope. "Dammit..."

I gulped, trying to stay calm and evaluate my options.

"Hurry!" I yelled down the shaft, failing on both counts.

"I'm trying, dammit!"

Windows blackened, and flames weren't just creeping, but engulfing the ceiling. I coughed a few times, then doubled over in a full-on coughing fit.

"Hurry!" Dobrov yelled to his men.

I wished Roux would, dammit.

Finally, the dumbwaiter lurched into motion and resumed its upward journey. I held my scarf over my mouth and eyed the ceiling. How long would it hold?

A beam creaked and shifted, setting off an avalanche of roof tiles. Some simply slipped into a new position, but others fell and slammed to the floor.

I looked around, growing panicked. This wasn't a fire. It was an inferno.

The dumbwaiter creaked into position. I stood back, studying it, then the windows. Surely jumping out was a better option?

The flames blazed higher, cackling something like, *Want to try, honey?*

"Mina!" Roux called. And, yikes. Even he sounded panicked.

Okay, so no windows. I stuck my upper body into the dumbwaiter, then wiggled around.

"Hey!" I yelped when it started moving. "I'm not in yet."

"No time," Roux barked.

The guy was merciless, and my shins and knees banged four or five times. On the (very slim) plus side, that forced every appendage into the tiny space, and I was on my way.

On my way, but suffocating. I heaved for air, but the fire was busy consuming it. Henrik's box poked into my belly, giving me even less space to breathe. My head started to swim, and my eyes watered. Or were those tears?

Both, probably. Tears for myself, tears for the paintings. Tears for my father, whom I'd failed, and my mother, who would be gutted if I didn't survive this. Tears for—

Something clamped around my foot and yanked. I felt myself falling, then being lifted. Henrik's box was pried out of my hand, and a faraway voice called.

Was I dying or getting rescued? If the former, I hoped I would at least get to see my father. If the latter... Well, I hoped my dress wasn't up over my ass, revealing everything.

As it turned out, I was being rescued, and — big bonus — my dress wasn't over my ass. Whew. I was bumping wildly, though, and upside down in a fireman's carry. Gradually, I worked my way from coughing to flailing to pitiful protests, which my rescuer ignored.

Then there was a roar, and I was torn from Rescuer One's arms and cradled in Rescuer Two's. And just like that, everything stopped. The bumping. The coughing. The urge to fire off dozens of questions. I sank into a warm, fluffy cloud, feeling totally, utterly at peace.

"Mm," I murmured, nuzzling my rescuer.

If it had been Roux or Bene, I would have been really embarrassed. If it had been Henrik, I would have been downright traumatized.

But, whew. It was Marius. And even if we hadn't yet figured out where the undeniable pull between us was leading, I knew one thing. I'd never felt safer or more grounded than when I was with him.

"Are you all right?" His obsidian eyes glinted anxiously.

I nodded. Using superhuman effort to resist the urge to kiss him, I pointed my feet toward the ground. He set me down gently, keeping firm hold of my shoulders in case I toppled.

I didn't, though I did sway.

"I'm fine," I said, then folded into another coughing fit.

Eventually, an invisible vise released its grip on my lungs, and I wiped away the accompanying tears.

"Really okay?" Roux asked, peering in from the right.

Rescuer One, I realized.

"Yes. Thank you." I looked around, then grabbed Roux's arm. "The paintings..."

He held them up wearily. "Got them right here. Both of them. And this thing." He showed me the box, clearly irritated.

"Dammit, Mina," Marius growled. "What were you thinking?"

A comment I might have taken offense at, but his hands and voice were shaking.

I held his hand to my chest. "I was thinking about the painting and how to get us all out of this. But you're right," I added before the angry spark in his eyes turned into an inferno like the one raging behind us. "It was dangerous, and I'm sorry. And grateful." I turned to Roux. "Thank you."

Roux muttered a reluctant, "You're welcome."

Marius crushed me against his chest. "Swear to me you'll never do that again."

Ha. Easiest promise ever.

"I swear," I mumbled into his pecs. And, oops. A totally inappropriate wave of longing swept over me.

Marius's growl dropped to a lusty hum, and who knew what we might have done if Roux hadn't cleared his throat and pointed behind us.

"Can I suggest we get away first and express undying affection later?"

Not a bad plan. Marius and I eased apart, but his eyes glittered with a vow.

Maybe not now, but soon...

My heart thumped, and I made my own vow. But Roux was right. We weren't in the clear yet.

Chapter Twenty-Seven

MINA

Marius, Roux, and I stared at the blaze. Fifty yards away, flames danced over the villa. Staff hurried to move vans and equipment away from the rear entrance — the side we faced — and a pair of women did their best with garden hoses. A doomed, but valiant effort.

"*Aquí! Aquí!*" *Over here,* someone directed them toward the front of the building.

Yes, over there, I agreed. *As far from the library as possible.* The faster that area burned, the better.

Party guests huddled a safe distance from the front of the building. Some stared at the fire in awe, while others jabbered into phones. One moron was actually filming the disaster.

"Have you seen Delphine? And what about Bene?" I asked, suddenly seized with fear.

Roux pointed. "Delphine is there, and I spotted Bene on the way out."

I exhaled. "And Henrik?"

Marius snorted. "First one out, probably. Self-preservation is his greatest instinct. Just like Celeste." And boy, was his voice bitter.

"I guess she made it out too?" I ventured.

"Unfortunately, yes," Marius said without the slightest hint of remorse. "But Henrik will make sure she doesn't talk."

A cry went out as part of the building collapsed.

"Wow," I breathed, staring at the enormity of the fire.

"Yes. Wow." Roux shot Marius the evil eye.

Marius pointed to me. "She wanted a diversion."

"I did," I said quickly. "And it definitely worked. It's just...just..." I looked to Roux for help.

He crossed his arms, mum.

"Just what?" Marius frowned, looking at the building.

"A little big," I finished in a bold understatement.

He looked at the burning villa, then shrugged. "I guess I didn't account for the flammable supplies in the catering truck."

I winced. Well, that explained the quick spread of the fire.

"I guess not," I said, choosing my words carefully.

Roux rolled his eyes.

"Not that I'm not grateful," I added before Marius got riled up. "But next time, could you maybe...um..."

He socked me with a dark look, waiting.

I thought of a similar exchange the night he'd torched a strip of woods in search of the intruder at the château and of everything that had transpired since. Time and again, Marius had come through for me. How could I be anything but grateful? And if his style was a little more *bulldozer* than *chisel*, well, that was just the dragon in him.

I flung my arms around him. "Forget it. Thank you."

"You're welcome," he said gruffly, wrapping his arms around me.

"I was the one who dragged her out of the fire. With the paintings," Roux muttered.

I eased away from Marius to give Roux a quick hug — a very quick one, lest another fight break out. "Thank you. Again. I really, really appreciate it."

There. Enough to stroke his tiger's ego? I turned back to the villa, whispering, "I just hope everyone got out all right."

Marius huffed. "Even Baumann and Dobrov?"

My answer should have been an indignant, *Even them,* but it was one of those times when empathy took effort.

"Even them," I finally said. "Gordon is sure to question us about the fire. If those two died on top of that... Well, the fewer questions we have to face later, the better."

"You mean, the fewer questions *we* have to face." Roux motioned between himself and Marius. "You were never here."

Right. Of course. I nodded quickly, though I felt a twinge of disappointment. I'd more or less aced my first super-secret mission—

Less, the back of my mind grumbled, considering all the near misses.

—but I wouldn't be able to take credit for the good to come of it, like recovering the Van Gogh.

Then I chastised myself. My father hadn't hunted great artworks for recognition. He only wanted to right wrongs and bless the general public with access to priceless masterpieces. Shouldn't I emulate him?

Funny how I had to remind myself this was a one-time deal. It wasn't like I was getting into the business of hunting down lost masterpieces.

"Well, mission accomplished," Roux said wearily. "Let's get out of here... and hope Gordon considers the fire a bonus."

God, I hoped not. If he did, I had really, really misjudged my godfather.

I hung back. "What about Delphine?"

"She knows the meeting point," Roux assured me, setting off.

Easy for him in his patent leather shoes. Not in the heels of doom, however, that he had somehow remembered to grab for me.

And boy, did that say a lot about Roux. High heels were the last item I would grab on my way out of a blaze.

At risk of seeming ungrateful, I yanked off the heels and started picking my way over the rough terrain. My stockings would be destroyed, but I would miss them about as much as I missed the heels.

Still, progress was much too slow. Any time now, the police were sure to appear.

"Here." Marius motioned for the shoes. I handed them over, and he snapped the heels off. "Better?"

I slipped one on, then the other. Not my trusty hiking boots, but better than barefoot.

"Much better. Thank you."

We picked our way through the surrounding brush, slipped into a fenced olive grove, and eventually emerged on a narrow track. Not far away, the rear lights of a four-wheel drive glittered.

"Delphine!" I rushed forward, spotting her by the car with Bene.

We hugged in relief, then stepped apart.

"Oh, your poor dress," I clucked, looking down at her.

To my surprise, she barely noticed. She just gazed back toward the blaze on the hilltop. "Henrik..."

Marius, Bene, and I exchanged uneasy looks.

"He'll be fine," Roux assured her. "He'll depart in the car he arrived in, but he'll have to wait a while to avoid arousing suspicion."

Ha. Suspicion was about the only thing Henrik aroused in me. Marius, on the other hand...

He touched my hand, and my body temperature ticked upward.

But Roux, drat him, turned to Marius with an order. "I need you to shift and keep an eye on things. Bene, you too. We'll meet you back at the *finca*."

Marius grimaced but didn't argue. He kissed my knuckles and stepped backward, pulling at his tie. "Sorry, but..."

I forced myself to nod and hold out my hands for his clothes. "Just be careful, okay?"

"You too," he whispered.

Seconds later, the clothes in my arms fluttered as he took to the sky in dragon form. I stared at his massive wings, long, tapered tail, and streamlined body. Then I sighed. I could live to one hundred and never get used to the magnificent sight.

"Heya, Mina. Can you take mine too?" Bene asked, totally ruining the moment.

I scowled at him, making sure to keep my gaze at eye level.

"Sure," I grumbled, letting him heap his clothes on top of Marius's. Then I looked up and swallowed hard. Marius was a mere shadow against the night sky. Much too far for comfort.

Not too long ago, I would have said the opposite. How things had changed.

For the better, a little voice assured me.

"Get going, Bene," Roux ordered.

I looked over just in time to see a tawny body slink into the bushes. Roux helped Delphine into the vehicle, then called to me softly.

"Mina..."

I took one last, longing look up, then slipped into the back seat.

Roux drove, with a very quiet Delphine in the front passenger seat. I sat pressed against the window, scouring the sky for a glimpse of Marius.

We bumped down a rocky track, then turned onto the main road, craning our necks to take in the fire. Flashing lights appeared in the oncoming lane, and emergency service vehicles rushed past us.

Forty minutes later, we were back at the *finca*. Bene appeared a good hour later, and Marius...

"He'll be here soon," Roux assured me.

"Uh-huh," I mumbled, keeping my face turned skyward.

An eternity later, the wind gusted, and a shadow loomed over us. I scurried back as it rushed closer...closer...

My hair blew across my face, and trees rustled as Marius swept in to a landing.

"Tell him ten minutes until our debriefing," Roux called to me.

"Debriefing at ten in the morning? Perfect." Bene sauntered off toward his cottage.

"No, I said..." Roux started, but his words faded to a frustrated growl.

"Nine in the morning," I suggested.

His tiger eyes blazed, but he finally relented — sort of. "Eight."

I nodded, already jogging out to meet Marius at the end of the road. Then I stopped, suddenly cautious. Maybe one didn't rush right up to a dragon. Maybe they needed a few minutes to transition out of deadly beast mode. Maybe—

Two huge eyes glowed at me through the darkness, a good five feet above my eye level. Smaller points of light blazed below them — the last vestiges of fire flickering in his nostrils. A long, thick tail lashed menacingly.

My heart stopped. Uh-oh.

He folded his wings in a surprisingly delicate motion and shuffled forward, lowering his head.

My knees wobbled.

"Good to see you," I squeaked.

The fire in his eyes flared, then dimmed, going from *red alert* to *warm and welcoming.*

Good to see you too, his voice rumbled in my mind.

I raised my hands, trying not to shake as he eased his muzzle forward. Rough, leathery hide came to rest over my palms, and his eyes swirled at me.

Wow. I was face-to-face with a dragon. Cupping his snout, even, or as much of it as fit.

Snout? he grumbled.

I gulped and felt around gently. "Um, nose?"

I'll give you a nose, he muttered, transforming in front of me.

I couldn't say if it happened in super-fast or super-slow motion, because most of it blurred and I only caught a few details. Huge chest plates compacted before me, and his claws slowly morphed to feet and toes that curled into the gravel driveway at a similar angle.

I found myself patting his shoulders, then touching his face.

"See?" he said gruffly, as if his vocal cords were still transforming. "Nose."

I chuckled, stroking it. "Nose. Cheeks...lips..."

His eyes glowed in a softer hue, and his lips moved. My focus zoomed there, and everything else in my mind blurred. And blurred and blurred, until nothing existed except my lips and his, and nothing waited to be done except meeting them in a kiss. And another and another...

I was barely aware of walking to the cottage, stripping out of my clothes, or sliding into bed with Marius. But I was blissfully aware of every kiss, every caress, every perfectly timed move as our bodies meshed.

"Oh... Yes..." I moaned, clutching the sheets as he moved over me. In me. With me.

His eyes shone, and his glistening skin rippled with muscle. When I clenched around him, his breath caught. Then he regained his rhythm with a vengeance, sweeping us both higher, higher...

I shuddered and cried out, hitting the zenith of a very steep curve with him. We hung on as long as we could, then slowly sank into each other's arms.

I shut my eyes, holding him close. God, what a night. What a couple of weeks. Weeks that had turned my life upside down in ways both thrilling and terrifying.

So, yikes. What would the coming weeks bring?

Throughout the summer, my life had been driven by one theme — *repairs and renewal* — of the château and, in some ways, of myself. Since Marius had entered my life, the theme had shifted to *truth versus lies* — in art, in love, in life — and all the gray zones in between.

Like our art heist. My father would be proud of the end, but not the means.

Like the passion that blazed between Marius and me, too. He was a good man, and he was very, very good to me. But was he good *for* me? Were we really meant to be?

Then there was Gordon, who had always looked out for me and my family. But his business dealings weren't as legit as we'd always assumed them to be.

Each of those issues was a boulder perched on the edge of a cliff that loomed over me. It was only a question of time until one — or all — of them came crashing down.

"Get some sleep," Marius whispered, snuggling closer.

I tried, but my eyes kept wandering over the room. There was just enough moonlight to make out the lumps of our clothing and the three shapes beyond them. Henrik's short, squat box, perched on the windowsill, and the two frames I'd propped against the wall earlier.

One was Monet's *Thaw*, though it was a forgery. The other was *The Painter on the Road to Tarascon,* and I was damn sure that was the real thing.

Marius curled his thick arm around me, and I stroked his skin gently, thinking. The Van Gogh was the real thing... What about what I felt for Marius?

"Good night," he murmured, kissing my shoulder.

I kissed his hand. "Good night."

It didn't take long for his breath to settle into the slow, peaceful rhythm of sleep. But as for me...

Tired as I was, I didn't close my eyes for a long time. I just lay there, thinking.

Chapter Twenty-Eight

MARIUS

Steam followed me out of the shower the next morning. I wrapped a towel around my waist and wandered out to the bedroom, where I found Mina perched on the edge of the bed, staring at the paintings propped against the wall.

"Are you worried they'll walk off?" I joked.

She shook her head, too deep in thought to laugh. "Just amazed at what I'm looking at." She gestured toward the painting on the right. "I can't get over the idea that that was in Vincent van Gogh's hands, and now it's in mine. Well, in a manner of speaking."

I strode over, picked up the painting, and thrust it at her. "*Now* it's in your hands."

"Careful!" she admonished, holding it like... like a priceless painting, I supposed.

Watching her made me grin, because her awe and wonder were a joy to behold.

Then my grin stretched, because she turned and looked at me in the same way.

Behold — something priceless. And it's all mine, her glowing eyes said.

Shifter eyes, my dragon whispered.

Maybe even dragon eyes, I realized. Someday, I would work up the courage to ask.

Maybe even someday soon, because a night spent holding Mina made one thing perfectly clear. There was no way I could leave her. Not now, not ever.

I had one burning question that couldn't wait, though. I just hoped it wouldn't ruin a nice morning.

"If I let you ask me anything, would you answer something for me?" I ventured, figuring that was a fair trade.

She looked at me, going quiet. I steeled myself for something like, *Depends on the question.*

After some serious — and seriously scary — consideration, she licked her lips and said, "Remember what you said about not letting this mean something?"

I gulped hard. Had I really been dumb enough to say that? But I had, so I nodded.

"I want this to mean something," she whispered, looking at my hands, not my eyes. "I want to give it a chance, at least."

My throat went dry, but I got the truth out. "I want that too."

Her eyes jumped to mine, full of hope — and fear. Then she nodded. "I'm glad. Really glad," she smiled shyly, then went serious again. "But if that's the case, we shouldn't need to make deals with each other. Just ask, and I'll answer."

My cheek twitched, because she was offering trust, raw and unguarded. Trust I would have to reciprocate. Both sides of that equation terrified me.

It scared her too. I could see that. And yet, she had enough faith in me to offer hers up like a tiny, defenseless bird. Something I could crush easily.

I swallowed hard, then nodded. "I wanted to ask about how you got into the library. The second time, I mean. Bene said he saw a sentry posted there."

She knotted her hands together. "There was."

"How did you get past him?"

More thinking, and finally, a nervous answer. "The same way I got past Henrik that night he was in my attic."

I waited, because that still mystified me.

She put the painting aside, then motioned for me to sit beside her.

"Have you ever heard of shadow-walking?"

When I nodded, she didn't say anything. She just looked at me, waiting.

Then it hit me. "Whoa. Wait. You can shadow-walk?"

She nodded slowly. "Sometimes. Also, he was distracted. And it was dark. And—"

"You can shadow-walk?" I repeated stupidly.

I didn't know much about magic, but I knew shadow walking was a rare skill. Rare, as in one in a million.

"Yes, but—" She tried playing it off, but I wasn't buying it.

"And you shadow-walked away from Henrik that time too?"

She nodded, looking miserable. "My grandmother taught me. I'm not very good at it, though. I've only ever done it a few times, and—"

I took her hand. "Why are you apologizing? That's amazing."

She snorted. "I only inherited a tiny bit of magic, and it comes and goes. I don't really have any control over it."

"Maybe you just need more practice."

She blew out an uncertain breath. "Not sure I want to."

A few seconds ticked by in silence, which I finally broke. "Well, I think you're amazing, and not just because of the shadow-walking." She opened her mouth, but I covered it gently. "Thank you for answering. I won't tell anyone, if that's what's worrying you."

She started to object, but I knew I'd touched a nerve there.

Bene hollered from outside. "Rise and shine, ladies and dragons. Our fearless leader has called an AAR starting right now."

I groaned. Mina cocked her head. "AAR?"

"After action review," I muttered. Roux *loved* going by the book.

"On our way," Mina called back. Then she faced me with a wry grin, clearly ready for a change in subject. "Well, I guess it was a good thing we didn't shower together. Separately turned out to be faster."

I made a face. "Faster, but less fun."

Her smile lit the room, and her eyes danced.

"What?" I cocked my head.

She blushed. "I might be corrupting you. Fun didn't seem too high on your agenda when we first met."

I snorted. "If anyone is doing the corrupting, it's me." Then I grew more somber. "As for having fun, maybe I forgot for a while. But now, I remember, thanks to you."

Fun. Pride. Honor. The list of what Mina reminded me of went on and on.

I kissed her knuckles, because I could see her eyes better that way. Amazing, sky-blue eyes full of joy, hope, and other dangerous things.

Then she took an extra-deep breath — her reset button, I was starting to learn — and stood. "We'd better get ready. The sooner we get this over with, the better, right?"

I reached for pants and a shirt, hoping it would be that simple.

∞∞∞∞

It wasn't. Meetings with Roux never were, and having Bene and Henrik around always complicated things.

Except Henrik wasn't there, and Delphine was beside herself.

The dining table stood in the morning sun, warm and inviting. A mountain of food crowded a shaded side table. Eggs, bacon, fruit, fresh juice... It would have been heaven if Delphine hadn't been in her own personal hell.

"Shouldn't he be back by now?" She paced around.

Bene set down a plate piled with food and flopped into the chair beside Roux. "I'm sure he's fine."

An uneasy feeling settled into my gut — a feeling confirmed when a car pulled into the drive and Henrik stumbled out like a man who'd long since lurched from *drunk* to *hungover*. And since vampires got drunk on blood, not alcohol...

Roux, Bene, and I exchanged grim looks.

"Henrik!" Delphine cried.

She ran over and flung her arms around him, then stepped back to look him over. His tux was askew, and the tie dangled listlessly from his hand. His pocket square was gone, along with one of his cuff links, and his hair was a mess.

"Oh, Henrik!" Poor, oblivious Delphine fussed. "Are you all right?"

The morning breeze carried the scent of blood, sex, and something else.

My nostrils flared, and I blanched.

Bene frowned and whispered, "I'm sure I know that perfume..."

Crap. I did too.

Mina wrinkled her nose and muttered, "'Good Girl' by Carolina Herrera." Then she went perfectly still.

Celeste, my dragon growled.

Delphine went stiff, and her face fell. She backed away from Henrik, all shaky in the knees. "You...you..."

Mina jumped up to support Delphine. With her free hand, she shoved Henrik — hard. "You piece of shit!"

"Good morning to you too," he muttered, stumbling toward a chair in the shade.

Mina guided Delphine toward the main house.

"Come on, Delphine. He's not worth it."

They disappeared into the house, but even then, I could hear Delphine wail.

No one at the table spoke, but the air zinged with angry energy. Me, most of all, which was weird. I hated Celeste. Why did I care if she slept with Henrik?

Because it's wrong, my dragon grumbled.

Apparently, I was developing a conscience. Maybe Mina really was corrupting me.

"What the hell were you thinking?" Roux finally burst out. "You know what Celeste is."

Succubus. The word ran through my mind like a curse.

I could only be so angry with Henrik, though, because I'd fallen for the same spell.

Never again, my dragon vowed. *Never again.*

"You were supposed to keep an eye on her, not fuck her, dammit," Roux ranted.

Henrik made a face. "I might have underestimated Celeste. Her powers are. . .rather overwhelming."

"Overwhelming? You're a goddamn vampire!" Roux thumped the table, making the silverware jump. Then he sniffed. "Fuck. You drank from her, didn't you?"

Henrik leveled a cold look at him. "And if I did?"

Roux fumed. "Idiot. Succubus blood. . ."

Henrik's eyes drooped as he savored the memory. "Delicious. Distracting. And rather potent, I have to admit."

"You're lucky you didn't wake up with a stake in your heart," I grumbled.

"Technically, he wouldn't wake up," Bene pointed out cheerily.

No loss to the world, I couldn't help thinking.

Henrik scowled. "Lucky? No. She tried. I stopped her just in time."

Too bad, I nearly blurted.

"Then what? Don't tell me you let her go?" Roux demanded.

Henrik flapped a hand. "It seemed like a fair trade."

Bene snorted. "Let me guess. You were too sluggish to stop her."

"I might have been," Henrik admitted, closing his eyes and settling back.

Mina reappeared alone, shooting daggers at Henrik.

"Dammit. Celeste could be heading for Gordon with a full report right now," Roux muttered.

Henrik shook his head. "Celeste won't talk. I made sure of that."

"How?" Roux demanded.

Mina made a face, muttering, "Do we want to know?"

"Simple," Henrik said. "I made it clear the way things stood."

I huffed. "Like what? That our original plan failed? That Mina is in Mallorca with us?"

Henrik shook his head. "Our plan was working. It was Celeste who nearly botched the job. She's the one who has to worry about *us* talking to Gordon, as I made perfectly clear."

Bene snorted. "Before or after she took you to bed?"

Henrik gave him an icy look. "Both, if you must know."

Roux's brow furrowed. "He's right. Celeste won't want to discuss the details of last night with Gordon any more than we do."

I grumbled in disgust, but the tiger had a point.

"She won't talk," Henrik said with whatever smug dignity he could gather. "So, a win-win in the end."

"Except for Delphine," Mina growled.

Henrik pretended not to hear. What an ass.

Mina went on pacing. "What about Baumann and Dobrov? You're not worried about them coming after us or demanding an investigation?"

"Nah. As far as they know, you three died in the fire," Bene said cheerily.

My dragon snarled viciously.

Roux didn't seem offended by the comment. "They'll assume the paintings were lost in the fire. And Baumann won't encourage a detailed police investigation, because he can't admit to keeping anyone prisoner or inviting an illicit art dealer to his party. That would ruin his reputation."

Mina scoffed. "Reputation? He's the worst kind of criminal."

"Well, that's the way the world works," Bene said, digging into his eggs and toast.

We absorbed that cheery message in glum silence. But birds sang from the trees, and the wind whispered through the olive grove. The sun warmed my face, and Mina's presence did too. So, maybe the world didn't run on such a shitty premise after all. At least, not entirely. There was peace and beauty to be found in it too. Maybe even love.

The next time Mina paced by, I caught her hand and held it.

She flashed a tiny smile and wrapped both her hands around mine.

"Anyway, enjoy the painting while you can," Bene mumbled to Mina while chewing away. "We'll have to hand it over to Gordon soon."

She glanced toward the cottage, murmuring, "Maybe not."

Uh-oh. Now what?

Roux shot her a long-suffering look. "I know it's important to you, but…"

She walked off. "I'll be right back."

The moment she was out of sight, Roux groaned. "God, she kills me."

Ha. I could say the same thing, but in a good way.

Bene laughed. "She's tough, smart, and unpredictable. What's not to love?" He shoved another forkful of food into his mouth. "Plus, life has been way more entertaining with her around. I think we should add her to the team permanently."

"No way," Roux, Henrik, and I all barked at the same time.

At least we agreed on the *what*, if not the *why*.

Bene shushed us. "Careful. Here she comes."

Roux groaned. "You sound like you're in fourth grade with a substitute teacher around."

"Fifth grade," I growled. When were they going to get that straight?

"Catch," Mina said, tossing Henrik the small wooden box she'd retrieved from the fire.

He snatched it out of the air and held it like a precious artifact.

"And remember our deal," Mina barked, looking at him sternly.

Deal? I didn't like the sound of that.

Henrik slipped the box under his jacket, muttering, "I'll remember."

"What's—" Bene started.

Mina shook her head. "Don't ask."

Then she held up two paintings — the blurry Van Gogh and whatever the other one was — and propped both on a windowsill.

"Van Gogh's *The Painter on the Road to Tarascon*. The real thing, I'm pretty sure." Then she pointed to the other painting, a wintery landscape. "Monet's *Thaw*. Not the real thing, but a good copy."

Everyone waited. And waited…

"And your point is...?" Roux finally said.

Mina flashed that *they kill me with their idiocy* expression she did so well.

"Gordon and his client will know that most of Dobrov's artworks were lost in the fire," she said. "But they won't know *which* art was lost."

Roux frowned. "What are you getting at?"

She pointed at the Van Gogh, then the Monet. "Tell him you did your best, but due to an unfortunate fire that you had absolutely nothing to do with—" she shot me a stern look "—the Van Gogh was lost. But the Monet could be saved, thanks to your bravery — and his and his." She pointed to Bene and me.

"And mine," Henrik muttered.

Roux stared. "You're saying, give Gordon's client a different painting? Not the one he asked for?"

Mina nodded.

"What if he doesn't want it?" Roux asked.

Mina scoffed. "How could anyone not want a Monet?"

I glanced at the gloomy painting. Well, me, for one.

Bene rubbed his chin. "It could work... unless they figure out it's a forgery."

"That's the beauty of this situation." Mina chuckled. "That would be Dobrov's fault, not yours. You were simply following orders."

"Except we were told to get that painting." Roux pointed to the Van Gogh.

"Painting? What painting?" Bene quipped. "Oh, you mean the one lost in the fire when we were bravely rescuing a much more valuable Monet?"

"Exactly." Mina grinned.

"All this so you can keep the Van Gogh?" Henrik asked.

Mina shook her head vehemently. "No. Well, yes, but only for a couple of months. Long enough that no one will connect it to what happened here. Then I'll use my dad's contacts to make an anonymous donation to a museum that will make the Van Gogh available to everyone."

Henrik stared. "You're saying you would give it away?"

Mina nodded.

"How very noble." Henrik's voice dripped with sarcasm.

Mina shook her head. "Not trying to be noble. Just trying to do the right thing."

Months ago, I might have scoffed at the sentiment. Now, I etched her words into my mind.

Roux cut in, getting back to the point. "If you can figure out the Monet is fake, Gordon's client could too. What then?"

Mina shrugged. "Again, not your fault, but Dobrov's — and it implies the Van Gogh was a fake too. No one will be able to disprove that, because Dobrov never let an expert appraise either work."

Roux thought it over, then shook his head. "Too many unpredictables."

True. But, hell. That applied to everything in our line of work. And if we pulled this off... Just a few more months doing Gordon's bidding, and I would be a free man.

"I'm in," I said firmly.

Mina's eyes bathed me in warmth.

Henrik sighed. "I'm in."

"I'm in," Bene said, then elbowed Henrik. "Pass the salt."

Roux ran both hands through his hair, making it spike. A good alternative to tearing it out, which he seemed close to.

"You're serious?"

Bene, Henrik, Mina, and I all nodded.

Roux gritted his teeth, then sighed and picked up his phone.

∞∞∞∞

Marseilles. Two days later...

"The contract was for a Van Gogh," Gordon grumbled.

Bene shifted from foot to foot, catching my eye.

"A Van Gogh. Not a Monet, a Manet, or even a Picasso. A Van Gogh," Gordon emphasized. "I don't expect you lot to have my goddaughter's taste in art, but this is really too much."

Bene muttered into my mind. *What would he say about his goddaughter's taste in men?*

I shot him a look to kill.

"Yes, sir," Roux agreed. "But unfortunately — might I say, tragically — the Van Gogh was destroyed in the blaze. We were lucky to get out with this."

"Not lucky. Brave," Bene added, laying it on thick. "Roux insisted we go back for it, even when the roof started to collapse." He patted the tiger shifter on the back.

Interestingly, the fire didn't seem to bother Gordon. He didn't say as much, but clearly, there was bad blood between him and Baumann. He'd even muttered, *That ass got what he deserved.*

So, we didn't have to explain the fire. But we did have to talk him into the Monet.

"Sir, if I may..." Henrik gestured to the painting. "This artwork has much more subtlety and depth than the Van Gogh. Surely, your client will appreciate that."

I wasn't so sure about depth, because both looked equally out of focus to me. But, hell. What did I know about art?

Gordon paced, regarding the painting from different angles. Eventually, he looked at Roux with a pained expression. "Monet, you say?"

"Yes, sir. Monet."

The room went very, very quiet as Gordon looked at each of us in turn. Roux, I sensed, held his breath. Hell, I did too.

Finally, Gordon grumbled and pointed to the door. "You're dismissed. Considering this is not the requested piece, you get three rather than four days off. Report to me from Auberre at this time Thursday for your next assignment." He checked his watch, then motioned for us to leave. "Oh, and I expect the next job to go more smoothly than this."

"Yes, sir," Roux said gravely.

"And not a word to Mina, you understand?" Gordon added ominously.

Bene looked at me. I stared at the wall. A vein in Henrik's forehead started to twitch.

"Not a word, sir," Roux barked, using sheer volume to wipe any trace of the lie.

"Good. You're dismissed." Gordon gestured to the door.

"Sir, about our days off. I really think—" Bene started.

"Not a word. Out," Gordon barked.

"Yes, sir," Bene said, sounding glum.

I could see his eyes dance, though. We'd pulled it off!

We filed down the long, echoing hall of Gordon's imposing villa a stone's throw from Palais Longchamp and out into the sun. The nearest Metro stop was only a few blocks away, and we managed to keep straight faces for most of the way.

Bene was the first to break into a grin. "Three days isn't four, but I won't complain." He smacked Henrik on the back in glee. "Three days off without you yo-yos. Paris, here I come!"

Roux muttered something about Toulouse, while Henrik slunk off, leaving us without a word. I joined the other two on the Metro to the main train station.

"You think Henrik will stay in Marseilles and try to make up with Delphine?" Bene asked as we pulled out of the station.

I had no idea. But one thing was carved in stone. I was heading straight back to Château Nocturne.

Chapter Twenty-Nine

MINA

Four days later...

"Wilhelmina!" Madame Martin called cheerily as I entered the *boulangerie.*

"Bonjour," I greeted her and the only other customer.

Madame Fontaine, the retired schoolmistress, echoed my greeting, then tut-tutted. "Running again? Young people these days..."

"No wonder she's still so thin," Madame Martin, the baker, lamented as if I wasn't even there. "And she still hasn't found a man."

Ah, but I had. A dragon shifter, no less. Not that I volunteered that news.

"Well, at least she has more color now," Madame Fontaine said. "Must be this fresh autumn air."

My cheeks flushed. No, that was a side effect of great sex, every morning and every night. Sometimes even in between.

Marius and the others had departed for their meeting with Gordon apprehensively, knowing any outcome was possible. So I'd been surprised, delighted, and relieved when Marius had appeared at my door late that very same evening. Touched, too. He'd come home — to me. He wanted to spend his precious time off with me. I'd practically squealed with glee.

But those three days were up now, and we expected the other guys back within hours.

"What can I get you?" Monsieur Martin asked.

"Two *pain au chocolate*, please," I started. "One for now, one for later," I fibbed, so they wouldn't think I was serving breakfast for two. "And four baguettes."

"Four? Are you expecting more clients?" Madame Martin asked.

I stifled a sigh. Everyone knew everyone's business in Auberre.

"Yes." I moved pointedly to the register. "How much will that be?"

I paid and snatched up my purchases before they could pose any more questions, like who my clients were and how long they were staying. Even so, my mind started calculating. Three weeks had elapsed since Marius, Roux, Bene, and Henrik had first arrived. My contract with Gordon ran three months. That left a little more than two months.

I bit my lip. How many more missions might they be sent on during that time? What would those entail, and what other dirty secrets about my godfather might they reveal? What would happen afterward — after their three months with me *and* after their time working for Gordon?

Above all, what about Marius? Would he disappear at the end of that time, or would he stay... and stay... and stay?

"Well, goodbye, everyone—" I whirled into a quick exit from those thoughts and the bakery.

The bell over the door jingled too late for me to react, and I crashed into the incoming customer.

"*Désolé.*" *Sorry,* a man said from an inch away.

"My fault," I started, then whispered, "Clem."

"Mina," he murmured, eyes aglow.

For a moment, our gazes locked, and a whole alternative life drifted through my mind. A nice, simple life, with a good man with a good, steady job. A stunningly handsome man free of crimes and links to the criminal underworld. A man who would be content to build a quiet life in this quiet place with someone like me.

But that vision was black-and-white, and it faded quickly, replaced by a different, brilliantly colored one. One of a life of blazing passions, and not just the kind found in bed. Life with Marius was life on the edge. Thrilling. Unpredictable. Sometimes even terrifying. But oh, so very alive.

Maybe my life didn't have to be a constant cycle of school semesters or home repairs. A life that didn't adhere to the standard framework, with education, marriage, and children all pre-programmed for certain times, followed by years of watching that life unfold in predictable ways.

Which wasn't to say I wanted to plunge headfirst into a world of danger, intrigue, and covert missions. Just hoping that Marius and I could find a middle ground.

"*Bonjour*, Clement!" Madame Martin called. "Doesn't Mina look well?"

I winced.

His eyes sparkled. "She does." But then his nostrils flared, and I steeled myself.

Clement was a wolf shifter, and wolf shifters had good noses. Too good for me to hide the scent of dragon, no matter how hard I'd scrubbed or how much I'd sweated while running.

His eyes went wide, and his expression hardened.

Ten awkward seconds followed. Neither of us uttered a word, but so much passed between us. Memories of the past, hints of a future. A whole fantasy world that sprang up, then faded away. The walls of a friendship, once solid, now crumbling, like my château. Could it someday be repaired the way walls or a roof could?

Clement's eyes filled with anger and jealousy, and for a moment, I worried what he might say or do. But all that ebbed away, replaced by deep sorrow.

Guilt stabbed at me, but what could I say?

"You look good too," I said with an undertone that added, *And I'm sure you'll find the right person soon.*

He stepped away.

"Good to see you," he murmured, a martyr whispering his last words.

I swallowed hard. Madame Martin was right. He was a good man. Just not *my* man.

It hurt me to hurt him, and words wouldn't help. But, oh! A new love interest might.

"Did I mention my sister and cousin are coming soon?" I asked. "Gen keeps asking about you."

Absolutely true, because my younger sister had been infatuated with Clement from about the age of five. Unfortunately, Clem was four years older and had barely noticed her.

But Gen — Genevieve, officially — had been an annoying chatterbox back then. Nowadays, she was poised, intelligent, interesting — and much, much prettier than me. Wasn't a good man just what she needed after a string of toxic relationships?

"That's good," Clem said, unenthused.

Then, yikes. His eyes started glowing, and his jaw clenched. His wolf side was prowling closer to the surface, and crap. It wasn't ready to accept defeat.

This isn't over yet, that determined glint said, then communicated something like *Let the best man win.*

Crap. Just what I needed — a wolf and a dragon shifter feuding over me. Flattering, but potentially fatal.

I could see and hear it now. The earsplitting howls, the possessive growls, the bared teeth. Marius would unleash his fire, while Clement could call in an entire wolf pack to assist. If I didn't find a way to de-escalate things, they could lay waste to lovely Auberre and burn my château to a crisp.

Not good. Maybe Gen could fly in a week sooner. Hell, tomorrow would be good.

Then again, knowing my sister, she would fall for Henrik instead.

The town clock struck the quarter hour, spurring me into action.

"Oops. I have to go. *Merci.*" I waved to Madame and Monsieur Martin, bid Madame Fontaine a polite *Au revoir,* then turned to face Clem.

My lips moved with two false starts before I finally got something out.

"*À bientôt.*" *See you soon,* I said, hurrying out the door.

"*À bientôt,*" he whispered.

Four pairs of eyes followed me out. Especially Clement's.

I always picked up the pace on my run back to the château, but this time, I really hit the gas, desperate to escape to the safe bubble of home.

A soon-to-be slightly less safe bubble, what with Henrik on his way, but still. Home was home.

I raced through the woods, ticking off my own private landmarks. The fallen oak... The pool in the stream... The scorched patch Marius had left the night of the intruder...

Eventually, I emerged at the tangled garden, then jogged across the lawn.

Beep! Beep! A vintage Citroën 2CV puttered down the drive, and the driver waved from the window.

We converged at the front door, and a slightly stooped, older gent emerged.

"Mina!" He opened his arms.

"Sid!" I ran over to hug my father's old friend.

His hair had thinned, and his frame was more gaunt than I remembered. Either I had grown an inch, or he had shrunk. But it was the same old Sid.

An ache settled in my chest, and I closed my eyes, imagining hugging my father. If he had lived to Sid's age, would I be wise enough to treasure signs of aging as a monument to all the years we'd shared?

I leaned back, keeping hold of Sid's hands.

"My God. Every time I see you, I see him," Sid murmured, experiencing his own moment of *what might have been*.

I laughed, touched and embarrassed.

"Thank you so much for coming," I said, moving things along.

His eyes twinkled. "Wouldn't miss this for my life. Now, show me that painting."

∞∞∞∞

Meeting Marius came first, however, and viewing the painting was further delayed by the early arrival of Roux and Bene. The fierceness of their hugs — and mine in return — was both moving and surprising. It had only been a few days, and a few weeks of knowing them at all, but they felt like old friends now. The brothers-in-arms effect of having survived a dangerous mission together, I supposed.

"Good to see you," I said, meaning every word.

"Good to be back." Bene grinned, and Roux did too.

Henrik appeared a short time later, beating Gordon's deadline by a good hour. So, hmm. Maybe these men, tough and capable as they were, had nowhere they would rather be — or, at least, nowhere else to go. Maybe they were coming to love the château the way I did. Like home.

A sad, but equally heartwarming thought. Slightly alarming, too, at least when it came to Henrik.

No hugs for him, though our handshake wasn't as forced as it might have been.

"Delphine sends her regards," he said, stiffly handing me a fancy bag.

I hid my surprise. Was there hope for the coldhearted vampire after all?

"How sweet." I peeked at the pastry box inside.

"Yes, I'm told they are," he said indifferently.

Not what I meant, but it sure beat him licking his chops and murmuring, *Yes, she is.*

A light lunch followed, because the arrivals had all started their journeys before dawn. I set out cheese, cold cuts, and bread, wishing Claudette were around to help, but also grateful she wasn't. We all sat around the dining room table, catching up.

"Maybe I should follow Marius's cue and spend my days off here next time," Bene teased. "You look so relaxed."

"It's the fresh country air," Sid said, blissfully oblivious to Bene's subtext. "It gives one a certain glow."

"Oh, they're definitely glowing." Bene laughed.

Marius growled, and I shushed him, blushing. As close as Sid and my father had been, my father had never let on about supernaturals, and I didn't want to explain dragons, lions, tigers, or vampires now.

"How did you and Mina's father meet?" Roux asked, changing the subject.

So, whew. I owed him one.

Sid chuckled. "Care to explain, Mina?"

I did my best to put it delicately. "My father was checking on a series of paintings that appeared on the art market in quick succession. The auction house that obtained them was sure the works were genuine, but my father suspected a forger."

"Did he get the guy?" Bene asked.

"Yes. Me." Sid pointed to his chest with a wry grin.

Bene's eyes went wide. "And?"

Sid shrugged. "The judge wanted to give me five years, but Thomas talked him down to three, and he eventually talked the parole board into releasing me after one. So I could get back to my children, you see..."

He trailed off sadly, and everyone grew quiet.

"Sid was the forger," I explained, "but it was a guy named Sutherland who drove the whole operation. He commissioned works, faked the provenance, and pocketed the money."

"He served eight years," Sid added dryly.

"Plus another six when a separate fraud case surfaced," I added.

My father despised Sutherland, but he had hit it off with Sid. Other than being on opposite sides of the law, they shared a love of art and art history.

"What do you do these days?" Bene asked.

Sid smiled apologetically. "I paint portraits in the style of any grand master a client requests."

"He does pets too." I scrolled through my phone, then turned it around to show off a portrait of a bulldog in a classic Napoleon pose.

Bene giggled. "That's priceless. Do you do lions?"

Roux kicked him under the table, but Sid didn't catch on.

"I haven't had the opportunity, but you never know." Then he looked at me. "Speaking of paintings..."

I stood with a crisp nod. "I'll get it. Meet you in the drawing room in a few minutes?"

Everyone stood, and Bene pointed to the pastries Henrik had brought. "Can I bring those?"

"Only if you don't insult my coffee machine," I shot back.

"Ha. It deserves every word. But..." He rooted around in his bag, then pulled out a huge box with a triumphant look. "Ladies and gentlemen, may I present the Breville Barista Pro X380." He held the box to his cheek and stroked it.

Marius whistled. "That must have cost you a couple of paychecks."

Plus savings, I figured, having learned that Gordon only paid each of them a paltry sum. I'd been incensed when Marius told me, but he'd just shrugged.

The real payment is having our records wiped clean when our contract is up. As long as Gordon sticks to his word on that, I'm good.

I was still of two minds when it came to the darker aspects of my lover's past, but he'd proven his loyalty and good heart too many times to count.

"Worth every penny." Bene planted a loud smooch on the box.

"Well, set it up, then. Meet you there," I said, setting off.

Marius wove his fingers through mine as we made our way up the spiral stairs. I was about to step into the upper hallway when he tugged me back.

"That coffee machine will take some time to set up, you know..." He leaned in to kiss me.

The moment our lips touched, my body heated, and slowly, I melted against the wall.

I tilted my head back, basking in the flurry of kisses he planted along my skin.

"Up these stairs, correct?" Sid's voice drifted up the stairwell.

We froze.

"Yes," Henrik said with a hint of glee. "Take those stairs. Up one flight, then turn right. The drawing room is above us."

"Fucking vampires," Marius growled as Sid's footsteps sounded below.

I grabbed Marius's hand and continued toward my suite. "Probably not the best time right now."

"Not the best time to kill a vampire?" he grumbled.

I kissed his hand. "Or to make out. But I promise you, tonight..."

"Kill vampire first, sex second. It's a deal," Marius said.

I laughed. "Just sex. For now, at least."

Fifteen minutes later, everyone gathered in the drawing room and watched Sid inspect the Van Gogh. Well, everyone except Bene, who was more interested in the coffee machine's hissing and sputtering — across the room from the painting, just in case.

Sid hunched over the painting with a small, handheld lens, mumbling to himself.

"And?" Roux asked impatiently.

Even Henrik looked curious.

"Shh," I cut in. "Let him concentrate."

Marius snorted. "We already know it's real. Mina said so."

I appreciated his faith in me, but my paranoia had grown over the past few days. What if the painting was a fake? There would be no celebration today, no silent pride when the news hit the papers in a few months. No glance at heaven to say, *I did it for you, Dad.*

A lump formed in my throat.

"Interesting," Sid murmured, then moved on to another section of the painting.

Bene sipped his first batch of coffee and kissed his fingers. "*Magnifique.*" He pranced over to sit on the couch, where he leaned back and raised his feet toward the coffee table.

"Don't—" I started, but he'd already pulled his feet back with a grin.

"Gotcha." He planted his feet on the floor and sipped, then moaned and started to speak.

"Not a word about my coffee machine," I warned.

He snorted. "It was a machine, but I'm not sure about the coffee part." He raised his cup. "*This* is coffee."

Roux chuckled. "Now we know what to get Bene for Christmas. Fancy beans."

Bene gave that a thumbsup. "Dark roast Akagera from Rwanda, please."

I made a mental note, then caught myself. My contract with Gordon only ran to the end of November. Where would Bene go afterward? Where would they all go?

My eyes wandered to Marius.

Once upon a time, my grandmother had hosted big, buzzing Christmas parties with live music, spiced punch, old-fashioned decorations, and countless guests. But the "biggest" gathering we'd had since she died was when my sister, cousin, mother, aunt, and I had met here for Christmas the previous December. But with the heating broken and empty, echoing halls... Well, it had been a little on the gloomy side.

I looked around at the people and the place, wondering what the coming Christmas would bring. More importantly, *whom* it would bring.

Sid leaned away from the painting, murmuring, "Incredible."

My pulse skipped.

He turned, eyes sparkling. "Your father would be so proud."

Marius squeezed my hand, telling me he was too.

"So, it's real?" Bene asked.

Sid nodded, and I grinned a mile wide.

"Wow. That's got to be worth millions, right?" Bene asked.

I groaned. "Way to spoil the mood."

"Spoiling the mood is your mom butts in on you during foreplay, or what Henrik does whenever he walks into a room."

The vampire flashed his fangs, but Bene ignored him, and Sid, thank goodness, didn't see.

"It might fetch millions, but it's priceless in other ways," Sid said.

I nodded. "Like knowing it will be displayed for anyone to see."

"You're an idealist, you know that?" Bene laughed.

Roux looked at me, then Marius, and a cloud came over his eyes. A cloud that implied I might be overly idealistic about the dragon shifter too.

Well, I could make up my own mind about that. And ultimately, time would tell, wouldn't it?

"Now, about that Monet. You're sure it's a fake?" Sid asked.

I showed him the picture I'd snapped before the guys had handed it over to Gordon. "I'm sure. Look at the signature and the brushstrokes."

Sid held his lens to my phone, then caught himself and laughed. "Oops. What about the back of the painting? Any clues there?"

I grinned. "Look at the stamp."

He scrolled to the next image and zoomed in on the mark on the back of the canvas. "*Sammlung Flechheim.*"

I waited, then prompted him. "Look again."

He did, then cracked into a grin. "*Flechtheim* should be spelled with a T."

I nodded, and we both broke into hoots.

Bene sipped his coffee, muttering, "Art nerds."

"Well, you're right again," Sid said. "Did I say your father would be proud?"

He had, but I would never tire of hearing those words.

"Just one thing," Sid said, growing somber. "I respect that you can't reveal the details of how you procured this artwork, or about the previous owner. But what happens when he or she discovers that *The Painter on the Road to Tarascon* has suddenly resurfaced in the art world?"

"I figured if I wait a few months..." I said hopefully.

Sid shook his head. "A year. At least."

"A year?" I yelped.

Hiding the painting for a couple of months was a necessity. Hiding it any longer came with risks. What if a fire broke out in the château? What if Clem stopped by for some reason — and I was sure he would find a reason, such as checking up on my clients — and spotted it? What if Bene splattered it with coffee or used it for dart practice by mistake?

Marius squeezed my hand. "It will be fine."

Sid chuckled. "Poor you. You have to live with your very own Van Gogh for a whole year." He patted me on the shoul-der. "I say, make the most of it. *Carpe diem* and all that, as they say."

"Yes. You should seize as many carps as you can in life," Bene quipped. "I certainly plan to."

"May I suggest a toast?" Sid said.

Roux found a bottle of champagne while I handed out glasses.

"To Vincent?" Bene proposed once every glass was filled.

Sid shook his head. "To a mission fulfilled."

He meant my father, but it applied to what we'd just been through in Mallorca too.

"To missions fulfilled," Roux agreed with a wink.

"And future missions," Bene added. "May they be as successful."

Warning bells rang in my mind. Future missions? Including me?

God, I hoped not.

Still, I added my voice to the others when they echoed, "And future missions."

We clinked and drank, but Marius held back, waiting for me.

He raised his glass an extra inch, toasting me, and whispered over the edge.

"To future missions."

Sneak Peek: Marked by Moonlight

Dragons rage, vampires thirst, and dangerous rivals covet a lost masterpiece as one woman battles for her heart's desire.

Mina's world is unraveling thread by magical thread. Her enigmatic dragon shifter lover has vanished without explanation. Her vampire houseguest is one bad night away from disaster. And her overprotective wolf-shifter friend — local cop, full-time temptation — is coming closer to uncovering secrets she can't afford to reveal.

Just when she thinks she can't handle another complication, her godfather offers her a tempting distraction: a trip to London, all expenses paid. All she has to do is help appraise a long-lost masterpiece. Simple... except the painting doesn't just attract art collectors. Dangerous rivals, ruthless power players, and her lover's sworn enemies all have their eyes on the prize — and on Mina.

As danger closes in, Mina and Marius are torn between duty and desire. Can they protect a priceless painting and outwit their enemies while finding a way back to happily ever after? Or will the shadowy shifter underworld tear them apart forever?

Books by Anna Lowe

Château Nocturne

Brushed by Moonlight (Book 1)

Marked by Moonlight (Book 2)

Touched by Magic (Book 3)

Spellbound in Sedona

Wind Whisperer (Book 1)

Fire Dancer (Book 2)

Dream Weaver (Book 3)

Sherwood Forest Shifters

Tempting the Sheriff (Book 1)

Tempting the Outlaw (Book 2)

Tempting the Maiden (Book 3)

Aloha Shifters - Jewels of the Heart

Lure of the Dragon (Book 1)

Lure of the Wolf (Book 2)

Lure of the Bear (Book 3)

Lure of the Tiger (Book 4)

Love of the Dragon (Book 5)

Lure of the Fox (Book 6)

Aloha Shifters - Pearls of Desire

Rebel Dragon (Book 1)

Rebel Bear (Book 2)

Rebel Lion (Book 3)

Rebel Wolf (Book 4)

Rebel Heart (A prequel to Book 5)

Rebel Alpha (Book 5)

Fire Maidens - Billionaires & Bodyguards

Fire Maidens: Paris (Book 1)

Fire Maidens: London (Book 2)

Fire Maidens: Rome (Book 3)

Fire Maidens: Portugal (Book 4)

Fire Maidens: Ireland (Book 5)

Fire Maidens: Scotland (Book 6)

Fire Maidens: Venice (Book 7)

Fire Maidens: Greece (Book 8)

Fire Maidens: Switzerland (Book 9)

The Wolves of Twin Moon Ranch

Desert Hunt (the Prequel)

Desert Moon (Book 1)

Desert Blood (Book 2)

Desert Fate (Book 3)

Desert Heart (Book 4)

Desert Rose (Book 5)

Desert Roots (Book 6)

Desert Destiny (Book 7)

Sasquatch Surprise (Book 8)

Desert Yule (a short story)

Desert Wolf: Complete Collection (Four short stories)

Blue Moon Saloon

Perfection (a short story prequel)

Damnation (Book 1)

Temptation (Book 2)

Redemption (Book 3)

Salvation (Book 4)

Deception (Book 5)

Celebration (a holiday treat)

Shifters in Vegas

Paranormal romance with a zany twist

Gambling on Trouble

Gambling on Her Dragon

Gambling on Her Bear

Gambling on Her Panther

Serendipity Adventure Romance

Off the Charts

Uncharted

Entangled

Windswept

Adrift

Travel Romance

Veiled Fantasies

Island Fantasies

www.annalowebooks.com

About the Author

USA Today and Amazon bestselling author Anna Lowe loves putting the "hero" back into heroine and letting location ignite a passionate romance. She likes a heroine who is independent, intelligent, and imperfect – a woman who is doing just fine on her own. But give the heroine a good man – not to mention a chance to overcome her own inhibitions – and she'll never turn down the chance for adventure, nor shy away from danger.

Anna loves dogs, sports, and travel – and letting those inspire her fiction. On any given weekend, you might find her hiking in the mountains or hunched over her laptop, working on her latest story. Either way, the day will end with a chunk of dark chocolate and a good read.

Visit AnnaLoweBooks.com